# Carolina Mercy

*Southern Breeze Series, Book 2*

## Regina Rudd Merrick

Scrivenings PRESS
Quench your thirst for story.
www.ScriveningsPress.com

Published by Scrivenings Press LLC
15 Lucky Lane
Morrilton, Arkansas 72110
https://ScriveningsPress.com



Paperback ISBN 978-1-64917-074-3

eBook ISBN 978-1-64917-075-0

Library of Congress Control Number: 2020940043

Cover by Diane Turpin, www.dianeturpindesigns.com

(Note: This book was previously published by Mantle Rock Publishing LLC and was re-published when MRP was acquired by Scrivenings Press LLC in 2020.)

*To my sister, Andrea Gail Rudd Peak – Annie. You not only read my stories before anyone else and encouraged me to write more, but you also gave me my favorite wedding story ever. Thank you, and I love you, baby sister!*

*He has shown you, O man, what is good; And what does the Lord require of you but to do justly, to love mercy, and to walk humbly with your God?*

— MICAH 6:8

# ACKNOWLEDGMENTS

As a writer, there are more people to thank than there are pages in a book. I have an amazing support system.

Thank you, God, for giving me stories when I get stuck, and putting a piece of scripture in my head at just the right time.

Thank you, Todd, for giving me your office, loving, and supporting me every step of the way, even when I make you stop talking to me.

Thank you Emily and Ellen for encouraging me to keep plugging along.

Thank you, Kathy and Jerry Cretsinger and the Mantle Rock Publishing family for having confidence in me. They never questioned whether or not second and third books were in me.

Thank you, Richard and Wanda Rudd, James and Margaret Merrick, for being so excited and supportive of me and my writing.

And thank you to my church family, friends, and extended family, and all the people that I've met and sold books to at odd places – book events, restaurants, parking lots, funerals, etc. You know who you are, and I love you all!

# CHAPTER ONE

*April*

Lucy Dixon wanted it to be a bad dream, but it wasn't.

Auto pilot. It was the only way she was getting through this. Daddy was dead. Two other workers lay in the hospital in critical condition because he'd pushed himself in front of them before the explosion. Grandmommy was burying her son, and she was burying her father.

Another group of friends reached the casket, and she braced herself for their condolences. If she had to do this much longer, she feared she would run from the room screaming.

And then he came.

Tom. She hadn't heard from him in eight months.

"Now who in the world is that tall drink of water?"

Lucy took a deep breath and tried to slow her heartbeat. "It's Tom Livingston, Grandmommy. The man I told you about from South Carolina. I guess he came with Sarah and Jared."

"Is Sarah's young man, Jared, the boy with the dark hair and eyes?"

"He is."

"Well, no wonder she's stayin' in South Carolina."

"Grandmommy, behave."

She was vigilant as they gradually made their way through the line that went all the way to the front door of the funeral home. She knew where they were at all times. In a way, she didn't want them to get to her. When they did, she would know it was all real. Tears pricked her eyelids all evening and overflowed when Sarah got to her and reached out for her.

They sobbed together.

LUCY'S HAIR WAS DIFFERENT. Shorter. But he could have seen her ten years from now and still known it was her, from the back. And it had only been eight months. But they hadn't spoken since she left.

When her head lifted and her eyes met his, she trembled. Was it the emotions of the day? Was she glad to see him? Or angry? He probably should have at least sent a Christmas card.

They made it to the casket where Lucy stood on one side, and an elderly lady sat in a chair on the other side. There were only the two of them, no one sitting on the front "family" row to act as backup.

Sarah got to her first. The two young women simply cried as they clung to one another, causing Tom to choke up himself.

"Are you okay?" Sarah had backed off enough to take the tissue Lucy handed her.

"I'm fine. I . . . ." She sniffed loudly and swallowed the emotion that welled upon seeing her best friend.

"I know. I can't believe it either."

Lucy shook herself and pulled away from Sarah. "Jared, thanks for coming. Tom." Her tears began to flow again as she reached for his hand.

When he took it and squeezed, he pulled her to himself and

enveloped her in a hug and whispered, "You couldn't have kept me away."

She simply nodded and pulled back, her cheeks flushed. "Grandmommy, you know Sarah, and this is Jared Benton and Tom Livingston from South Carolina."

Sarah hugged Elizabeth Dixon. "I'm so sorry."

"I know, Sarah. When you get to be my age, you sure don't expect to bury your children. At least you hope you won't."

"Thanks for coming over." Lucy tucked her feet under her legs on the overstuffed sofa and nodded when Sarah handed her a box of tissues. "I don't think I could face the thought of only Grandmommy and me in this big barn of a house."

She looked around at the opulent family room. Her father had given her carte blanche to redecorate it when she moved home from college. His one request was that she stay there with him for a little while after graduation. Not forever. He had missed her while she was away.

"Where did you dump Jared and Tom?" Lucy gave her best friend a grin along with a hefty sniffle and relaxed a bit when Sarah chuckled.

"They're at Mom and Dad's house. Mom always secretly wanted boys, you know." Sarah's eyes sparkled almost as much as the brilliant diamond on her hand.

"Let me see that thing again." She sighed as she grabbed Sarah's left hand and turned it different ways in the light, watching as the flashes of color created a rainbow in the room. "It's so beautiful. Beautiful like you."

"Oh, Luce. This is going to be too much, isn't it?"

"Absolutely not. I'm going with Grandmommy to Atlanta to bury Dad next to Mom, and then I'm heading to you. The show must go on, you know." She put all the stoicism she could find into her voice. She had to.

"I don't want to put more pressure on you. I mean, it's only a wedding."

"Only a wedding?" Lucy snorted. "Young lady, this is only the wedding of my best friend, who is marrying the man of her dreams." She stressed the word "only" to make her point. "Get real, here. I'm the maid of honor, don't you know?"

Sarah giggled at her last phrase. "You're channeling Mrs. Watson, 'don't you know?' Where did she get that, anyway?"

Lucy laughed. Her first real laugh since she got news of her father. It was cathartic. "From what I hear, Mrs. Watson, a native Kentuckian, picked it up when she married a Canadian. I guess the phrase stuck." The strict, high school business teacher knew everything there was to know about typing the perfect document, and she was exceedingly strict when it came to the English language. It was one of Lucy's favorite things about the lady.

They stared into the gas fireplace for a few minutes, resting and thinking. "I'm all alone, Sarah. No Dad, Grandmommy living in Atlanta, no other family around, you getting married and living in another state."

"I know. Have you thought about what you're going to do? You'll have this house."

Lucy looked around, her eyes lingering on this and that family picture or piece of art. "It's home, but it's not, you know?" A tear ran down her cheek and dropped onto her hand. "And tomorrow, after the funeral, it'll be full of people."

TOM AND JARED sat on the front porch, out of the way of family and friends who had come to pay their last respects to Mr. Atwood Dixon.

"Some house, huh?" Tom had to say something. The silence was killing him.

"He speaks." Jared chuckled. "Yeah, it's nice. Surprised?"

"A little. What am I doing here?"

Jared leaned forward. "You're here because Lucy's father died, and she's someone you care about. Don't you?"

Jared's level stare unnerved Tom. "I think Lucy would probably rather I hadn't come." Tom looked down at his hands, clasped between his knees.

"Why?"

"Maybe because I haven't talked to her since she left South Carolina last July?"

"Wondered when you would tell me. Sarah was wondering about that too."

"I mean, look at this place. You've seen where I grew up."

Jared looked at Tom, one eyebrow cocked. "Yeah. Pretty bad. An antebellum house full of family history, your grandparents next door, cousins and aunts and uncles in and out all the time, and parents who were more focused on raising good kids than on making money. Rough life."

"Well, they're not having much fun now."

"I know. But you've made sure your mom doesn't want for anything, and you're there for her. And someday, when Ms. Right comes along, she'll be right there at your side, loving your family as much as you do."

"Don't you think that's asking a lot? It's like asking them to marry not only you but your family."

"Hey, I'm marrying Sarah's family. I think I fell in love with them at almost the same time as Sarah."

Sarah chose that moment to step out the screen door. "I'm sure my brother-in-law will be delighted to hear it." She leaned down to meet Jared's lips in a quick kiss. "I missed you guys."

"How's Lucy?" Tom didn't want to revisit the previous line of discussion if he didn't have to.

"Wondering when you're going to address the issue of not calling her since she's been home. Eight months, I believe?" Sarah straightened and put her hands on her hips as she gave him a pointed look.

Jared arched a brow toward his friend. "Straight for the jugular. You can get away with a lot, but not if you're messing with a girl's best friend. Fair warning." He reached for Sarah's hand and kissed it. "I think I'm going to see if there's any more of your mom's potato salad."

"Do you have to?" Tom blanched a little at the idea of being left alone with Sarah.

"You're a big boy. She doesn't bite too hard." Jared's wink through the screen didn't make Tom feel any better. The slap of the wooden door was like a nail on his coffin. Which was a very bad analogy, considering the circumstances.

"Sarah—"

"Tom, I don't want to butt in, but—"

He held his hands up. "Let me start over. Sarah, I didn't want to lead her on."

"What do you mean? She liked you, Tom. She really did. Probably still does."

"I liked her too. Still do. But you know about my family. They need me. Mom—"

"Your mother, who I love dearly, would be furious at you for even thinking that her needs would keep you from finding the one God has for you. Isn't that a little short-sighted?"

"Sarah, look at this place. I can't compete with this."

"Who's asking you to?"

His thumb pointed to the doorway. "All those people in there."

THE GRAND HALLWAY was empty of guests. Grandmommy hugged Lucy once more before heading upstairs. "I knew your daddy was a good man, but it does my heart good to know how much people thought of him."

"It helps, doesn't it? I didn't know a lot of the people from work, but nearly the whole church was here. Brother Mike did a good job with the funeral, didn't he?"

"For a young un', he did a fine job. I could tell he loved Atwood." She kissed her granddaughter. "Don't stay up too late, you hear? Your friends are here to comfort you, not wear you out."

"Don't worry. We can sleep in tomorrow. You get some rest. Love you, Grandmommy." A tear rolled down her cheek about the time she smiled.

"Love you, too, baby. You think about what I said earlier."

"I will. Sleep well." Lucy watched as her grandmother ascended the stairs.

Lucy rubbed her arms. It wasn't chilly, but the friction felt good. Her eyes on the floor, she startled when she looked up to see Tom standing in the doorway.

"Are you okay?" His eyes bored into hers and she couldn't look away. The look in his eyes . . . it was almost like pain. Why would he feel hurt? He was the one who had broken off contact. She was the one mourning the loss of her father.

She twitched her eyebrows, irritated at the question. "I guess I'm as well as can be expected. What about you?"

"I'm sorry, Lucy. I really am."

"For what?" Her chin went up a bit in defiance, every bit of her five-foot-two frame on alert. She would not let her small stature take away from being in charge of the situation. Not this time. "Are you sorry that my father is dead and you never had a chance to meet him, or that you let me think you . . . liked me and then didn't call or even email me in eight months?"

He looked down at his feet, put his hands in his pockets, and took a deep breath before looking her in the eye. "Yes."

Her chin quivered. Why now? Those stupid overactive tear ducts. You'd think they'd be depleted by now. She could feel her face getting hotter and took a deep breath. She didn't want to meet his eyes, but he didn't look away again. "Where are Jared and Sarah?"

"They're in the kitchen fixing snacks. She said you had hardly eaten today."

"Who had time?" She stared at him, unsure what the glint in his eye meant.

"Well, you do, now. Time to let us take care of you." He caught the tear before it made it halfway down her cheek.

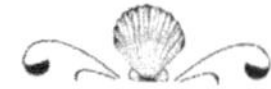

LUCY JUMPED when the doorbell rang. 9:15. Who would be stopping by at this hour? Everyone knew this was a house of mourning. Sarah flew past, aiming for the door.

"I don't want the doorbell to wake up your grandmother."

She couldn't have missed Tom's tender ministrations. Feeling her face flare up once again, she stepped back, her eyes on Tom's.

"Thank you. I need to see who it is. Maybe—"

"I know. I'll be here."

A male voice came through the doorway, and Lucy's eyes widened then closed in defeat. It was Ben. Why now, Lord?

"Lucy!" He strode toward Lucy, ignoring Tom and Sarah. Jared came into the hallway in time to see him grab Lucy in a bear hug. "We got back tonight, and I just heard. You should have called me."

"You were in the middle of Land Between the Lakes. You know there's no service there." Lucy frowned as she stepped back. "Um, Ben Maxwell, you know Sarah. This is her fiancé,

Jared Benton, and a family friend, Tom Livingston. They're from South Carolina."

Ben shook hands with the two men. "So this is the guy who convinced Sarah to leave the good old hometown?" He put his arm around Lucy's shoulder and pulled her to him in a good-natured hug as he kissed her forehead. "I'm hoping to convince Miss Dixon here to stay in hers."

Lucy caught a glimpse of Tom's face. He was pale. Honestly. Like he expected her to pine away for him for eight months. Eight months! Ben was a nice guy. A really nice guy. He was a member of her church, sang in the choir, helped little old ladies across the street, and had been promoted to head football coach. She missed a little of the conversation, stewing, as it were, on the motivation behind Tom's coming to her father's funeral.

"Congratulations, Ben. I know it's always been your dream to be a head coach." Sarah kept glancing at Lucy.

"Yeah. That's why I'm only now finding out about Mr. Dixon's accident. I was with the team at survival camp. Kind of a bonding thing, you know."

Bonding. She thought that was what had happened between Tom and her on the boardwalk of Myrtle Beach. It was one kiss, little more than a peck on the cheek. One kiss can tell a girl a lot about a person.

Especially if it's the kiss to which you compare every kiss you've ever had and the others all come up short.

# CHAPTER TWO

*May*

"You're sure you won't stay here with me?" Elizabeth Dixon's eyes looked sad but not surprised. "You know you're welcome."

The tears wanted to stay on the surface. Aggravating things. Surely, soon they would be dried up? "I know, Grandmommy. I think it's time to be out on my own. I'm almost twenty-nine years old, you know. Practically an old maid." She liked to kid her grandmother to see her bristle.

"Not one of my grandchildren will call themselves a spinster. Marriage isn't the only estate to achieve, you know. Why I was past thirty when I . . ."

Lucy laughed at her little Bantam hen of a grandmother. She liked to think Grandmommy was where she got what she liked to call "grit."

"I'm messing with you, and you know it. I'll miss you. Are you sure you feel like coming over to Litchfield Beach for the wedding?"

Grandmommy patted Lucy on the cheek. "I wouldn't miss it for the world. Sarah's been the sister you should have had."

"I'll come back for a visit after the wedding. Promise."

"I'm counting on it. I love you so much. You know that, don't you?" The elderly woman looked deeply into her lone chick's eyes, sad in the realization that they both were alone, together.

"I love you too." She kissed her grandmother on the cheek and hugged her tightly, willing herself to push the tears back in. Enough. "I'd better go, or I'll be late getting to Sarah's. It's already past one."

"Be careful. And call me when you get there or if you get sleepy along the way."

"You know I never get sleepy driving."

"It's been a long week. There's always a first time. Humor me?"

Lucy smiled at her fiercely independent grandmother putting on the traditional grandmother role. "I will. And you, no doing anything crazy like jumping out of an airplane or climbing a mountain, okay?"

Elizabeth Dixon winked. "You never know. Us old people have to get our excitement where we can, you know."

WHEN LUCY GOT about two and a half hours down the road to Augusta, Georgia, right on the state line between Georgia and South Carolina, she almost grinned. The weight of the events of the last few weeks began to lift off her shoulders.

"Thank You, God. I've been giving You the silent treatment, haven't I?" Her lips twisted a little, embarrassed at her own behavior. "I know Dad's there with You and that it's a much better place than down here, but did You have to leave me alone, without my father?"

Unwanted tears were returning, and she gently hit the steering wheel of her sky blue 1964 ½ Mustang, her dad's labor of love for her. "No. I will not cry anymore. And I won't be angry.

"But You know I'm angry, and deep down, I blame You a little bit. You could have saved him, Lord. I know he was used to save others, but You could have saved him."

She let the tears fall and began taking deep breaths as she pulled into the first rest area east of the South Carolina line.

"Why, God? Why didn't You save him?" She sat in the driver's seat, parked well away from other traveling motorists as her dad had taught her to do, and rolled down her windows to allow the soft Southern air to wash over her.

As much as she knew God loved her and that He loved her father, she also knew bad things happened to good people. After all, who was better than His son, Jesus? And what happened to Him?

She closed her eyes and thought about her dad. His life was a sacrifice. He was all she had, and it was snatched away from her.

But she had a Heavenly Father, didn't she?

"Forgive me, Father, but sometimes all I want is someone I can touch and feel and joke around with, You know? Somebody like my dad."

Enough. This conversation, albeit with God, would have to continue another day. She wanted peace. She wanted comfort. She looked around the rest area: families picnicking for supper underneath the shelters, a large building holding restrooms, brochures, and an information desk. A vending machine area. Lucy knew what she wanted, more than anything else.

She wanted a Coke and a candy bar.

"Jared! Look at this one!"

Sarah held the shell up, beckoning with the other hand for Jared to come to her. He jogged to her, taking the shell from her with a smile.

The wind had kicked up in the night, making the surf rough and the cleanest beach on the Eastern Seaboard a little more marginal than usual. There was more trash and seaweed littering the beach, but the shells had arrived as well. Shell seekers were out and about, hoping for that one pristine conch shell that seemed always to elude them in this part of the country. Sometimes, when the tides were ideal, a perfect shell was bestowed upon a fortunate early riser.

Sarah Jane Crawford smiled as she thought about her life since an eventful summer changed it completely. An unexpected inheritance had brought her to Litchfield Beach, South Carolina, and an unexpected love kept her there.

"Nice one, Sarah." He turned it in his hands to inspect it.

Oliver, Sarah's dog, tried to sneak up on a sea gull on the beach. The bird was worrying a dead jellyfish, slinging the dried animal, making Oliver think twice before playing tug-of-war with the seagull's lunch.

Frowning a little, she looked closer at the imperfections of the shell. Taking it back, she pointed at a line on the broad part of the shell. "It's cracked . . . and the tip is broken."

He laughed as she talked herself out of her excitement. "If you want perfect, I know a nice little gift shop down the road where they import shells from the Caribbean."

"Very funny," she said, twisting her lips in a smile.

"Hey. I know something that is perfect." Jared dropped the shell at their feet as he pulled her closer to him.

She arched an eyebrow at him. "And what might that be?"

"You."

"Oh, Jared, you're so silly sometimes." She focused her attention on his shirt buttons to avoid his eyes.

"I'm not silly, I'm in love."

"I love you too." She eased her glance up to his face and smiled as delicious embarrassment welled up inside her. There was a flutter in her stomach each time she heard him declare his love for her and wondered if she would ever be immune to it. She hoped not.

He grinned. "I could get used to getting up early and spending Saturday on the beach with you."

Sarah sighed as she wrapped her arms around him and snuggled into his arms. "Mmm, yes. It's been a long week. I'm glad Lucy's coming."

"Me too. I was afraid I was gonna get roped into choices like variations in the color pink, tulle versus satin, and all that."

"I wouldn't do it to you. You're wonderful, and you have an amazing eye for décor, for a man, but I saw the glazed-over look you had when it came to picking out china patterns for the wedding registry." Sarah shook her head with a smile. "I'll let you decide the important things, like the honeymoon. Gonna tell me where we're going?"

"Nope. It's a surprise. Tom doesn't even know." Jared looked at his watch. "What time is Lucy coming? I wanted to go by and see if there's anything I can do for Tom's mom."

"She'll be here by four or five, I think. Do you have time to buy a lady some breakfast before you go?"

"I could probably be convinced." As he bent to pick up the shell she had dropped at their feet, she called out to Oliver. The Schnauzer-mix seemed glad to leave the seagulls behind.

Dog and shell in tow, Sarah was quiet for a few moments as they walked to her little beachside cottage where Jared had left his car. She was examining the shell Jared had handed her. "I think I'll put this shell on my coffee table."

"I thought you said it was cracked" His eyebrow arched.

She shrugged her shoulders and gave him a little grin. "I know. I guess I need a reminder, every once in a while, that beauty isn't in perfection. It's in how you turn out after you've been tossed about in a stormy sea. Know what I mean? It kind of, I don't know, speaks to me."

"Lucy's sure been tossed about, hasn't she? Losing her dad so suddenly."

"I know. Atwood was fun. He let Lucy and me do whatever we wanted to at their house, within reason. I admit, I was a little jealous, but now? Bless her. To be all alone. I mean, when she gets married, who will be there for her?"

"You will. You're a good woman, Sarah." There was a mist in his eyes as he smiled at her. He had been holding her hand, and as they made their way to the house to retrieve Sarah's shoes, he stopped her on the patio for another kiss. He wiped away the stray tear running down her cheek.

"And don't you forget it, mister," she whispered, pressing close to him as she tickled him in the ribs before turning to slip inside the door of the pink-clad beach house.

"You'll pay for that, missy."

She winked at him as she reached for the door handle. "I should hope so."

"DID I ever tell you about the assistant football coach back home?" Sarah looked at Jared over her coffee cup. They had enjoyed their breakfast. After a week of Danish, toast, and cereal, both Sarah and Jared were ready for the traditional Southern fare of eggs, bacon, biscuits and gravy.

"Are you going to eat your grits?" He had been eyeing the small bowl ever since the waitress brought their meal.

"Which do you want, the scoop or the grits?" Sarah tilted her head.

"Both. I met the guy, remember? At Lucy's house. As for the grits, I wanted to claim them before they were taken away."

Sarah giggled at the look on his face. It was a mixture of jealousy and desire. Jealousy there had ever been an assistant foot-ball coach in her life and desire for her grits. Wrinkling her nose, she said, "You know I won't eat them. When I told her I wanted grits, I was thinking of you."

"Thank you kindly, Miss Crawford," he said, reaching over to get the grits as the waitress arrived to take empty plates and refill their coffee cups. "I will take that as a compliment. Now, about this muscle-bound-has-been football player?"

Twisting her lips at his description, she said, "His name is Ben, and Lucy was sure she had finally found a match for me."

"Ben," Jared said, as if weighing his name to test his mettle. "Hmm."

Sarah laughed. "I met Ben about two years ago, when he got the job of P.E. teacher and assistant football coach at our high school. Lucy couldn't wait to throw us together."

"And did she?" he asked, arching an eyebrow and looking somewhat disgruntled.

Sarah shrugged her shoulders slightly. "We went out a few times after Marc and I broke up."

"And?"

"I told Lucy that jocks and chorus geeks didn't go together."

"Why not?"

Sarah could tell Jared was interested in her reasoning. He gazed at her, seeming to forget the cooling grits in front of him.

"Eat your grits. They'll get cold." Sarah smiled tenderly. "He was one of 'those guys.' The ones that dated the cheerleaders. Not mousy musicians like me."

Jared snorted into his coffee. "What did Lucy say to that?"

She rolled her eyes. "She said I always sell myself short, I didn't have to know a man from birth to date him, and that I should go out on dates to 'test the waters,' so to speak." She shrugged and stirred her coffee.

"Well, Lucy was right about one thing," Jared said, staring at her across the table, a little frown on his face.

"Which one?" She was curious. He wasn't reacting the way she expected.

"You do sell yourself short. Why wouldn't any man be proud to have you by his side?"

"Jared, I—"

"Not to belabor a point, but, well, at one time, I would have been considered a 'jock.' Would that have kept you from going out with me, if we'd met in high school or college or if I'd grown up in your home town?"

Sarah twisted her lips ruefully as she considered what he was saying. She had been prejudiced, as an adult, in the same way a high school student would be prejudiced. "I don't know. I really don't know," she said in surprise.

Jared grinned at her, a teasing glint in his eyes. "Well, it's a good thing I'm not just a 'jock' anymore. Who knew girls could be so particular."

Leaning her chin on her hand, she gave in to the contented sigh she had been trying to hold in, lest he thought her a simpering fool of a girl. "Lucy may or may not have been right, but I was right too."

"About?"

"When God showed me the man he had for me, I knew it."

"Even if you hadn't known him from birth?"

"Definitely."

Jared studied her face. She wondered why he had never asked why her engagement ended. She knew it didn't matter to him, but she still had moments of uncertainty, worried that it was all too good to be true. That's where faith came in. She was still working on that, and probably always would.

Jared finished his grits as Sarah sipped on her warmed-up coffee. They were quiet for a few minutes, and as he scraped the last remaining morsel of grits onto his spoon, he looked up with a look of contentment on his face.

"I think that will keep me going for a little while." He laid his napkin on the table beside his empty plate and picked up the check. "Ready?"

"I think so. Can we drive by Huntington Beach before you take me home?" She grinned and batted her eyelashes.

"You want to see Atalaya."

"What girl doesn't want to memorize every inch of her wedding venue? Actually, I brought my tape measure, and I want to take a few measurements of the water tower in the center of the courtyard. I'm still pondering where I want the focal point."

He grinned and touched her forehead. "You have that little line between your eyes. I'm still up for eloping, if it would make you worry less about the details."

"Good grief, no. If we did, I'd be worrying about all the people we cheated out of seeing us get married. Our mothers would never let us forget it."

"I know." He put some bills on the table for a tip and pulled Sarah's chair out for her before going to the counter to pay the bill. "I wasn't serious. Okay, maybe a little, but I know my mother, and I don't think she would ever forgive us. Atalaya it is."

AFTER WALKING around Atalaya Castle and along Huntington Beach, Sarah was quiet. Jared pulled her down on the sand beside him and squeezed her hand. "What's on your mind?"

"Work. Wedding. Open House. You. Stuff." She leaned her head on his shoulder. It wasn't stuff she was thinking about. It was those doubts that crept in every time she let them.

"I'm a good listener of stuff."

She smiled and hid her face on his sleeve. "I know." She sat up and looked into his face. "Sometimes when the stress-level goes up, the doubt-level goes up too."

"What kind of doubts?"

"Name one. No, not about you. I've never had fewer doubts in my life than about you. I mean, even with Marc . . ."

"You know, you've never told me why you broke off your engagement. You mentioned you wanted to be anywhere but Summerville and that he got married last summer."

Sarah looked out at the pounding surf, seeming to look through the tourists and locals enjoying a sunny day on the beach. "Well, to begin with, I didn't break off the engagement. He did."

"You've got to be kidding me."

"Before you start in on him, it was his wisdom that brought me here." She looked at him and shrugged her shoulders. "We had always known one another. We dated a little in high school and went to different colleges. When we both ended up back at home, we started going to things together, and before we knew it, we were a couple. We had fun, our parents were friends, and we had church in common. It was easy."

"Too easy. I know how that is." Jared put his arm around her shoulders.

"Exactly. I was happy. I was ready to be married and to have a home of my own. I had a plan, after all. Within five years of graduating from college, I was going to teach, get married, and have my first child."

"You and your lists."

"Yep. Me and my lists. We got along great, and finally, he asked me to marry him. There weren't any fireworks, but I thought it was because we were comfortable together. We were planning on about an eighteen-month engagement and our wedding was going to be perfect."

Jared held her away from him and looked at her closely. "That's crazy. No man wants a long engagement. At least nobody I've known."

She shrugged. "I agree, now. It was crazy. But not. God was looking after us. About six months into our engagement, Marc seemed distant, and he was becoming more insistent with the physical side of our relationship. One night he left, angry when I wouldn't comply. We were engaged. We were going to be married. But I wanted to wait." Tears threatened to fall. "It was horrible. We didn't talk for a week." She leaned her head back on Jared's shoulder.

"He called a few days later and said we needed to talk."

"I'm sorry, Sarah." Jared leaned down and kissed the top of her head.

"He had met someone. He didn't want to cheat on me, but he knew that if he could feel what he did for her, he couldn't marry me. It wouldn't be fair to either of us. I was devastated. He apologized for being aggressive. He was trying to gauge his feelings for me even while he knew it was wrong."

"That was rough."

"Compared to what you went through? It was a blip. At the time it hurt. Still does sometimes."

"When?" Jared's eyes narrowed as he looked at her tenderly.

She hesitated and looked out at the waves. Sometimes his love was more than she could bear, and she had to look away for a moment, to mentally pinch herself to see if this was real. "It made me wonder if I was enough."

"Oh, Sarah. I'm glad he's not here right now." He shook his head in anger.

Her smile widened as she reached up and laced her fingers with his as he tightened the hold he had around her shoulders. "I am too. I want to get past that part of my life."

"How far along were you in the wedding preparations?"

"Not too far. We had set the date and ordered the invitations and picked out the cake. I had ordered my dress but was able to cancel it, thank goodness. The hardest part was facing everyone. Especially at church. Thank goodness for Lucy. She stuck by me like glue."

"I'll bet. Lucy is a good friend."

"She's the best a girl could have. She made me get out and about, helped me find and move into my house, and fixed me up with the assistant coach." With the last phrase, she poked him in the ribs and giggled when he jumped.

"You could have gone all day without mentioning that again." Jared pulled her into his arms for a tender kiss. It reverenced her, but teased, as well. When they pulled apart, her eyes were shining.

Sarah looked at her phone when she heard the "ding" of notification. A text from Lucy. "**In SC. Stopped for a break. See you @5**."

She looked up at Jared. "Lucy's on schedule. Check us out for supper?"

"Who's cooking?" He winked at her.

"Funny guy. I'll have peanut butter on hand if it's not up to your standards." She raised an eyebrow, daring him to say something.

"I will look forward to a feast of culinary greatness."

# CHAPTER THREE

$\mathcal{A}$ police detective in a small tourist town was not what Tom had envisioned for himself when he graduated from high school. His original plan was to join the Air Force, much to the dismay of Jared's father, an Army man through and through. He would graduate from Clemson, do a stint in the Air Force, then join either the FBI or NCIS. Either would do. It would marry his love of organization and leadership to crime-fighting, but on a higher level than he could ever hope to achieve, even in the state police or state-level bureau of investigation systems.

He drove down the boulevard that was State Road 17 that ran from Pawley's Island to past Murrells Inlet, observing the travelers rubbernecking as they looked for a good place to eat along the main drag. Tapping on his steering wheel, he thought of Lucy. She was arriving today. Might already be here.

And what was he going to do about it?

Nothing.

He'd go to his ancestral home, make sure his sister Charlotte had plenty of groceries, check on his mom, and get the yard mowed. Typical Saturday for him.

At least for the last year it had been. There wasn't as much to mow these days, fortunately or unfortunately.

He drove up the gravel drive, more sand than gravel, to the old house. It wasn't so much "broken-down aristocracy" as the kind of house regular people lived in. If you lived in 1854. He was proud of the house and embarrassed by it at the same time. His mother was always a spotless housekeeper, but these days things always looked a little disheveled, as if no one had been home in a long time. His mother's housekeeping skills gave his sister little hope of ever feeling like she measured up. She always joked that in the housekeeping department, Tom was their mother's favorite daughter. This only pleased him when they had a bake-off and his biscuits turned out taller and fluffier than hers. That was before the changes came to their happy household.

It looked like he was going to have to get the trimming done today.

Arriving at the house, Jared was finishing putting the large, zero-turn mower on the trailer behind his SUV. Tom approached his best friend. "What's going on here, bud?"

Jared climbed down off the trailer and sat down on the side bar. "I had a couple of hours to kill and thought I'd give you a hand."

Tom raked his hand over his face. "Aw, Jared, you know you didn't—"

"I know, Tom. I also know Sarah's going nuts getting ready for Lucy and her family coming, and I thought the better part of valor was to help you out instead of being in the way."

"Or getting roped into something like china patterns?" Tom grinned. He and Jared had been friends since high school, and nothing either of them had been through could change that. "Thanks, Jared. Did you see Mom?"

"I did. She fussed, too, but when I told her they were trying to make me decide which shade of pink tulle would be best for the underskirt of the punch table, she laughed. She seems better today."

"Want something to drink?"

"I wouldn't turn it down. I saw Charly earlier. She said she had something to tell you."

They walked side by side onto the wrap-around porch and to the side door.

Concern washed over him. His little sister had recently graduated from high school, and since the death of their father, they had been so busy grieving and keeping the home fires burning that there had been a wall between them. Being a man didn't help. When she needed a dad, all she had was a brother. He knew the day would come when she would leave them. And then who would help Mom? And who was he to expect her to stay?

"Tom!" Charlotte Livingston's long, blonde hair whipped around as she turned, bowl in hand. Setting it down, she wiped her hands on a nearby towel and held her finger up. "Don't move." She ran into the other room.

"Okay." Tom looked at Jared. "Did she say what it was about?"

"Not a clue. Seems pretty excited, though."

"Yeah. Wonder how much that excitement is gonna cost me?"

"Thomas Sumter Livingston, it's not going to cost you one red cent, you hear me." She had entered the room behind him, and Tom had the grace to look sheepish.

"Sorry, Charly. I was kidding. You know that."

"No, and I'm in too good a mood to let you mess with me now. Look at this." She handed him a piece of paper on Coastal Carolina University letterhead. "Read it."

He took the paper, surprised that it was addressed to their mother.

"They're offering you a full ride?" He looked at her, his

mouth slack. "To study Special Education? I thought you wanted to go into broadcasting?"

"I've been thinking a lot about what I want to do with my life, especially since Mom started losing her sight. I started noticing kids at school having trouble with different things. Sometimes they have learning disabilities, and other times it's a health issue. Like the girl who graduated with me, with MS, or the guy a year behind me who got hit with a baseball, it messed with his vision and hearing, and had to have special accommodations while he healed up."

"But—"

"I know, you thought I wanted to go to Clemson, like you, big brother."

"Well, yeah." He peered at her closely. Had his baby sister turned into a woman overnight?

"Listen. I need to be here. Mom needs me. You need me. I can commute to Myrtle Beach every day if I need to and be home in the evenings to help Mom. I can't just leave."

Jared looked like he felt a little out of place. "Listen, I'll—"

"Don't you move, buster. I need you to take my side against him." Charlotte linked her arm in his and squeezed. "I have two big brothers, you know. How I would have survived childhood without both of you, I'll never know."

"I'm not going to argue about this. One question. Are you sure?" Tom leaned both hands on the kitchen table and bent to her level, looking her straight in the eyes.

"I'm sure."

Jared shook his head and blinked his eyes. "Hey, if there's anything I've learned, especially in the last year, when a lady is sure, you don't mess with her." He cut his eyes to Charlotte and gave her a wink, grinning when she smiled back.

"Does Mom know?"

"Not yet. I wanted to run it by you first."

"Come here." Tom held out his arms, and Charlotte went into

them, hugging her brother around the waist as he cradled her head against his shoulder. At five foot four inches, she was a full foot shorter than he.

"Let's go see Mom."

"But, sweetie, I thought your dream was to be on TV?" Mary Ann Livingston leaned forward from her seat on the sofa, her hands wringing together, confused.

"I know, Mom, but I've learned a lot the last few years."

"You can't live your life around what's happened to me, sweetheart. My being blind doesn't mean you have to sacrifice your dreams to stay and take care of me. I'll be fine. I'm getting around better all the time."

"Mama, you don't understand." Charlotte took her mother's hands and squeezed them. "I'm doing this because I think it's what God wants me to do, not because it's what I think you want me to do or need me to do. He's in control, not me, not you, and not Tom."

"It's just such a shock."

"I know. To tell you the truth, the last few news anchors they've hired on the local station have made me rethink that whole line of work. I mean, I'm smarter than that, you know?"

The huffy look on her face made Tom burst into laughter. The sound of his laughing made their mother smile.

"Well, that's never been in question." Mary Ann kept Charlotte's hand in hers and reached for Tom's. "Jared, if I had a third hand, I'd pull you in here, too, you know."

"I know, Ms. Livingston. You've got two great kids."

Tom looked at his friend and sent him a crooked grin when he noticed the mist in his eyes. He knew Jared missed his folks. But at least he had them to miss. He would miss his dad every day of his life.

"I guess this means we prepare you for commuting instead of dorm life?"

"I guess so." Charlotte stopped and shook her head. "Wow. It's really happening. I've been doing so much research online of different programs and this one seemed to fill the bill. I can help kids or adults, and Mom, do you know what the best part is?"

"What's that?" Mary Ann's sightless eyes didn't move, but her eyebrows quirked up in curiosity.

"I get to try out all the vision accommodations on you!"

She patted her daughter's hand and grinned ruefully, her dry wit floating to the surface. "Well, dear, at least you're not training to be a brain surgeon."

# CHAPTER FOUR

*L*ucy drove up to Sarah's little, pink beach bungalow and breathed a sigh of relief. She'd been involved in her own version of Jacob's wrestle with the Lord for the last four hours, and she was ready to change topics.

As soon as she stepped onto the porch, Sarah flung the door open and wrapped her in a fierce hug. "You're here! You're finally here!"

"I am, and I'm beat." Her stomach growled loudly. "I guess I don't have to tell you what my next question is?"

"I've got a chicken casserole on the stove, waiting for you." Sarah went with Lucy to retrieve her things from the car. "Didn't you stop between here and Atlanta?"

Lucy snorted. "Only once. Cola and chocolate break at a rest stop."

"That definitely does not count. Put your stuff in the guest room and come to the kitchen. I'll get you fixed up."

"I have one question."

"What's that, Luce?"

"Who are you and what have you done with my non-cooking best friend?"

JARED ARRIVED as Sarah was putting the casserole on the table. As he was leaning in to kiss his fiancée, Lucy walked into the kitchen with a sigh and grinned.

"Well, look what the cat dragged in."

"I followed my nose. How are you, Lucy?"

"I'm fine, and it's probably more likely you followed your stomach. Am I right?"

"You are. You know, once Sarah started practicing on me, she found out she was a pretty good cook."

Sarah looked pointedly at Lucy. "I'll never be a Lydia Mitchell."

Lucy shrugged and shook her head sadly. "Who will?"

Jared raised his eyebrows, and the girls burst out laughing. "Who is Lydia Mitchell?"

"She's the home economics teacher where Sarah and I used to work. Did you know she's dating Ben again?"

Sarah stopped laughing. "Okay, hold on. First, I know I used to work at Summerville High, but I thought you still did?"

Lucy had the grace to look sheepish. "Well, with all the stuff to do with Dad's estate, I decided to take a leave this year. I haven't decided if I'm going back or not. I have a lot of thinking and praying to do."

"I understand. But there was a second thing. What about Ben? When we were there for the funeral, I thought you and Ben were dating?" Sarah narrowed her eyes. "I know Tom thought so too."

Lucy chewed on her bottom lip before answering. "Ben was great. Don't get me wrong. I missed you terribly, and then there was the whole 'Tom' thing, so we dated for a little while. After Dad died, I broke it off. I knew it wasn't going anywhere, and I didn't want to lead him on. And I could tell he was too much of a traditional male to put up with me. I mean, I'm not going to cook two pounds of meat every day, along with potatoes and gravy. Honestly. Can you imagine what a diet like that would do to me?"

Sarah laughed out loud. "He does like to eat, doesn't he? Well, maybe Lydia can drag him down the path to matrimony and healthy eating. But are you okay with it? I mean, you broke up with him, right?"

Lucy's smile was tender as she looked into the concerned eyes of her friends. "Oh yes. I'm great with it. After Dad died . . . well, I knew it wouldn't work. That's all."

"That's all?" Sarah glanced at her sideways.

Lucy avoided Sarah's probing gaze. She grabbed a napkin and put it in her lap as Sarah took her seat.

"That's all."

Tom wiped his hands on a greasy rag. The oil in Charly's car had been changed and the tires checked. He shook his head.

There was no way he was going to let his little sister commute to CCU in the rust-bucket she affectionately called "Rachel." Yes, it was only 35 miles, but a 1978 Olds Caprice, while great at hauling teenagers up and down the road to the beach, was not the most economical or safe mode of transportation to his way of thinking. His dad would laugh at him. "Drive it into the ground. You won't wear this baby out!"

Tom grinned as he thought of his fun-loving dad. Hayden Livingston kept them all laughing, no matter the circumstance. He wouldn't have thought twice about sending his youngest chick to school with a 250,000-mile-vehicle.

His attention shifted to the side bay of the shed. There she was, his dad's 1956 sky-blue Ford Thunderbird. It hadn't been moved or started since his dad died. It was his "courtin' car," he had said, and was old when he got it and started working on it.

He always said it would be a lifetime project to get it back in shape to drive, but he was up for it. Little did he know his lifetime was shorter than that of the classic automobile.

But he wasn't his dad, and he was the man of the family, now. Tinkering and rebuilding the engine on his sister's car was not a priority for him. Maybe he was too protective, but his mother was in no position to advise him. Tonight he was going to start doing research. His sister might be attached to "Rachel," but she was going to be replaced with a newer model. Maybe a "Monica," or a "Caitlin?"

"Tom? You out there?" His mother called from the back porch.

"Yeah, Mom, do you need me?"

"No, but come in when you get done, please?"

"Yes, ma'am. Be there in a minute."

Tom sighed. He loved his mother, and she wanted so badly to be independent. The blindness that gradually overtook her weighed on her mental state as well as her physical coordination and general health. Dad could have handled it much better. Making Mom smile was what his dad loved to do more than anything. The disease that took her vision in tandem with the loss of her husband had taken the smile away except for brief glimpses. More often, yes, but not often enough.

He dropped the heavy hood down on the front of the car and pushed the side down that tended not to catch ever since the minor fender-bender Charly had been involved in at the Food Lion parking lot where she worked part-time. He placed the containers of used motor oil in a box in the trunk of his car for disposal and pitched the used filter in the trash when he took the funnel to the garage. Everywhere he looked, Dad had left his mark: the outlines of tools on the pegboard, all the tools here and there on the bench below it. He would get to it eventually. It messed with his idea of tidiness, but at least it was, for the most part, out-of-sight, and out-of-mind.

Jared's helping with the mowing was a God-send. Since he didn't have to mow, he was able to work on the car. As he made his way to the house, he surveyed the property in the glow of a setting sun. It was pretty. The columns on the front of the house might be peeling in places, but in this light, in the lengthening shadows of evening, they looked like a movie-magic image of Tara.

"Thank You, Lord. You gave me a great childhood here. You gave me a family that pointed me to You. Give me the strength to give myself up for You and for them." His sentimental smile faded when a fleeting thought, or was it a God-whisper, came to him.

Lucy.

Did he have to give up everything?

"MOM, YOU CAN'T BE SERIOUS." Tom sat at the kitchen table with his mother, his mouth hanging open in shock. "I mean . . . how long . . . we can't . . ." He knew he was sputtering, but this was out of the blue.

"Tom. I've given this a lot of thought. I know, this is my home place. I can't hang on to it for sheer sentiment's sake."

Sell the house? The house that once had been in the middle of a 300-acre plantation? Small by plantation standards, but a plantation nonetheless. Part of this house was built before the Revolutionary War.

"There has to be another way." Tom knew his mother couldn't see the pained expression on his face, but he could see the one on hers.

"I know, sweetie. It's been in my family for a long time. I don't want a house to own me, or you. Property can be a blessing or a curse." Mom groped toward Tom's voice, reaching for his hand. A touch. Something to ground them both. "I've prayed ever since your daddy died, and my sight started going. At first I thought staying here would be easier because I know every inch of the property in the dark. I thought my sight would come back. I thought God wouldn't take away something else so important to me. I was wrong."

"Mama, you've got me to depend on. I can help with the place."

She squeezed his hand. "I know, and you're doing a great job. But you know what? I'd rather have grandchildren to love on than a big, old, drafty house."

Tom was glad his mother couldn't see the red he sensed infusing his complexion. "There's plenty of time for that."

"Don't give me that. I know exactly how old you are. To the minute, if you give me time to do some figurin'. I've sensed something different about you lately."

"You're imagining things. When would I have time to find a wife with my job and . . ." He stopped. He was about to say "and two places to see to."

"Exactly. That's why Charly and I have been talking."

Tom stood up from the table. "Behind my back?"

"Yes. And sit back down. We've been talking behind your back because you would keep this place going and die an old man with nobody and nothing like old Alex Crawford did. That is not what I want for my baby boy."

Tom snorted. Alex Crawford. Sarah Crawford's unknown uncle who left them an estate and business partnership worth millions. Old Alex had done all right for himself and blessed his extended family to boot.

"Money doesn't buy happiness. You know that."

His mother sat there and waited for Tom's breathing to even out.

"Okay, what have you and Charly been plotting behind my back?"

"You make it sound like we're planning a murder. You are so much like your daddy." Another wistful smile lit her face.

If giving up the home place of her own ancestors would put a smile on her face, who was he to argue?

"Well, thank you for the compliment. Maybe one day I'll be as laid-back as Dad. He could make everything seem right with a grin and a wink, couldn't he?" He squeezed his mother's hand.

"I think it's time to sell the place, and Charlotte and I can find a smaller house, on one level, that would be easier for me to take care of. I don't want Charly tied to this place either."

"I don't think she minds."

"Not now, but what about when she meets 'Mr. Right?' He might not be ready to take on a mother-in-law and the family history."

Tom pulled his mother's hand to his lips. "I don't think she would marry a man who didn't appreciate her heritage, and yours."

"Face it. It's a heritage of broken-down aristocracy. We never recovered from Reconstruction, and then the farm depression and the Great Depression had us losing more than we could ever gain. Now we're down to this house and twenty acres. Not much to show for a plantation, is it?"

"Have you thought about where you'd like to live?" As his mother perked up, he laughed. "Of course you have. Why did I have any doubt?"

"Don't worry; we're not moving in with you."

"You could, you know." Tom was dead serious. He was prepared to give it all up. The dream. The family. Look at Paul in the New Testament. He never married, and in fact, told the churches in his letters it was better not to marry, if possible.

But could he? Into his reverie, his mother's voice came through.

"Charly's been reading me listings from Crawford Real Estate."

"Of course she has. Please tell me you haven't gotten Jared in on this."

"Not yet. We're not that underhanded." Her emphasis admitted her secrecy.

"The jury's out on that. So, condo? Beach house?"

"We're thinking North Litchfield or Murrells Inlet. Maybe one of those 'patio homes?' I know it gets pricier the closer you get to Myrtle Beach, but I don't want Charly to have too much of a drive to school."

"You don't think you would regret it?" He knew how regret could color every aspect of life. It was the last thing his mother needed. "Don't you think you would get bored in a little one-story house and a patio when you're used to all this space?"

"Oh, I don't know. The idea of not worrying about stairs, maintenance? That doesn't sound boring to me." She dipped her head and sighed. When she raised her face toward him, she gave him a gentle smile. "I think I would regret more saddling my children with a burden. You don't think of it as such now, but later, you will. Your daddy was proud to be connected to the place, even by marriage, but unlike Scarlet O'Hara's father, he knew it wasn't 'the land' that was the legacy. It was his children and his faith in his God. There were times even he wished we weren't tied to this place."

Tom considered her words. His father wished for freedom?

"Did you know when your daddy and I were younger, we planned to go into mission work?"

Tom stared as his mother left that bit of information on the table. "What happened?"

"We were living in a little apartment, expecting you, excited about going to seminary to learn how to be missionaries, when we got the news that my daddy had died." She shrugged. "Mama couldn't stand the thought of leaving the house, so we moved in with her, and I'm still here. Oh, we made a good life, and your daddy made the best of it, but there were times I wish I had stood up to my mama and talked sense into her about her situation."

"You mean like I'm trying to do?" Tom looked at his mother with a wry smile. He wondered, sometimes, how much his mother's vision loss affected her understanding dry humor.

"Very funny."

It was apparent that Mom's blindness was not a communication issue between mother and son.

"Tom, my sweet boy." She closed her sightless eyes as she held his strong hands in her slight ones, rubbing the backs with her thumbs. "If I thought it would be a blessing to you or to Charly, I would stay here. I think God's trying to tell me to let go. Let go of all the stuff that makes up what we call life, stuff that isn't real life at all. We think of heritage as something almost spiritual, but the only heritage that counts for eternity is the one we have through our Lord Jesus Christ."

There was silence in the room as Tom looked down at his mother's hands, once strong enough to pick him up and fix whatever was wrong. Now it was up to him to care for her. It was his job, wasn't it? He was the man of the family. He squeezed the slender fingers and sighed.

"Mama, I'm here to take care of you."

"No, son, you're not. I love you, and I depend on you for too many things, but I have to depend on God, not my children. He's got things for me to do, blind or not. And more importantly, to me, He's got things for you to do."

Tom started to speak.

"Son, I've made up my mind. I've been in a funk for too long. I can't see, but I can feel myself coming out of the fog of grief that's ruled me ever since your daddy passed. There's an excitement in me that I haven't felt in a long time. Let me have this. It'll be hard to give up the old place, but you know, now that I can't see, it doesn't really matter where I am. I'll have the memories of this place with me for the rest of my life, as will you and Charly."

"I don't want you waking up one day and regretting it."

Mary Ann smiled. "I won't. I've had regrets in my life. I don't think this will be one of them."

Tom sighed and leaned back in his chair. "All right. Should I call Jared?"

"That would be nice, son. How about we have Jared and Sarah over for dinner, and we can talk about it with them? And doesn't Sarah have her friend here, getting ready for the wedding?"

His heart started beating a little faster. He was glad his mother couldn't see his face that was no doubt getting redder. "Uh, yeah. Sarah might not be able to make it . . ."

"Nonsense. Invite her friend too. I want to meet this girl. Anybody that makes you stammer like a schoolboy must be an interesting person to know."

Tom stared at her. "Mom?"

She smiled. "Seriously, Tom. You're going to have to get a little smoother if I'm ever going to have grandchildren."

# CHAPTER FIVE

"Would you relax? You're going as my best friend, not a woman who wants to throttle her son." It was obvious Sarah was trying to pull Lucy out of the nervous state she was in. "Mary Ann is a wonderful lady. You'll like her, and you'll love the house. I can't wait for you to see it."

"I feel weird." Honestly, the nerves had more to do with being with Tom on his home turf than intruding on what seemed to be "family time."

Sarah's phone buzzed, and when she saw the display, her face lit up. Lucy quirked an eyebrow at her friend's bemused expression. "Jared, I presume?"

Sarah nodded as she answered. "Hi, Jared. I'm putting you on speaker."

"Okay. Are you girls ready? I'm about to leave the house."

"Ready when you get here. Lucy's being weird about it."

Lucy glared, which scored her a wrinkled nose from Sarah. She whispered intensely. "I am not."

Jared's snort was heard over the telephone. "Tell her if it helps, Tom's being weird too."

Lucy leaned toward the phone in Sarah's hand and spoke loudly. "It doesn't help."

Sarah laughed. "Never mind her. We'll be on the front porch waiting. Love you!"

She pushed the button to end the call and turned to Lucy. "I think—"

"I know what you think. Let me get my purse. Weird? Humph."

WHEN THEY DROVE up the drive to the Livingston place, Lucy's breath caught. Was this how Sarah felt when she first saw Pilot Oaks? The lengthening shadows gave the house a mysterious, other-worldly look that could have been any time in history. Or at least until two cars and a satellite dish next to the house came into view.

"This is amazing." Lucy was in awe.

"Isn't it? Part of it is pre-Revolutionary War. Much older than Pilot Oaks." Sarah sighed. "I love when a house has such history, and to think that the last two hundred years that history has been tied to Tom's family. I don't know if I could sell it or not."

"Sell? They're going to sell this piece of their family?" Lucy's mind raced with emotions as she compared this to her house in Summerville. It was her home, but it wasn't part of her heritage. This? This was heritage.

"Mary Ann is legally blind, and Tom's sister, Charlotte, is about to start college. It's too much for them to deal with." Jared gave her a sad little smile. "They've never had a lot of money. When Tom's dad, Hayden, died, they realized how little there was."

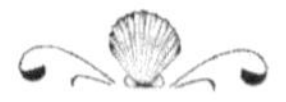

JARED PARKED the car in the drive that circled next to the front walkway. Tom tamped down his nervousness and came out of the house to greet them. Lucy was here, at his ancestral home. What would Mother think of her?

"Come in, come in. Mother's been looking forward to this all week." Tom held the screen door for them. "Charly's outdone herself. Mother talked her completely through pork roast and green bean casserole."

"Tom, honey, is our comp'ny here?" Her erect back and slender frame held pride and breeding, her sightless eyes dim but beautiful.

"Mother, Jared and Sarah are here, and I'd like to introduce you to Lucy Dixon."

Lucy took his mother's hand. "It's a pleasure to meet you, Mrs. Livingston. Thank you for inviting me into your home."

"Oh! You're a little woman like me, aren't you? My daughter and I are both small, and Tom took after my Hayden. Big, strapping men. Handy to have around when you need to reach the top cupboard." Mary Ann gave a little laugh, and her smile transformed her face.

"The women in my family were all taller than me. I must be a throwback."

Mary Ann patted Lucy's hand. "That's all right. It's all about quality, not quantity, right?"

Lucy laughed. "Yes, ma'am, it is. You have a beautiful home."

"Bless you, Lucy. It's a bit much for me now, as you can tell, but in my mother's day? Oh my, it was a showplace." She paused and squeezed Lucy's hand. "I was sorry to hear about your father's passing."

Tom was interested in her interaction with his mother. She looked up and captured his glance, and she blinked as she turned back to his mother. "Thank you. It was sudden."

Tom stopped staring and came to himself. "I think Charly's

got dinner on the table, if you'll join me in the dining room? We pulled out the good stuff for you guys."

Sarah smiled. "You didn't have to go to so much trouble for us. We'd be happy with a paper plate on the front porch."

Mary Ann waved a hand. "Nonsense. We've got this china, and I'm determined to use it while I can. Too many folks have good stuff and they keep it packed away to 'save' it, but I say, use the good stuff and enjoy it." With a gesture, she gathered them to the table and made her way to her seat at the head of the table.

Charlotte brought in the pork roast and set it proudly on the table. After wiping a bit of perspiration from her forehead, she smiled at her brother and their guests. "Welcome to our feast! Oh! You must be Lucy!"

"Nice to meet you, Charlotte?"

"Call me Charly. Everybody does, especially family."

Tom's lips curved in a grin at these two girls together. They were close to the same height. Charlotte's hair was a shade lighter and much longer than Lucy's. When he looked at Lucy, he might be looking at Charly in another ten years.

He seated Lucy at his left at the long table, with Charly across the table on the other side of Mother. It had become second nature to make sure she wanted for nothing, Charly filling her plate and quietly telling her where each item was on her plate, and Tom paying attention to her glass, a dropped napkin, or anything he could help her with. No one would ever know that the beautiful blue eyes weren't taking it all in.

As they finished the meal that everyone proclaimed to be delicious, Charly started clearing the table, Sarah and Lucy working alongside. When they came back in with dessert and coffee, Mother straightened her spine and directed her attention to Jared.

"Jared." She spoke and then paused. She looked emotional as she cleared her throat.

"Yes, ma'am?" He spoke softly and cordially.

"Jared, I think it's time to make some changes in our living situation."

"So I've been hearing. Tom said you've got the idea you'd like to sell your place." She had Jared's full attention. He glanced at Charly and Tom from time to time.

"Yes." She cleared her throat gently and took a deep breath. "There was a time I would have imagined living here long enough to have my grandchildren around me, as my mother did, but practicality skipped her generation and landed on me." She laughed and then sighed. "I used to think I had to keep it up for posterity. My posterity is in my children. My heritage isn't here, it's in Heaven. Nobody can take that away from me. A house, on the other hand, can be a burden if you let it."

"I understand, Ms. Livingston."

Tom had to speak. "I don't want you to do something you will regret later."

"A house is stuff. And stuff isn't permanent. You know that."

"Mother has spoken." He squeezed her hand. "What would Grandma say?"

"Well, she's been turning over in her grave ever since I first thought it." She crooked a feisty eyebrow and harrumphed. "When she was confined to her bed toward the end, her main concern was that your children grow up in this house like her children and her daddy's children had done. She was the most impractical woman I've ever met. I loved her dearly, don't ever think I didn't, but I realized a long time ago that broken-down aristocracy is nothing to take such pride in like she did."

"I know, Mother. I was teasing, a little." There was a tinge of pain at the thought of losing the homestead. But he hadn't lied. He was teasing. A little.

While Mom talked to Jared and Sarah about the house and their upcoming wedding, Tom offered to take Lucy on a tour of the house before it got dark.

"Are you sure you don't need to be in on the conversation?" Lucy was concerned. She had observed him through dinner and the ensuing discussion. He winced a little. He was troubled, she could tell.

Tom gestured toward the porch swing. "No, we've talked about it, and she wants to be independent while she can. That includes finances." They sat down on the swing, Tom keeping it moving slowly with one foot while Lucy's crossed feet dangled.

"That's one thing I didn't have to deal with. My mother died when I was thirteen. Dad was all I had, and he took care of all the details." The heaviness around her heart was beginning to grow as she talked about him.

Tom shifted toward her and reached for her hand. "Here I am, worrying about my mother selling out and moving away from the home place, and you . . . you've lost everything."

She gave him a sad smile. "Not everything. I still have Grandmommy and Sarah. And most of all, I have a great big God. Sometimes He feels a little far away, though, you know?" A tear began to drop, and it irritated her. "Oh, bother. Why do these pesky tears stay so close to the surface?" She shook her head vigorously and took her hand from Tom's to smooth out her tissue for another run.

He chuckled. "You amaze me, Lucy. You have a strength I don't know if I have."

Her head tilted, and she gazed at him. "You do, you know. You make people feel safe. Like they matter." She arched her eyebrow. "And sometimes they wonder if they made any impression at all."

"Oh, you made an impression, all right. A lasting one."

# CHAPTER SIX

"What did you say to that?"

Sarah and Lucy were sitting cross-legged on the antique iron bed in the guest room where Lucy had taken up residence.

Lucy raised an eyebrow and gave her a disgusted look. "I said nothing. He's going to have to work for it if he wants to win me over." She shook her head at Sarah's incredulous stare. "I mean it. He's a great guy, but talk about somebody needing to get in touch with his feelings."

"Okay, you're much braver than I would have been. I'm still in awe that I have this rock on my finger and am marrying Jared."

They both stopped to sigh over the ring once more.

Lucy tilted her head. "With everything that's happened, I realize I've been wrapped in cotton-wool all my life. Daddy made everything easy. Now I don't have him to run things by, and I don't have him to make everything turn out the way I want it to."

"You're pretty tough, you know." Sarah smiled at her friend and reached for her hand.

"I'm really not. I'm a big marshmallow inside."

"And a Bantam hen on the outside."

Emotion washed over her as she thought about Dad and how he laughed when she stood up to him. Her stature was never as tall as when she was trying to get her way or win an argument. Lucy swiped a tear from her cheek and laughed. "True. I think I've got my Granny to thank for that one."

"How long can you stay?"

Lucy hugged her knees to herself, happy to be there with Sarah. "Long enough to make sure you don't put me in a bridesmaid dress that makes me look like Mary Todd Lincoln."

Sarah laughed. Lucy's greatest fear in formal wear. She found out early on that poufy ball gowns and short girls were a bad idea.

She held her hand up. "I promise. I suppose I could do the cake testing after you leave."

"Uh, no. That is the main part I want to have a say in. I've seen way too many wedding shows to miss out on that part. What about flowers?"

"I don't want a lot, but it would be nice to have you around for the selection. Tell you what, I'll talk to Jared, and I'll take the rest of this week off. I would rather take time off now than later, when the open house will be upon us."

"True. What about your classes?" Lucy knew Sarah was trying to fast-track her real estate classes to get her certification.

"I've turned in the paper due next week, so I'm good for a couple of weeks. I'm not concerned about getting it all done before the wedding. In fact, I'm not taking any classes this fall. I've got three now and two in the summer, and that will leave me fifteen courses." Her eyes widened. "It's a lot, but I like the classes, and I like working at the firm."

"I love it. 'The firm.' It makes me think you're in a John Grisham novel." Lucy giggled.

"It does sound weird, doesn't it?"

"Yeah, but in a good way." Lucy smiled at Sarah. She was proud of her. To change careers, to move hundreds of miles from home, took courage and trust. Trust in God and in herself.

Sarah looked at her phone. "On the off chance we were able to get it in while you're here, I made a few appointments for us."

"How many appointments?"

Sarah grinned. "Well, tomorrow the bridal salon, Saturday cake, and Jared's joining us on that one. He insisted."

"Of course he did. Why don't best men do all this stuff?"

"Would you really trust Jared and Tom to select your bridesmaid dress? You would either be dressed like Beyoncé or Mary Todd Lincoln, depending upon their mood."

"Very true."

Sarah gave Lucy a calculating look. "Now, I could invite Tom to accompany us to the cake-tasting session if you'd like."

She could feel the heat rising to her face as her heart picked up the pace. Of course she'd 'like', but she wasn't going to admit it, even to Sarah. Not now anyway. Picking at the quilt on her bed, Lucy shrugged. "Whatever."

"Tom, you have icing on your nose."

Lucy was trying her best to be friendly but not too friendly. Tom was being impossible. She could have sworn his eyes lit up when he saw her and then? Nothing. The shutters came down. He was painfully polite. So polite it would be easy for her to burst into tears.

"Thank you."

That was all she got. Thank you. She raised her eyes in a silent prayer of frustration. "Lord, who is this man and where is the man who kissed me on the boardwalk last summer?"

"What do you think?" Emmaline Quincy, the wedding coordinator, had observed each of them as they tasted ten different cake and frosting combinations.

"About what?" Lucy realized the question was directed at her, and she was not asking about her opinion on one Tom Livingston. Heat rushed into her cheeks as she struggled to get herself under control without nervous laughter.

Sarah sighed and poked her. "The cakes, silly."

She had to switch gears. "Hmm. I liked the banana cake with chocolate buttercream, and I liked the lemon cake with the lemon curd and white buttercream too. But there was also the Devil's food with chocolate ganache and praline buttercream . . . I'm glad it's your decision."

"That's the problem. There are too many choices." Sarah laughed. "I love all the chocolate, but the lemon would look really pretty."

"Maybe swap the layers?" Jared spoke up. "I liked the chocolate with the mocha frosting. What about you, Tom?"

He hesitated and glanced at Lucy so quickly that she almost thought she imagined it. "I liked the banana too. But the mocha icing was exceptional. Like a cup of really good coffee."

"That settles it." Sarah looked at each of them. "I officially can't decide. Emmaline, what do you think?"

Emmaline chuckled. "I think I can make the decision for you based on your comments. Now for the design."

LUCY DREADED the long drive back to Kentucky. She thought about going back through Atlanta and visiting her grandmother but decided she needed a little time on her own. It still didn't seem real that Dad wouldn't be there to greet her when she got home and to fuss over her calling when she left and along the way. Now she was alone.

The bridesmaid dresses had achieved her approval. She

chose simple, wispy chiffon that would suit all of the brides-maids, even the height-challenged ones.

The cake testing was more of a test than she had anticipated. Not only was there a myriad of flavors to choose from, but also the Tom factor. He agreed to go along with them. Did he show the slightest bit of interest in her? None. He avoided being alone with her at all costs. She may as well have been invisible or his sister for all the attention he gave her.

Well, if that was the way he was going to be, he could be alone as long as he wanted. He didn't deserve a girl like her.

"Wow. That was humble. What was that verse, God? *He has shown you, O man, what is good; and what does the* LORD *require of you but to do justly, to love mercy, and to walk humbly with your God?*" She blinked the tears away. "I'm sorry. You ask so little of me, and here I go, expecting You to put it all on a silver platter like Daddy did."

"And I guess You did, didn't you? Help me, God. Help me know when I'm thinking too much of myself and too little of everyone around me."

om was a grouch. He knew it. He knew why. He knew there wasn't one thing he could do about it. Well, maybe one thing. Maybe not treat Lucy like she was nothing to him, because she was. She was everything, but she could never know it. He knew he had hurt her when they went with Jared and Sarah on the cake-tasting expedition. She was angry and confused, and he knew whose fault it was. And now he had to face Jared at the tuxedo store.

He drove across the Waccamaw and Pee Dee Rivers to Georgetown, running late. He had a last-minute report to complete, and then the sheriff brought a new guy around to introduce him. Sam Watson was a new state police department detective and was acting as a liaison between the state, the sheriff's office, and emergency management throughout Georgetown County. Seemed like a nice guy, but it slowed down his departure. Sarah wouldn't be happy.

He pulled in to the parking lot, grimacing when he noted the tuxedoed mannequins in the front windows. His throat constricted at the very thought of the bow tie. But Jared was his best friend, and he would do whatever he could to make their day the best it could be.

He knew he was in trouble. Upon entering the shop, there was an impatient Sarah tapping her foot. Good-natured Sarah was beginning to exhibit "bridezilla" tendencies, especially since her mom hadn't come yet, and Lucy had gone home.

Tom held his hands up in surrender. "I'm sorry, Sarah, it couldn't be helped. Got hung up at work."

She sighed and gave him a nervous grin. "I figured it was something like that. Jared went ahead and started trying on. You haven't missed much."

He chuckled. "I guess I could have used my lights and siren to get across the bridges faster."

"Could you have done that?" Sarah was dead serious. When she realized he was joking, she gave him a dirty look.

"What color are we to be graced with? Powder blue? Lavender?" He winked at her.

"Basic black or charcoal grey. I like my men to look classic. Think James Bond."

"Which Bond? I mean, they are all different in their own way."

"Sean Connery Bond, of course. He will always be the perfect Bond in my opinion. But then Daniel Craig looks pretty good in a tux as well." Sarah was loosening up. "And no tails. Totally unnecessary."

"Good. I didn't want to get mistaken for a waiter."

Jared came out in a black tux a shade darker and blacker than his hair. "Hey, Tom. Sarah, what about this one?"

She put her hand to her chin and walked around him, pulling on this and tugging on that. "I like it. Do you like the vest or the cummerbund better?"

Tom and Jared spoke at the same time. "Vest."

Sarah laughed. "Well, I guess that's settled. Vest, it is. Now go try on the gray one."

Tom grinned.

"Both of you."

His grin faded. "Do I have to try on the tie?"

Jared laughed and clapped his friend on the shoulder. "The whole enchilada, brother."

He followed him into the dressing area after being measured by the sales person.

"You know, Jared, they have courthouses for occasions like, say, weddings."

"Ha. Believe me, I mentioned it. We both agreed that our mothers would put out a hit on us. Not to mention her sister. This is the least I can do to have the blessing of having Sarah for the rest of my life. You'll see. One of these days you'll be hit with the same lightning bolt."

"Some people survive that lightning bolt and live to tell it." Tom struggled with the collar of the shirt.

"It seems to me you haven't let the bolt do its thing. What about Lucy?" Jared seemed like he was avoiding Tom's eyes.

"What about her?" If Jared wanted information, he'd have to drag it out of him.

"Seems to me that lightning bolt hit you when you met her, or was I mistaken?"

How do you tell your buddy to mind his own business?

"Maybe we were both mistaken."

Jared stood next to his friend in front of the mirror. Both of them were looking at themselves with a critical eye. "I don't think we were. She really likes you, Tom."

"Well, maybe she shouldn't." He was beginning to feel trapped, the red beginning to infuse his neck and face. Looking in the mirror, he not only felt the heat, but saw it as well. He blamed his Scottish heritage.

Jared turned toward Tom. "You don't know a good thing when you see it."

"Jared, you don't have to worry about Sarah. She comes

from regular folks, like me. You? Well, you're rich, man. I have no problem with gender equality, but a man wants to feel like he's providing for his wife, not the other way around."

Tom could tell Jared was getting angry. "That's about the most stupid thing I've ever heard you say. You know I don't come from any different economic background than you."

"Jared, she's wealthy. You saw Lucy's house. You met her grandmother. You really think her dad, if he were living, would like the idea of his princess hooking up with a cop in a small town in South Carolina? What do you think her grandmother would think? I'm done, Jared. You can reach for the stars because you're already there. Me? I know what I'm worth, and when I look at my bank account, I know it's not much."

"Guys, what's taking so long?" Sarah's voice came floating through the hallway to the dressing rooms.

Jared called out to her. "We'll be there in a minute, Sarah." He turned to Tom. "You're wrong, you know. Dead wrong. Lucy's not like that, and I have a feeling her family isn't, either. From what I've heard about her father, he would have been proud to have a son-in-law like you. Now let's get out there and put on a smiling face for Sarah, and agree to disagree. For now."

"Sir, yes sir." Tom raised his hand in grim salute and walked out of the dressing room. He'd said it. He told Jared what was holding him up, and his closest friend had rebuked him.

He at least expected sympathy, because he wasn't wrong.

"Cupcakes?"

"Check. And punch, finger sandwiches, fruit, veggies, and more food than anybody needs at a bridal shower." Susan looked over the list. "It will be perfect."

They stood at the island of Susan and Mike's newly-remodeled kitchen. The inheritance that had moved Sarah to South Carolina had benefitted her sister and brother-in-law as well, with their income from Crawford and Benton being invested in their house and a college fund for their twin girls, Trudy and Abby.

Lucy sighed. "It has to be. She's the closest thing to a sister I've ever had."

Susan laughed. "What do you know? Me too!" That put the smile back on Lucy's face.

Lucy hugged Susan tightly. "I'm glad to have you for a big sister."

Susan hugged her back and gave her an extra squeeze. "I am too. I'm glad my little sister has good taste in friends."

"And in husbands."

"Definitely. Marc was great, but Jared? He's the one we prayed for, isn't he?"

"Yes. Now you can start praying for me. I wish I knew what the Lord has in store for me." She sat on a bar stool, picked up the pen, and tapped it on the notepad that had the list on it. "Maybe I'm supposed to be alone. D'you think?" She looked wistfully up at Susan.

Susan gave her an extra hug around the shoulders. "I can't speak for God, but I've heard there's someone in South Carolina that might have caught your eye?"

Lucy blushed. The familiar leap of hurt, pride, and anger at Tom Livingston simmered near the surface. "Well, it seems it wasn't reciprocated."

"Don't worry. God has a plan for all of us. For me, it was Mike and twins. It was easy. Well, except for the twins, but I survived, and so did they. For Sarah, it involved a lot more heartache than I wanted for her. Sometimes we have to survive the heartache, like we have to survive the pain of having premature twins. I don't pretend to understand His ways, but God has it all under control."

"I know. At one point I thought maybe Tom was 'the one.' Then it was like it never happened. How do you get around that?"

"By being patient. Not your strong suit, I know." Susan patted her arm. "Things have a way of working out. If He doesn't give you what you want, if you're willing, He will change your heart to closer match His."

"IT'S time to let go of the past, son." Tom wasn't happy and for a number of reasons. This one as personal as the others. His mother wanted to sell off the family antiques, some of which had been in the house since before their family took possession in the early 1800s.

"I understand, Mama, but I see no reason to get rid of things that mean something to Charly and me. And what about your grandchildren? Don't you want them to have things that belonged to generations before them?"

"Yes, I suppose. It's getting harder to be sentimental about things I can no longer see. Almost like the act of doing something outweighs the value. But what will any of us do with a nine-foot-tall wardrobe?" Mom sighed and laid her hand on the smooth wood. "Remember when you read *The Lion, the Witch, and the Wardrobe*?" She chuckled. "You were forever hiding in this thing, hoping one of those times the back would lead you to Narnia."

Tom smiled at the memory. "Yeah. I fell asleep in there once, on top of all those quilts, and had a dream the back really did lead to Narnia, except our Narnia was hot and humid. Charly tried it a few times as well."

She laughed. "Only a boy from the South would dream about Narnia like that."

"I think it was because I was smothering in there." Tears pricked at him. He didn't want to get sentimental about "stuff," but this was his childhood, his mother's, and his grandmother's.

"Tell you what, Mama, How about I rent a storage unit, and when the time comes that you sell the place and move to a smaller one, we'll put it in there and you'll have a lot of furniture to choose from. If you want to buy all new stuff, that's fine. We'll cross that bridge when we get to it."

"I suppose that would be the wise decision. When did you get to be so smart?" She reached for his hand.

He took hers and squeezed it. "I guess I take after my Mama."

"I've always been so determined to not be like my mama, I'm afraid I may have kept you and Charly from being proud of your heritage. It isn't that I'm not proud; it's that I don't want to worship it like my mama did. Does that make sense?"

"Yep. It's like me being a neat-freak. I loved Dad and learned many important things from him, but he never put stuff away, remember?" He smiled at the memories. "When I was a teenager it always made me mad when he asked me to clean things up, because his workbench was always a mess."

"Still is, isn't it?" His mother pursed her lips in good humor. "When he passed, I went out there and noticed all the tools on the bench, out of their places on the peg-board. You fixed that for him, and he was so proud of it. But did he use it?"

"Occasionally I would go and put all the tools on it, but after Dad died, I didn't have the heart to put it in order. I wanted to think of him coming in and out, throwing a tool down and picking up another one."

"Like he was still here. We're both a little sentimental when it comes to our people, aren't we?" Her lips trembled with her smile. "Well. I think we must wait on the Lord to see what He has for us. Who knows? There may be a home out there that will house a nine-foot-tall wardrobe for my grandbabies to play in."

"Now you're talkin'."

"Course, that means I'll need to have some grandbabies."

Tom's face warmed. "Yes, ma'am." Emphasis on "have" noted.

KENTUCKY WEDDING SHOWER AN UNMITIGATED SUCCESS? Check. Surprise South Carolina shower planned? Check. Bridal shower and bachelorette day planned for the weekend before the wedding? Check. Constant communication between Lucy and Sarah all summer long? Check. Any possible word from Tom?

Nothing. Absolutely nothing.

Juggling. Lucy was juggling, and clumsily, she thought.

Juggling her dad's estate, of which she was the sole beneficiary. Sarah's wedding was tossed in there, and she was determined to be the best maid of honor in maid-of-honor history.

Then there was her peace of mind. She didn't have much of that. She was praying. Oh, how she was praying. But where was God? Did He really have a plan? Was she even a part of His plan?

When those questions came, she decided to clean out another closet. She couldn't deal with it when there were so many other things on her mind. She needed concrete tasks to do. Something with an end to it.

Having Sarah home for a few days for the shower was great, and now she was back to packing up the house and going through things. Organizing for better living was much more fun than organizing for leaving your home for the past fifteen years.

"God, why didn't Sarah plan her wedding for July instead of October?" She heaved a sigh.

# CHAPTER NINE

*July*

"It's so hot the ice cream truck melted."

His mother laughed at her son's answer to the usual July question in South Carolina – how hot is it?

"I imagine it is, son. We're needin' rain, aren't we?"

"I'm not complaining. Haven't had to mow the yard in two weeks, but Charly's doing a good job of keeping after the garden." Tom sat down at the kitchen table, took off his baseball cap and wiped the sweat from his brow.

"Well, I guess we'll see rain when hurricane season hits. I do want it pretty for Sarah and Jared's wedding." She set a glass of ice water in front of him, careful to feel of the edge of the table and calculate the placement of the glass. She could see shadows and outlines, but other than that she did everything by feel and by memory.

"Thank you, Mama. I'm parched." He had trimmed around the "for sale" sign that made him sigh every time he drove up the driveway. Between what little yard work there was and rinsing dust out of the air-conditioning unit it was about as much outside work as a man could do on what was forecasted to be the hottest day of the year.

"How are the wedding plans coming?" Mom always asked about the wedding. For his part, Tom would be glad when it was over. Things had been a little strained between himself and Jared.

"They're coming, I reckon. I try to stay out of the way."

"Tell me you're not planning one of those bachelor parties." It was a statement, not a question, and it made Tom chuckle.

"No, Ma'am. Jared told me at the beginning he wanted nothing of the kind. I was glad." Really glad. Getting married was no reason for a man to indulge in what went on at traditional bachelor parties. "Maybe we ought to invite all the guys to a party and have a prayer meeting, instead."

His mother laughed. "That would serve 'em right, wouldn't it?" She sobered. "You know, it wouldn't be a bad thing."

"No, it wouldn't. Tell ya what. When I get married, I'll tell Jared that's what I want."

"Maybe you should do that before you decide to get married. Maybe pray up a bride." His mother was being funny now. They hadn't talked about the topic of his matrimonial prospects in a while.

"I'm sure you're covering that."

"Yes, son, I am." She paused. "I really like Lucy. She seems like a sweet girl."

Here it was. "Yes, ma'am, she is."

He didn't say more, and he took a long swig of his water to keep from having to talk. They sat there a minute, not saying anything.

Dead air. Silence, in a room with his mother, had never been a problem, but this time he wanted to scoot the topic off of Lucy, which meant he had to come up with the next topic.

"Any bites on the house?" There. Maybe that would get her off the topic of marriage.

"Not since the first week. Maybe we're asking too much. Maybe such an old house scares people off.

"I'm sure Jared will have his people on it."

"I know he will. I don't want him worrying over it with the wedding coming up."

Tom laughed. "Believe me, everything that can be planned to the –nth degree has been planned. That's Sarah for you. She's got this four-inch binder with every wedding detail known to man. Except for the honeymoon."

She chuckled. "Where are they going?"

"No clue. Jared won't tell anybody. I hope it's not because he doesn't have a plan yet."

Her eyebrow raised in speculation. "I doubt it. He can be cagey, that one. He's got something up his sleeve."

# CHAPTER TEN

*August*

The Crawford and Benton company open house was at hand. The weather was iffy and the drought broken as August and September marked the rainiest months on record in South Carolina. So far, everyone had said their prayers for good weather, and had been busy sprucing up properties all over Georgetown County.

Working at her desk on homework for her last real estate class before the wedding, Sarah grinned as she typed, sensing a tall, good-looking business partner and fiancé standing in the doorway, waiting for her attention. "I know you're there, Jared."

"Sorry. I didn't want to interrupt."

"That's okay. I'm almost finished." She clicked on "save," backed it up on her flash drive, and looked up from the computer. "What can I do for you?"

"Want to ride out to look at a house with me? I got a lead on a property coming available, and thought we might want to check it out." His eyes glittered with excitement.

"Sounds like fun. I'm done with my paper, my inbox

contents have turned into outbox filler, and until you put more in there, I'm officially caught up."

"Good. I thought I'd lost you to paperwork there for a while. You do know you don't have to complete a week's worth of paperwork in one—" Jared stopped to look at his watch then looked at her with an arched brow, ". . . morning."

"I know, but I also figure the end of the week will be completely crazy with the open house, I have a dress fitting tomorrow, and Lucy's coming the next day. With all that, I won't get anything else done. Am I right?"

Jared smiled at her warmly. "You're right. We'd better escape while we can, maybe mix a little business with pleasure?" he asked, leaning across her desk and wiggling his eyebrows.

"Why, sir, whatever did you have in mind?" She smiled at him, batting her eyelashes for good measure.

"I was thinking maybe we pick up some lunch and go for a picnic before we check out the property. How does that sound?"

"I could definitely eat. What is it about writing a paper—no, let me rephrase that—finishing a paper that makes a person feel like she hasn't eaten in a week?" She leaned down and reached into her desk drawer for her purse.

"Relief? I remember when I completed the licensing courses, I was so relieved. I had graduated from college with honors, and yet these classes had the potential to impact my life, which made me a complete wreck."

Walking down the corridor of the office, he put his hand on the small of her back, winking at her as she tossed her head around to flash him a brilliant smile. "I guess that's it. So, where's this property?"

"That's for me to know, and for you to find out," he said mysteriously.

"Hmm, a surprise, huh? I'm game. And I'm hungry. KFC?"

Jared chuckled at her as he shook his head. "Sounds good to

me. You can take the girl out of Kentucky, but you can't take Kentucky out of the girl, huh?"

"You got that right, mister!" She beamed as she swept out the front door, Jared holding it open for her.

RIDING IN JARED'S "WORK" vehicle, the luxurious, black, Ford Expedition he used during the week, Sarah relaxed in the comfortable leather seats and sighed as she took in the sunny day. She was glad to get out of the office for a while. The week before had been rainy, and there had even been reports of flash flooding in Charleston, with people working in the downtown area having cars flooded out, stranding them at their place of business until they could be rescued by individuals driving larger vehicles. When it was not raining, it had been gloomy, and she had suffered a bout of nerves as she began her second big project of the licensing course. Could she handle the career she had chosen?

But today, the sun was shining, the surf had gentled, and she was done with her first real estate course. Wedding plans were on track. It was a good day. As they went through the drive-thru at Kentucky Fried Chicken, she leaned her elbow on the arm rest and smiled as she looked across the vehicle at Jared, thinking back to that first picnic they had shared.

It had been an impromptu lunch date, the first day she had visited the offices of Crawford and Benton, and the day after she had met Jared Benton on the steps of Pilot Oaks, the antebellum mansion she and her family had inherited from a distant relative.

Taking the bag of food from him as he waited for his change, she opened the bag and inhaled the aroma of the fried chicken and biscuits. Her mouth watered as she smelled the spicy goodness.

"Everything look okay?"

"I don't know about that, but it smells dee-vine," she said. "Did you get coleslaw?"

"Of course."

She smiled as they headed back onto State Road 17. They passed Brookgreen Gardens on the left and the entrance to Huntington Beach State Park on the right. This familiar territory was beginning to feel like home. "So, where's this property?"

"You'll see." His face had a pinkish cast.

"You seem awfully excited. I know you love real estate, but you don't get this pumped about a new property."

They were going to Murrells Inlet, to the summerhouse at Pilot Oaks for their picnic. Sarah's curiosity and Jared's excitement made the picnic much shorter than usual.

After clearing away the wrappers and bags and stowing them back in the SUV for disposal later, Sarah looked across at him as she buckled her seatbelt again. "Okay, the suspense is killing me."

"I know."

He chuckled when she rolled her eyes and released a loud sigh. Jared pulled away from the brick gates of Pilot Oaks and instead of accelerating, he slowed down.

Sarah whipped her head around in surprise. "There's a property available on this road? And I didn't know about it?"

Jared laughed as he pulled into the driveway of a large white house.

"It's your house! Jared! This is the property you were talking about?" Sarah bounced in her seat, leaning forward in excitement.

"I had told the owner a while back if she ever decided to sell, that I would appreciate it if she would give me an option to buy it, and now Miss Alma is thinking about selling."

She sat, mute, as they drove up the long drive to the white frame house with red brick trim and rambling red rosebushes on either side of the wide, welcoming steps.

"It'll probably seem smaller to me now."

She sensed a hesitation in him. He was worried she wouldn't like it. Who wouldn't love this beautiful house? "I can't wait to see it."

Jared looked across at her with a tender gaze. The teasing expression of earlier had given way to a look of love and longing that set her heart aflutter. "I want to show you every inch of this place. One day, I want to show it to my children and to my grandchildren."

The lump in her throat threatened to choke her, and tears threatened to fall as she reached across to take his hand in hers before they left the vehicle. "I love you, Jared."

"I know, and I love you too," he said, leaning in to kiss her on the lips as he squeezed the hand she had grasped. Smiling joyously, he quirked his eyebrows up and said, "Shall we?"

Sarah laughed and her face warmed as thoughts of their home and future came to her unbidden. She knew she would follow this man anywhere, and a request as simple as this one was easy to fulfill. Nodding her head, she smiled as he gestured for her to stay put as he got out of the vehicle and circled around to open the passenger-side door.

After smoothing out her skirt from the ride over, she nodded her head when his eyes asked her if she were ready. Taking her hand, he led her up the walkway, and into what could very likely be her future.

# CHAPTER ELEVEN

The scent of old-fashioned roses wafted across the porch as they mounted the steps. The elderly lady who opened the door took one look at her guests and started smiling as she pushed to open the screen door in order to give Jared a hug. "That sure didn't take long," she said, quirking an eyebrow on her well-worn, thin face.

"Miss Alma, I would like you to meet Miss Sarah Jane Crawford, my business partner, and Sarah, this is Miss Alma Ruth McGinty. She's been taking care of my house for the last fifteen years or so," Jared said.

"It's a pleasure to meet you, Ms. McGinty," Sarah said, shaking the frail hand that held a firmness unexpected in such a small woman.

"Call me Miss Alma, dear. And do you go by Sarah, or Sarah Jane? When I was a girl, my mama called me Alma Ruth, but since I got old, I'm plain old Miss Alma."

"Please, call me Sarah. I only get called Sarah Jane when I'm in trouble."

Miss Alma gave Jared a pointed stare. "Well, son, you've

kept this young lady hidden away from me. What do you have to say for yourself?"

Jared grinned. "I apologize, Miss Alma. Sarah came last summer but didn't move here until fall."

"And you wait until now to bring her around? And if I hadn't called you about this big old house, who knows when I would have met your young lady?"

"She's got a point, Jared." Sarah batted her eyelashes at him in acknowledgement of this lady's assumption that Sarah was more than a "business partner."

"I know when I've got two women ganging up on me." Jared held up his hands in surrender.

"Good boy. And so you know, I had heard a little bit about your new business partner from Prudie. I hear there's to be wedding bells soon."

"I had a feeling you had heard." Jared pursed his lips in good humor. Turning toward Sarah, he said, "Prudie and Miss Alma have been friends for over fifty years and have talked each other out of getting married more times than I want to think about. For some reason, if Prudie thought she liked a man, there would be something about him Miss Alma didn't approve, and if Miss Alma thought she'd found 'the one,' Prudie considered herself beholden to find a flaw in the poor guy."

"And we were right about every one of those ya-hoos," Miss Alma said with a determined shake of her head. "That is, until Harold came along. We had held out hope for marriage and a family, and I found marriage for a short time. It was hard losing him, but you know, Prudie and I found happiness in lots of other ways. God is good."

"All the time," Jared completed. "Since Prudie never married, and Miss Alma has been a widow for as long as I've known her, they've decided it's their life's call to find me a wife. You never know how prayers are going to be answered, do you?"

Sarah smiled.

"That's right, boy. You never know." Miss Alma grinned at the blush on Sarah's face and patted her hand. She seemed to sense it was time to change the subject. "Now, I think I called you over here for business-talk, not matchmaker talk. Am I right?"

"You are, and that's why I'm here. I do apologize for not coming around sooner."

Miss Alma nodded. "All's forgiven. Here's the deal, Jared. I know you think I'm going to live forever."

"You mean you're not?"

"Who would want to? No, I'm ready to meet my maker, I can tell you. Oh, calm down." She waved a hand, dismissing his objections. "I haven't gotten a death sentence. I'm old. I'm in better health than my mother was at my age, but I can tell I'm slowing down. This big house is getting to be too much for me, and I'd like to see a family living here that loves it while I'm still around to bug 'em."

"What are you planning to do?"

"You may think I'm too old to think for myself, but believe it or not, I've got my eye on a sweet little first-floor condo up the road toward Litchfield Beach. There's an ocean view, no upkeep, and I would be able to soak up the sun on my own private patio. I think my knees would thank me."

"Now, Miss Alma, you know I never said you couldn't think for yourself. Have you been talking to Mary Ann Livingston?"

"I may have had a conversation with her at the Missionary Union meeting. She told me what she had planned, and it gave me an idea it might be time to ease things up for myself a little bit. She may be blind, but I'm just plain old."

Jared chuckled. "I'm wondering if there's something in the water, all you ladies wanting to downsize."

"I could see you were wondering if I'd thought this through."

"Can't blame a guy for looking after his women folk, now can you?"

"No, I can't fault you for that, and I appreciate it. Sarah, honey, watch out, or he'll have you wrapped in cotton wool so fast it'll make your head spin."

"Are you trying to say I'm overprotective?"

She laughed out loud. "Yes, sir, I am, and you may as well face that fact, and she may as well too. Now, are we going to talk business, or are we going to spend what's left of my life sitting here gabbing?"

Smiling, Jared took out his notebook. "Business it is. What were you thinking of asking for the property?"

"How much do you want to give me for it?" Miss Alma narrowed her eyes and smiled at him. "I know you want it, and I know you're a fair man. What do you think?"

Jared looked over at Sarah, who had been sitting back, enjoying the exchange between the two, and quirked an eyebrow at her. "I think I need to think about it, and I need to show Sarah the house. Would that be all right?"

Smirking a little, Miss Alma looked from one to the other and said, "I wondered how long you could wait to show her your old homestead. Make yourselves to home."

THEY HAD ENTERED the house by the front door, passing across the large front porch that held a porch swing on one end and a conversation area of rockers on the other end. He could tell she was a fan of the roses.

When Jared got up to show Sarah around, he looked around at the living room. The house, built in 1916, showed its age, but overall, it was a sturdy, well-built house. The original gold tile on the fireplace and hearth was still intact, the dark-stained oak woodwork virtually untouched except for periodic cleaning and polishing, and the quarter-sawn oak plate rail in the dining room held pictures, plates, trays, and other mementos of Miss Alma's life.

"It'll need work." Jared glanced at Sarah to get a feel for what she thought about taking on a project like this.

"Yes, but Jared, this house is over a hundred years old! I mean, you couldn't build a house like this for less than a million dollars these days, and you can't get wood like this anymore." She ran her hand along the door facing that held pocket doors between the living room and dining room.

"If I recall, the kitchen and bathrooms will need major renovations." He pointed out the negatives, trying to keep things neutral, but he couldn't help but feel confident at her reaction.

Sarah laughed. "Don't they always? When I bought my little house in Kentucky, I had to renovate the kitchen. Of course it was tiny," she said as they peeked into the kitchen at the back of the house. She grimaced. "And this one is too."

"Yeah, this was the one room my mom hated when we lived here, but she could never convince Dad we needed to gut it and start over."

"You're right. It's a big project." She looked back at him with a tender smile. "But, Jared, think about what we'd have."

He grinned as he observed her taking in all that the house could be. It was no mansion like Pilot Oaks, but it had been a fine home in its day.

"I know." Leading her down a hallway, they came to a small bathroom and office area in the back corner. "This used to be a porch, and they enclosed it, from what I've been able to figure out, around 1935."

"It's tiny, but usable. Good powder-room size." Sarah nodded as she looked at the dated bathroom.

As they came back through the house, Jared looked out the French doors in the front to see Miss Alma sitting on the porch swing with her knitting, tapping a foot to the floor to keep the gentle movement going. She was determined not to interfere with this decision. Reaching for Sarah's hand, Jared said, "Let's go check out the upstairs."

WALKING up the sunny stairwell hand-in-hand, Sarah couldn't help but compare it to the stairwell at Pilot Oaks. Where the staircase in the antebellum mansion had a graceful curve and a stained glass window, this one had a simple window in the landing to let the morning light shine in and light up the entire hallway on the second floor. "Oh, Jared, this is beautiful," she said, taking in the perfectly proportioned stairs and the mixture of painted balusters and more oak on the treads and handrail.

The upstairs was painted a sunny yellow and held three bedrooms and a bath. The bath was large, and as with many bungalows built at that time, there was a little alcove for the toilet, and the plaster on the walls was etched to mimic subway tile and painted with glossy yellow paint. She reached out to touch the cool, shiny plaster wall. Such an interesting texture. "I've seen pictures of plaster work done like this."

Sarah turned and walked to the middle of the roomy hall, looking at each of the three roomy bedrooms, imagining a young Jared running up and down the stairs. She was deep in her thoughts when she felt a hand on her arm.

"Hey, that back bedroom? It was mine and my brother's." They walked to the end of the hallway and into the room that had not two windows, which would be the norm for a modern house, but seven large double-hung windows. Jared pulled her to the windows facing east. "If you look through the trees right there, you can see the water. And in the wintertime, the view is amazing."

"I can imagine." She could imagine their own children playing in the floor, running back and forth between the two smaller bedrooms, and in and out of the master bedroom in the center. Sarah smiled and turned to Jared. "This is a beautiful home, Jared. I can see why you love it so much."

"I do love it, but I don't have to have it."

"Why not? I thought acquiring this house was one of your main goals in life?" She inserted a teasing note into her voice, unsure of the look in his eyes.

He shook his head. "Maybe at one time, but my goals shifted a little bit recently."

"Oh? When?"

"Around the middle of last June."

Sarah knew she would melt if he didn't kiss her, and soon. And he did.

# CHAPTER TWELVE

"Slow down. Now tell me again. He bought you what?" Lucy was sitting on the floor in the middle of her dad's office, going through papers. She wanted to get this done before she left the next day for South Carolina. The open house was coming up, and she had volunteered to help keep Sarah from going nuts. Jared's words, not Sarah's.

"He bought me a house, Lucy. The house he grew up in. I can't believe it. Here we are, getting ready for the wedding, and he buys us a house!"

Lucy couldn't tell if she was excited or if she was overwhelmed. Probably a bit of both. "Are you okay with this? I mean, did he talk to you about it?"

"We went and looked at it. Lucy, I fell in love with it like I knew I would. I can't wait to show you."

"Well good. I was wondering if you were upset or happy about it. Tell me you're not moving in immediately. I thought you were moving into Jared's house until you found another one."

"That's still the plan. There will be lots of renovations, and we didn't want Mrs. McGinty to have to move out until she found something. She's a sweetheart, best friends with Prudie! I admit I was in overwhelm-mode for a bit. Oh, Luce. I'll be glad when you get here. It's all getting so close. Any bites on your house?"

"I've had a couple of people looking at it. One seems pretty serious."

Sarah was quiet on the other end of the line. "How do you feel about it?"

Feel? She was beginning to feel numb about everything. She took in a deep breath. "I'm okay. I mean, I'm a little sad about it, since I've lived here longer than any other place in my life, but it's just a house, and without Daddy, it doesn't feel like home."

"I get it. Are you still planning to come this week? You've got a lot on you right now; I hate to add to it."

Lucy could hear the reticence in her voice. "Don't worry about me. I've got a real estate agent. I've heard a good one is worth their weight in gold." She laughed. "I plan to leave first thing in the morning and be there by nightfall. Has Jared got me lined up with a job for the open house?" A change of subject might get Sarah back on track.

"He has. You'll be my flunky."

"But aren't you Jared's flunky?"

Sarah's laugh came trilling over the phone. "Yep. That means you are 'flunky, grade 2.' Or maybe Assistant Flunky? Flunky-to-the-flunky?"

"Hey, whatever gets me inside those pretty houses works for me. I gotta go. I'm knee-deep in Dad's paperwork and want to get this done before I go to bed tonight."

"Okay. Be careful tomorrow, and let me know how you are along the way."

"Yes, Mother." Lucy's voice flattened in good humor. "Talk to you tomorrow. Love you, friend."

"Love you, too, friend."

Lucy pushed the disconnect button on her phone and put it down with a sigh. Would Tom be around? She wondered if his mom had sold that amazing house. For some reason, she hoped not. She really wanted to have Sarah and Jared's shower in that wonderful place.

One pile down. Bank statements from the last five years. Sure, you only had to keep three years' worth, but her dad believed in covering all his bases. She put them in a cardboard banker's box and labeled it with a marker. Underneath all the statements, in the bottom of the last drawer, she found a box. It was fire-proof.

Strange. The deeds, insurance papers, and all the other important stuff had been in the safe. This wasn't locked, so it was not something in danger of being stolen.

She opened it. As she did, photographs spilled out. It was packed full to overflowing. It was a wonder the latch even kept it closed. On top were the most recent pictures of herself and her dad at a church event. As she worked her way through the stacks of images, she found her school pictures, family pictures of when her mother was still with them, and at the bottom, her baby pictures mixed with wedding pictures.

These were his precious memories. Not the deeds, not the insurance papers or wills, but his family. She had often been a little jealous of Sarah and the fact that she had her family all around her and was settled here. Dad was settled in a different kind of way. He might not be sentimental about "stuff," but he was about his family. He didn't want to take the chance of any of his memories of his family being destroyed by fire. It was a legacy she could take with her and make a home wherever she was. Life is short.

"Oh, Daddy. Why did you leave me?"

She was mopping up tears and blowing her nose furiously

when her phone rang. She looked down at it and sighed. Not who she had hoped. That would be too much of a miracle. It was Ben. She waffled over answering long enough that it stopped. Whew. That was a close one.

As she put her phone back down on the floor beside her, she heard a quiet "ding" indicating voicemail. Great. What about Lydia? Weren't they seeing one another now? Listening to the voicemail, she was torn.

"Lucy, this is Ben. We need to talk. Dinner tonight? I'll call you back in ten minutes. If I don't get you, call me back? Bye."

BEN WAS A NICE GUY. Really nice. Sometimes too nice.

When he called her back that night, she couldn't say no to dinner with him. He was the perfect gentleman tonight, treating her like a princess. She could almost be convinced a bird in the hand, but she didn't feel anything.

"Lucy, I know before you left after your dad's funeral you said there wasn't a future for us, and I respected that. You've heard of 'fight or flight?'" His look of intensity made her a little nervous.

"Yes, Ben, I have." Great. He was going to analyze her using sports and animal metaphors. Why did she suddenly feel a giggle longing to surface?

"It's all about adrenaline and endorphins. Adrenaline can do weird things to your mind when you're in crisis mode. Sometimes you make rash decisions."

"I've heard that. Look, Ben—"

He put a hand up to interrupt. "Hear me out. I know you think you made the right decision breaking it off with me, but are you sure? Luce, I'm still attracted to you."

He reached over to take her hand that was resting on the

table. Her heart beat a little faster. God? Is Ben who you have for me? I'm so confused. "What about Lydia? I thought you two were dating."

His face got redder. "We decided to cool it for a while. I'd like a second chance with you, Lucy. You're all alone. I can't stand the thought of that."

Her eyes flickered up to his and realization hit her. Wait. She wasn't all alone. She had a great big, wonderful God with her all the time. She had friends like Sarah. She was blessed. So blessed and loved by God that she had no business settling for a husband for whom she had no passion. Oh, they could have a future together, but was it the future she wanted? And Ben wasn't in love with her.

"Ben, you do me a great honor, and believe me, I appreciate it. You see, I'm not all alone. I have God. He has the very best in mind for me. He sent you to me when I was lonely, but he sent you to me so I would have a friend, not a boyfriend. I see that now."

"But Luce . . ."

She tilted her head and gave him a rueful grin. "Ben, I saw the look on your face when I mentioned Lydia. You need to get things straight with her. She's a wonderful woman." She could have laughed when she saw the sheepish look on his face.

"She is." He looked at her intently. "Are you sure?"

"I'm sure. As a matter of fact, I've met someone. I don't know if he feels the same way I do. If he doesn't, God is in control, not me."

"I do love you, Lucy. Maybe not in the way you want to be loved, but as a friend, you are tops."

She smiled at him through a mist of tears and squeezed his hand. "You are too." She chuckled. "Hey, I could never have gotten Josh Scott to do anything if you hadn't let him work out with the football players."

"That's no big deal. It was good for the guys to have someone to look after. He's their mascot now."

Bless his heart, he looked relieved.

Now it was up to her. She was going to get answers, one way or another. No turning back.

# CHAPTER THIRTEEN

"You know, Emmaline, this wedding planning thing is fun. I really think I'd like to do this."

Lucy had been tasked with being the liaison between the bride and the wedding planner, and she loved every minute of it. Her love of organization, of interpreting what people say and what they mean, and design all spoke to her like nothing outside of education ever had. Working with special needs teenagers had prepared her to work with anyone.

Emmaline Quincy, of Quince Wedding Designs, laughed and answered in her slow coastal drawl. "Oh, it has its moments, believe you me, but when a weddin' turns out perfectly, you can't help but bask in the beauty of it all. This one is gonna be a humdinger."

"Sarah has loved everything you've put together."

"I couldn't have done it without you. Poor Sarah. Trying to take those real estate classes, her mama hundreds of miles away, and moving to a new place? That can be a recipe for disaster." Emmaline pulled her pearl-studded watch pendant around to read the hands. "I've got a meeting in thirty minutes, and in an hour I have to pick Sophie up from soccer practice." She looked sideways at the younger woman. "Now if I had a business pah'tner." She raised an eyebrow at the surprised look on Lucy's face. "Forget I said that. Just tuck that thought away for later."

"I will. I never considered doing anything but teaching. What am I saying? I've got a teaching degree and an estate to settle, and Sarah's wedding to boot." Could she? Yes, Lord, all I need is another issue to pop up in my life.

"Teachers have summers, you know. That's the busy season. Just a thought. I've got to run. Let me know what Sarah decides on the centerpieces, and we'll get the stuff all ordered."

"Will do. I'll try to sway her to the one I like."

"That's what a weddin' planner does, dearie. You'd be great."

Lucy laughed. "Well, I can be persuasive when I want to be."

Except when it comes to a certain six-foot-four-inch tall police detective.

"I THOUGHT Lucy already gave Jared and Sarah a shower?" Tom scowled as he helped Charly scrub the porch and hose down the furniture.

"That was in Kentucky. This one is for people here, and it's a surprise, remember?" Charly threw a soapy sponge at him.

"Watch it, kid. I have a lot better aim than you." He grinned and threatened her with the same sponge.

"I need you to get that corner with the sponge." She made sure he was doing it to her specifications. "You haven't said anything to Jared, have you?"

"If anybody can keep a secret, I can."

"I know. We want this to be a surprise."

"It will be. Tomorrow night they will come for a casual supper with family and find fifty people here."

"What about the cars?" Charly looked worried.

Tom raised a hand. "All arranged. Pastor Bill is going to run a shuttle from the church parking lot to here, and the happy couple will be none the wiser."

"Good. I knew you would take care of it. Lucy was worried."

He glanced at her studied avoidance of his face. She was determined to bring Lucy into every conversation they had. "Is this a straight-up shower, or are there silly girl games we men will have to endure?"

The dirty look on her face rivaled the actual dirt on her face. "Watch it, Bub. Lucy and Mom are in charge of food and decorations, I am in charge of games. And I've got some good ones."

"Not spin-the-bottle, I hope."

She gave him 'the look.' "Good grief. What are we, seventh graders?"

Mom opened the screen door and walked out on the porch. "Well, I can't tell if it's clean or not, but it sure smells good out here."

"Mama, we could eat off of this porch, it's so clean." Tom got up and kissed his mother on the cheek.

"That's what I like to hear, son. Charlotte, when you get to a stopping point, I need you to pull out the good linens to use for the shower. They may need to be cleaned and pressed."

"Yes, ma'am."

Mom turned to go back in then turned. "Oh, and Charlotte, Lucy is coming over later to start movin' stuff around. Tom, can you stay and help?"

He drew in a deep breath. Thrown together yet again. He was almost getting used to having her around. "Yes, ma'am. I'll be your strong right arm." And he would get to see Lucy again.

"Very well then. I appreciate it."

"You're more than welcome."

LUCY WAS BEAMING. There were close to fifty people at the shower, including Jared's parents. Everyone was outside eating the sumptuous low-country supper she, Mary Ann, and Charly had put together: fried chicken, shrimp and grits, crab cakes, coleslaw, cornbread, and all of that topped off with a five-layer coconut cake with fruit salad, and pecan pies.

"Y'all did great." Tom had walked up on the porch behind Lucy while she was basking in the success of yet another event in Sarah's honor.

"Thank you, kind sir." Her cheeks warmed at his proximity. "This was fun. And this house. It's beautiful and cozy at the same time. I keep thanking your mother and sister for helping, but they seem to be having as much fun as I am."

"They are. It's good for them to get to do this. A year ago, Mom wasn't doing so well. She could see better than she can now, but she was down."

"She's a great lady."

"She is. You would have loved my dad." Tom leaned on the porch post and looked out over the crowd in the lengthening shadows underneath the bistro lighting he had strung between the porch posts and the live oak trees in the front yard.

"I'm sure I would have." Tears pricked as she looked up at him. He looked relaxed for once. She hadn't seen him like this in a while. Since last summer, in fact. "When did he die?"

"It will be two years in August."

"You never mentioned it last summer." Finally, she had breached the "last summer" topic. What would he do with it?

"It never came up. I guess it was still pretty fresh." He grinned. "Not a good ice-breaker with a pretty girl you've just met."

She raised her lips in a smile. "True. I guess I didn't tell you all my woes, either, did I?"

"No. I didn't know your mom had died when you were a child until Sarah told me. That had to be hard."

"It was, but I had Daddy. He worked hard so I wouldn't know the difference. He was both Mom and Dad to me." She gave him a half-smile. "Now I think about how lonely he must have been. It's no wonder he was willing to do anything to get me to move back home after college."

They stood there, a little apart, listening to the chatter amongst the guests. A marshy, salty breeze whispered through, lifting her short blonde waves. She crossed her arms as if chilled.

"Cold?" Tom frowned.

She laughed. "Goodness no. It's still 90 degrees. Somebody walking over my grave, I guess." She smiled then sobered. "Charly told me your mom started going blind last summer." She searched his face, looking for answers to unasked questions.

He looked straight ahead and stood tall. "She did. The three of us went on a trip to the Smokies and Biltmore Estate, and it was while we were gone that she started having the headaches. She didn't say much, but she didn't feel right. When she went to the doctor, she got her diagnosis. It's been downhill since."

"I'm sorry."

Tom looked down at her, surprised.

"Really, I am. I wish I had known." She looked him full in the face.

Timing was everything. As they stood there, staring at one another, Lucy was distracted by Charly's voice. It was time to open presents.

GIFTS AND PEOPLE filled the living room and dining room of the old house. Mary Ann Livingston looked as happy as Tom had seen her in a long time. Charly and Lucy were in charge of making sure the gift opening went smoothly and that each gift was acknowledged promptly as details were documented for the later thank-you notes.

He couldn't help but smile at Lucy flitting from Sarah, to Charly, and to his mother. She fit in so well. Too well. She was in her element.

As tissue paper, bows, and ribbons were collected into a large garbage bag, Charly stepped to the middle of the room.

"If I could have your attention, please." Talking continued.

"People!" Lucy got their attention. "Charly's got something to say, and y'all need to listen up or you won't know what's going on." He had a feeling, by the look on Sarah's face, that Lucy was using her 'teacher voice,' and it brought with it a laugh from the crowd.

"Thank you, Lucy. I guess I need to start working on that, don't I?"

"Yes, ma'am."

Sarah piped up. "For Lucy, it was natural."

"Ha. Ha. Better be good, or I'll conveniently lose the ring come wedding day." Lucy made a face at her best friend.

"You wouldn't," Charly whispered to Lucy, her eyes round as saucers.

"Of course not. I've worked too hard on this wedding to mess it up." She winked back at Sarah and gestured to Charly to take the floor.

"Okay, every good wedding shower needs three things: good food, presents, and games." When she heard a groan, she held up her hands. "Hold on a minute. I promise not to embarrass anyone, and I promised my big brother we would not play spin-the-bottle." She gave him a smart look.

Lucy lifted a delicate brow at him. He could feel his face getting hotter and raised his hands in surrender.

"The first game is a kissing game." Hoots and whistles from the crowd had her holding up her hands. "No, not one where you actually get to kiss somebody. I know better."

"I would hope so, young lady." Mom laughed.

"Yes, ma'am. Now this game is different. It's called 'Worst

Kiss, Best Kiss,' so be thinking about what you want to share. Nothing graphic, please."

"Shall we start with the bride and groom?" Lucy gave Sarah a batting-eyelash look.

Jared spoke up. "I think it's only fair, don't you, Pookey?" He pulled Sarah close to him as she gave him a bewildered, and slightly hostile, look.

"Pookey?"

He laughed out loud. "I'm trying out pet names."

"Well, you can stop with that one." She shook her head. "Pookey, my foot."

Jared's father raised his hand. "I don't mind starting this off, if it's all right with you, Charlotte."

"Why, Mr. Benton, I would love to have you volunteer."

"All right then. Worst kiss first." He thought a few seconds. "I have to say my worst kiss was with my sweet wife."

"Conrad Benton!" His wife jabbed him with her elbow.

"Now, Lizzie, hold on right there. Remember our second date?"

She giggled like a schoolgirl. "I do. I guess I should say that's my worst too. It so happened I had agreed to go out on a date with one of the cadets in my father's unit, unbeknownst to me. Our first date was a dance, and we met at the rec hall. On our second date, we were on the front porch, Conrad leaned in for a kiss, and the front porch light came on. When my daddy said 'ten hut, soldier,' Conrad almost took my lips off when he straightened and saluted."

The room burst into laughter. Jared was flabbergasted. "Why have I never heard that story before?"

"You weren't old enough, son." Conrad Benton gave his son a jaunty salute as they laughed together.

The ice thoroughly broken, dating and kissing stories swirled around. Finally, it got to Tom. Great. That's all I need. To have the whole community know my dating history.

"Tom, you can't get out of it. You're the best man, after all," Jared teased, but there was a glint in his eyes.

Sarah nodded in agreement. "And Lucy will be next." The engaged couple looked at one another and nodded in unison.

"Fine. Okay . . . worst kiss. Seventh grade hayride, Jenny Adcock, braces on both parties. Get the picture?" Groans all around.

"What about best?" His baby sister had ended up next to him, and she slid her hand into the crook of his arm.

He looked down at his sister, at the crowd, and after surveying the group, his eyes went straight to Lucy. "Best kiss. Last summer, Myrtle Beach boardwalk, Lucy Dixon. And no braces."

All eyes joined his as they looked at Lucy, waiting for her story. Would it match his? He wanted to look away from her, but he couldn't. It seemed she was mesmerized, as well. Were there other people there?

Finally, after chewing her bottom lip for a moment, she spoke. "Worst kiss. All of them except one. Best kiss? Last summer, Myrtle Beach boardwalk, Tom Livingston. Definitely no braces."

# CHAPTER FOURTEEN

*September*

Saturday, the day of the agency-wide open house dawned to sunshine but with a hint of storm in the air. Charleston was under a hurricane warning, but it was predicted to stay south of Georgetown County.

By 10:00, the starting time for the open houses, Sarah and Lucy were doing all they could to help out with limited experience.

They were in the golf cart traveling between open-house homes in the Litchfield Plantation development, taking boxes of supplies back and forth to the different houses. As a realtor-in-training, Sarah couldn't technically show houses, but she could make sure the licensed realtors had everything they needed to have a great showing. Flyers, business cards, shoe covers, restroom supplies, giveaways. All this was part of it.

Sarah slowed the silent vehicle to a stop next to a Crown Victoria. Lucy didn't know who it could be. When the window rolled down, a jolt rattled her heart. It was Tom. She hadn't seen him since the wedding shower at his mother's house, and she didn't know how to talk to him for some reason.

"'Morning, Tom!" For today, anyway, anti-morning Sarah had turned into Little Mary Sunshine.

"Sarah. Lucy, nice to see you." Tom flickered a look her way and then looked at Sarah. "Y'all are keeping an eye on the weather, aren't you?"

Sarah held up a walkie-talkie. "We're all connected, and all have our weather apps on standby. Do you think it will be bad later?"

"It's looking like it might be. Tropical storm watch south of here, and that could change pretty quickly. I'll be in the area, and we've got everybody working this weekend. This would have to hit on Labor Day weekend." Tom shook his head as he kept an eye on traffic around them. "Both of you be careful."

"We will. See ya, Tom." Sarah waved and put the vehicle in gear. "Never seen you so quiet, Luce."

"Just don't feel like talking, if you know what I mean." She gave Sarah a look that did not bode well for a certain police detective. "I can't keep up with him. He's too changeable for me. One time I meet him and he seems interested in me and the next, he turns into Mr. Darcy and shows no emotion whatsoever."

"Ah, Mr. Darcy showed plenty in the end, didn't he?" Sarah laughed.

Lucy and Sarah had watched the PBS mini-series of *Pride and Prejudice* by Jane Austen more times than they could count. Mainly because of Mr. Darcy. And a young Colin Firth.

Lucy sighed. "Yes, but I want a fairy tale like yours and Jared's. One look and Cupid's arrow had you both at the same time."

Sarah laughed. "It wasn't quite that easy. At first I wondered if Jared was interested in me for my inheritance. I mean, it should have all been his, but Uncle Alex decided to leave my family the bulk of the business. I didn't think I, a school teacher from Kentucky, was nearly enough woman for Jared."

Lucy snorted. "You're nuts, you know that? Jared knew a good thing when he saw it. I would have thought, being friends with Jared, that Tom would have the same smarts when it comes to women." She crossed her arms in what could almost be considered a pout.

"Well, you are a good thing."

"Right? That's never been in question, has it?" Lucy's lips twitched in a smile, and a laugh gurgled up. "I've been working on that 'walk humbly' part."

"I can tell."

By 3:00, Sarah and Lucy were tired but pumped. The agents had shown houses to more people than the year before, possibly because of the rip currents and winds keeping beach-goers off the beach. Her phone buzzed as she drove the golf cart down the street of a development that had several homes to show.

"Sarah here." She answered as she surveyed the skies.

"Hey, it's Ron. Could you bring a box of shoe covers down to Beachside Bungalow? We've run out."

"I'm not surprised. That's an awesome house. I'll be there in ten minutes."

"Thanks, Sarah. You're a life saver."

Sarah sighed. It wasn't exactly what she envisioned when she decided to go into real estate, but she was only half-way through her real estate licensing courses, so at this point she was a glorified go-fer. A gust of wind hit the vehicle and made her swerve. The weather wasn't looking promising for the afternoon.

"Hey, watch it there!" Lucy held on to the bar next to her seat.

Sarah grimaced and concentrated on the road and the skies. "Sorry. That gust surprised me."

"Me too. There's the supply truck. You stay here, and I'll run out and get what you need."

Lucy sprinted to the truck and pulled out a box of shoe covers to take to the beach house that seemed to be the hit of the season. It was new and the star piece of property. Local designers had been sought to plan and decorate the interior and the land-scaping. The shoe covers were designed to keep the floors in the pristine condition they were in when the open house started.

As Sarah drove into the drive of Beachside Bungalow, her phone buzzed again, this time with a weather alert.

"Luce, what does that say? I need both hands to drive."

"Yikes." Lucy's eyes rounded as she looked over at Sarah. "We were in a severe thunderstorm watch as a result of the impending Hurricane Rosa to the south, and now we're under a tropical storm watch, one step away from a warning. Possible hurricane force winds. No kidding, huh?" The golf cart shud-dered a little with the next gust.

Jared was across town in another development. Sarah pressed Jared's number, and he answered immediately.

"Jared?"

"Sarah, I got the weather alert. How does it look over there?"

"The wind is getting up. The sun keeps peeking out."

"That's not good. It makes the weather more unstable. I'm going to call the agents and tell them to close down early. Did you figure out your storm shutters at your house?"

"I think so. As soon as we get the golf cart back to the office, I'll run home and take care of it and pick up Oliver. Don't worry. We'll be fine." Hearing the worry in his voice made her nervous, but she held it together. He had the weight of this entire event on his shoulders. As a partner, the least she could do would be to take care of a few things on her own.

"Keep an eye out for the weather. I was afraid of this."

"I thought hurricanes were forecast weeks in advance?"

"They are, but even if you're not in the eye of the storm, it can wreak havoc with beachfront property and beyond. Tornadoes, lightning strikes, high winds. You name it, we could have it. Listen, if they call for an evacuation or for people to take shelter, get to the church. Promise?"

Okay, this was getting scary. Having never lived through a hurricane, Sarah only knew what she had seen on television. Jared, on the other hand, had been here.

"O-Okay. I'll keep my eye on the sky, and my ear to the weather report."

"Good. I'll be in touch as soon as I can. Call me when you get to your house."

"I will. Jared?" Her voice was shaking along with the rest of her.

"Yes? Do you need something?" He was quick and to the point. Problem-solver mode.

"I need you to be careful too." She could feel nervous tears gathering.

There was a pause. "Don't worry. I love you, Sarah." His voice gentled.

"I love you, too, Jared. See you soon."

They ended the conversation. Sarah stared at Jared's picture on her phone for a second before another wind gust threatened to blow them out of the golf cart. Time to get to the office and batten down the hatches both there and at her house. No time to linger.

JARED SURVEYED the churning clouds as he drove from north of where Sarah had called him. The weather report had not improved. North of Georgetown, across the river, they had been included in a tropical storm warning, which meant the probability of Pawley's Island being threatened was imminent.

The open house signs had been stacked in the back of various SUVs, and he got word the storm shutters on the office had been closed, thanks to Sarah getting there ahead of most of the veterans. She should have gone straight to her house. He was more worried about her than the office.

Traffic was getting heavy going away from the storm but light headed south, as he was. Not a good sign. Cell phones were getting spotty. He had tried to reach Sarah's phone several times, to no avail. Too many calls.

Jared slowed as Tom flashed the headlights on his unmarked cruiser, and they met side by side as the rain began.

"Where are you headed? We're trying to get everyone to safety, and here you are going the opposite direction of where you should be."

"I wanted to check the new house. It's close to the office and shouldn't take a minute." When the weather notification on his phone signaled, he looked down briefly and saw the word "Warning" before it went out. Severe thunderstorm? Tropical storm? He would have time to check on Beachside Bungalow, and head to Sarah and safety.

"Okay, but be quick. We're under a warning now. High-level tropical storm."

"Thanks, Bud. My phone died."

"Yeah, my cell did too. Probably a wind gust got a cell tower."

"Great. I'll get to the church as quick as I can. I told Sarah I'd meet her there."

"Good. Check on you later. Stay safe."

"Hey, you too."

They both put their vehicles in gear. Jared stopped and looked at Tom soberly. "Are we good?"

Were they? Was Tom willing to let things go to let a friend give him sound advice?

Tom looked away and back at his best friend. Tom nodded. "We're good. Later, dude."

Jared smiled and drove away.

"Yes Mom, I'm fine. We're under a tropical storm warning." Sarah closed the door behind her. Between them, she and Lucy had locked all the new storm shutters Jared had insisted upon installing before she ever moved in. The power was out when she arrived, so they gathered Oliver, his dog food and bowls, and any perishables to take with them to the shelter.

"Shouldn't you be at the shelter? Oh, Sarah, please don't take any chances."

"Mom, I have my emergency kit with me, and we're getting in the car to head to the church right now. I need to get off the phone in case Jared calls."

"All right. Keep me updated as best you can."

"Don't worry, I will. I love you, Mom."

Her mother ended the call on her end, and Sarah checked her "missed calls" in case she hadn't heard the electronic notification for all the wind. Nothing. She didn't want to worry her mother, but now she was worried, herself, about Jared.

"He should have called by now."

"Maybe there are too many calls to get through. Or maybe cell service is out?" Lucy was trying to keep herself and Sarah calm.

Sarah tried his cell. Nothing. Straight to voicemail. She frowned into the phone.

"Let's pray, Sarah. It's the best thing we can do."

Sarah nodded. "God, I know you said many times in the

Bible not to fear, but I'm getting a little freaked out. Can You please, please take care of Jared for me?"

"And us," Lucy added.

She squeezed Lucy's hand. "Thanks. If we have to have a first hurricane experience, I'm glad we're together."

"Me, too." Lucy seemed to shrink into the bucket seat of Sarah's car.

She put her car in gear and headed out of the driveway. She didn't speak as she drove. The wind and the sudden bursts of rain made driving a bit dicey, but safety was at the makeshift shelter at the church, not a house right on the beach.

Calvary Church's nominating committee had approached her about helping out with the Disaster Preparedness Committee, and she'd said yes. Her background as a teacher and her proximity to the church was a plus. Having come from Tornado Alley, disaster relief looked much different from here. At home, in Kentucky, tornado activity could pop up in the middle of a thunderstorm, leaving devastation in its wake with less than an hour's warning.

Tropical storms and hurricanes had more notice but could, and probably would, impact an entire region. Collecting food and supplies, making sure there was a safe, hurricane-resistant building to shelter in, and keeping the people there calm was the tip of the iceberg, she had learned. They partnered with the Red Cross and other organizations to provide a place for people to come who couldn't leave the area. Calvary Church was one such location. It would serve the Murrells Inlet area and the area south of Litchfield Beach. Across the river, Georgetown had a shelter, and there was a church a few miles inland from Pawley's Island that served their area.

Sarah handed Lucy her phone. "Try Jared's number again."

"Nothing." Stuck in traffic, all they could do was pray. Call on God. "What about Tom? Maybe he will know something."

She scrolled through the contacts on Sarah's phone, found his number, and pressed "call." On the fourth ring, right before voicemail, his voice came through. She put it on speaker.

"Sarah? Where are you?"

"It's Lucy, on Sarah's phone. We're stuck in traffic on the way to the shelter at church. How is it?"

"It's getting bad. I took Mom and Charly to the church. They're fine." She heard him pull the phone away from his face and yell instructions into the wind. "Did the open house get closed down?"

"As far as I know. Litchfield Plantation's did. Have you heard from Jared? He was going to check on the new house and then head to Sarah's house, but he never arrived."

Her voice was starting to quiver with the gusty wind buffeting her car.

"He was headed toward the new house, but he promised he would head straight to the shelter after that. He probably got stuck in traffic like you."

"Sarah can't get him on the phone, Tom, and she's getting pretty scared. If you are in that area, would you check on him? She wants to make sure he's okay."

As Sarah listened, the sick feeling in her stomach was getting worse.

Tom's phone started cutting out. They could barely hear him but did catch, "check on him" before it went dead.

Sitting there, stalled in traffic consisting of locals trying to get home and nervous tourists trying to get out of town, Sarah's tears started, and she let them flow. These tears were between her, Lucy, and God, and she knew they would both understand.

JARED ARRIVED at the new house about the time the outer edge of the tropical storm hit.

Shaking his head in frustration, he decided to pull into the garage and try to wait it out until it slacked off a bit. He looked at his phone and read "no service" up at the top where he should have Wi-Fi and several bars of service. This house had every state-of-the-art tech item that it could hold. But could it hold up to hurricane force winds?

"I guess I'll find out."

He went into the house and confirmed the storm shutters had been closed before the agents closed it up after the open house. Good job. It was a beautiful house. In other circumstances, he would have wandered from room to room admiring the craftsmanship and design that had gone into the building of a dream house.

Today, he was preoccupied. Had Sarah and Lucy made it to the shelter, or were they still waiting for him at her house? He hoped not. Both their houses were right on the beach, as was this one. Great for nice days. Bad for storm surges.

A weather alert on his phone cut through the wild, screaming wind outside. "Tropical storm warning with the potential to be upgraded to a hurricane warning as the winds escalate. Stay tuned for weather alerts."

"Why can I get that on my phone and no signal to call?" He shook his head and looked up in prayer. "Am I getting selfish? I know You can calm the storm and tell the sea to lie still. Right now all I want is for Sarah to be safe."

THE SKY DARKENED both from the storm and the time of day. By dark the wind was still howling, and the surge was coming in.

When they arrived at the church, there were already several people from the community there, taking shelter. Lucy was glad to have something to do. The wind screaming outside was unnerving.

"Okay, Lucy, I'm in charge of keeping the little ones occupied, so, since you're here, we'll transition them between games, songs, and crayon and paper activities, with a craft thrown in. We can tag team. While one keeps the kids occupied, the other will put together another activity."

"Look at you, all organized and everything. I thought that was my thing." Lucy grinned. She couldn't keep from wondering where Tom was. As a county detective, he was on duty. She had to keep busy or her nerves would get the best of her. As it was, her stomach was tied in so many knots the thought of eating anything made her feel sick.

"We've gathered old Vacation Bible School materials in tubs for emergencies and summer day-camp activities, and they sure do come in handy in times like this."

Lucy was impressed. Sarah was doing an excellent job hiding her concern for Jared. She checked her phone every few minutes but had a smile for the children and their parents. The last thing anyone wanted was for a child to be traumatized by a storm, so when she could see them getting scared, they would stop, pray, and play a noisy game that helped to shut out the howling wind. It helped the grownups too.

She knew Tom had a reason to be absent, but where was Jared? He should be here.

# CHAPTER FIFTEEN

As night closed in and the screaming wind abated, the children began sorting themselves out amongst their parents and their cots or air mattresses. It was getting quieter. Everyone was wondering what had happened to their property. Some of the people there were vacationers in rental homes and condos.

Lucy, Sarah, and Charlotte—Charly to everyone except her mother—had stacks of blankets and bottled water in their arms. They went to different people, focusing on the elderly, to make sure they were warm enough. When they finished, they ended up with Charly and Tom's mother, Mary Ann, in the corner of the fellowship hall.

"Are you doing okay, Mrs. Livingston?" Lucy had grown to love this woman.

"I'm fine. I can't see how many people are here, but it's a full house, isn't it? Are you all right? You sound worried."

Her lack of vision had no effect on her intuition. "Sarah hasn't heard from Jared since this started."

"Tom, either. They're big boys, and they've gone through this before."

"I know. But we haven't." Lucy chuckled quietly. "I guess Sarah will have to get used to this, living on the coast."

"You never really get used to it. We're fortunate it doesn't happen every year, and the good outweighs the bad most of the time."

"Except for the humidity and mosquitoes." Charly had plopped down on a mattress next to her mother. "Other than that, it's pretty near perfect, don't you think?"

Sarah sank into an adjoining air mattress.

"Definitely. And it's home now." Sarah smiled at the teen.

Mary Ann put out her hands. "Let's pray for our boys, shall we? Our Gracious Heavenly Father, we praise Your Name. We thank You for the safety of these people here and in other places. We pray safety for those outside these walls. And, if we're honest, and You know our innermost thoughts, we pray a little harder for mercy and care for our boys, Tom and Jared. Keep them safe, Lord, in the palm of Your hand. In Jesus' precious name, Amen."

"Thank you." Lucy and Sarah wiped the tears from their faces.

Sarah straightened her back in the dim light. "I believe and trust God for their safety. He's got this."

Lucy sniffed loudly, and chuckled. "Of course He does." She wanted to believe it. Right now, she wanted to see Tom, make sure this maddening man that had her turned upside down and inside out was safe.

WHEN THE WINDS began to calm down to a roar instead of a scream, Jared fell asleep in the dark house. He had survived the storm.

When he woke, it was still dim in the shuttered house, the house quiet. He could hear sirens in the distance, but the house was standing. When he had finally fallen asleep the night before, the wind was screaming all around. He opened the shutters to survey the damage. There was debris all over the patio, but the wall of glass doors was intact. The pergola, however, was in pieces, leaning on the side of the house. Two of the new palm trees that had been planted a few weeks ago were on the ground. He calculated how much it would cost to replace them. Since they were not native to the area, losing one tree was losing money on a property.

He walked out the front door to inspect the damage on that side. No movement in the neighborhood. He assumed everyone had either evacuated or was still asleep. The wind was still gusty. Still dangerous to the trees and structures on the rain-and-storm-surge-soaked land that was more sand than dirt or rock. You had to dig deep to build a house on the beach. Fortunately, they had.

Jared smiled, remembering a verse from Matthew. *But those who hear my instructions and ignore them are foolish, like a man who builds his house on sand. For when the rains and floods come, and storm winds beat against his house, it will fall with a mighty crash.* Seeing the damage to other properties, his smile faded. He had to get out of here so he could help. It had been foolish of him to not go straight to Sarah's house or to the shelter.

The large palm still stood in front of the house, but it was leaning. That would have to come down or be re-planted, and soon. He went back through the front door after seeing the drive was where he could get out, if he were careful. He locked up and manually opened the garage door.

He backed out of the garage. Out of habit, he stopped and looked down both sides of the street. As he looked up the street, his main thought was to get to the church and check on Sarah. What if the roads were closed? He hadn't thought of that. He sat there a minute, thinking.

As he swung his head around to look down the other end of

the street, the last thing he thought of was Sarah, and the last thing he saw was the large palm tree coming down on the sunroof of his SUV.

# CHAPTER SIXTEEN

Power was out. Landlines and cell towers were out. The only communication was satellite radio and emergency communication devices.

When the sun came up the day after Tropical Storm Rosa, which had at moments pushed at the level-one hurricane scale, it was all any of them could do not to run out of the church and look at the devastation. They were instructed to stay inside until emergency services reached them. The men began opening the storm shutters, which gave them a glimpse of the church yard and the highway beyond the parking lot.

The lot was littered with debris, and the cars were there, but it looked as if a giant hand had been playing with them. No longer in straight rows, they were staggered, and there would be damage from the vehicles bumping one another. At least the storm surge hadn't reached this area.

Sarah wondered about Pilot Oaks. Prudie Matthews and Alma Ruth McGinty had come to the church as soon as it opened. She was glad to not have to worry about these ladies. They were too special to her. Prudie had taken over the kitchen first thing. The food was good, and she kept it coming.

Through all of this, one person remained on her mind. Jared. Where was he? Had Tom been able to find him? And was Tom okay? She knew Mary Ann was worried, but she never let on. Lucy had been very quiet all night.

When the door to the family life center opened, she didn't look up, thinking it was one of the men working on the shutters. Tom's voice broke through the chaos. Finally. She immediately handed the toddler she held to Charly and went straight to him.

"Tom! Have you heard from Jared?"

Tom had a grim look on his face that did nothing to alleviate her fear. He had been through a hurricane, on duty. He did nothing more than squeeze his mother's hand and kiss her cheek before he came directly to her.

"Sarah, there's been an accident."

Lucy came up and put an arm around Sarah.

"Jared." Her knees weakened, and her hands begin to shake. "Is he okay?"

"He's alive."

Lucy held on to her, and Tom grabbed her arms before she could fall. She closed her eyes, took a deep breath, and made her knees stop shaking. This wasn't the time.

"Where is he?"

"The ambulance took him to Georgetown General. They should be getting there about now. He's unconscious."

"I need to go. Now."

"I'll take you. Let me give instructions to the leadership here, and then we can go. Power's still out all over the county and beyond. The storm surge did a lot of damage, and a lot of these people will be here for a few days, I'm afraid."

Lucy spoke up. "Go. Take care of it. I'll keep the kids occupied."

Tom nodded at her in approval. He knelt by his mother and sister, assuring them he was fine, and updating them on Jared. He found the Red Cross sergeant overseeing the shelter and gave him an update on what was going on outside the walls of the church.

Sarah was trying her best to keep a "stiff upper lip," but at the look on Charly's face, she almost broke down. "Charly, I need you to help Lucy with the kids. I've got to go to Jared." A stray tear worked its way down her cheek. "I have to."

"I know. Take care of my brother, will you?"

"Tom? He's fine." Sarah was confused.

"No, Jared. He's like another big brother to me." She went into Sarah's arms and sobbed for a moment before pulling away and drying her eyes. "I'll be okay. It's just scary, isn't it?"

Sarah smiled through her tears. "It is. But we know Who is in control. We have to remember that." She squeezed the teen with another hug and nodded at her in approval. "You've got this."

Charly grinned. "I've got this."

Lucy, overseeing a paper-and-pencil activity with the children, paid attention to Tom as he interacted with his mother. She missed her parents. What must it be like to have a parent that needed you so much? She never knew her dad to "need" her, except in the way parents like to have their children near them. She always wanted to be more involved in his life than he would let her.

Had she been spoiled? Yes. Her dad made sure she never wanted for anything. He was the fun, snuggly dad. The dad that didn't scold. A pointed look from him was scold enough. But she was used to getting her own way.

Tom? She wasn't sure. He certainly looked after his mother and sister. An irritating thought came to her, unbidden. He had convinced himself, with his family to care for, that he didn't have time to have a relationship.

"Lucy, I told Sarah I would help. What do you need?" Charly had walked up and surprised her in her reverie.

"You startled me, Charly. Okay, if you would, set up those table-top easels over there and get the watercolors and paper out. We'll have them paint one another's portrait." For an idea off the top of her head, she didn't think it was too bad.

"Awesome! I love art, and watercolors are my favorite."

"Great. You can be in charge of that one while I check on something, if that's all right with you?"

Charly laughed and pulled her long hair back into a ponytail. "No problemo. I'll see that the rug rats paint one another on the paper, not on each other."

Lucy squeezed her arm and smiled. "Thanks. I think I'll sit with your mom for a few minutes."

"Please do. It's driving her crazy not to be able to help in the kitchen, where she would have been, in the past. She's trying to pat the Jones' baby to sleep, so she's feeling semi-useful."

She made her way through the maze of air mattresses until she could get to the corner where Mary Ann sat on the mattress next to little Carly Jones. She was almost asleep, and Mary Ann was singing softly to her. When the child relaxed in sleep, she smiled, and lifted her hand slightly.

"Hi, Mrs. Livingston." Lucy whispered as she lowered herself down on the mattress next to hers.

"You must call me Mary Ann, dear girl. We don't stand on formality around here, especially in these circumstances."

"Very well. Mary Ann, it is. Aren't you worried about Tom in all this?" This was the easiest way to turn the conversation to Tom. She had to know more about him. What made him tick? Was he as good as he seemed?

Mary Ann smiled and sighed. "I'm a mother. Of course I'm worried. I learned a long time ago that worrying didn't gain me anything but a headache, so when my sight started going, the only way I could get by every day was to leave it all on the altar. Jesus has this under control."

"I never worried about my dad. He was always strong and in control, and I never thought anything could happen to him. Until it did. Then it was too late."

"Sweet girl, do you feel guilty for not worrying about your daddy? From what I've heard, he died a hero."

"How did you know?" Lucy looked at Mary Ann's clouded eyes in surprise.

"Tom told me. Told me all about the funeral, your grand-mother, about the sermon the preacher shared, about your house and all the people that came to grieve with you. Said it reminded him of his daddy's funeral. Except for the hero part."

Lucy looked down at her hands. Tom had told his mother all about the funeral. She knew he cared a little, or he wouldn't have come. She wondered, though, did he care as much as she did?

"Tom told you all that?"

"He did. He told me about you the first time you met too. I knew a little about you before that 'kissing game' story he told. He was quite taken with you, I believe."

Lucy would swear Mary Ann could look into her soul, blind or not.

"Humph. I don't know about that. He's not as communicative with me as he is with you."

"I know. He's a little moody like me, but he feels like he has to even everything out, like his daddy. His daddy used his sense of humor. Tom uses organization. After you left, I was diagnosed with a fast-progressing glaucoma. His daddy had died the year before, and when that happened, it was like he turned his back on his own life to take care of Charly and me."

TOM WAS careful as he drove Sarah from Calvary Church to Georgetown General. The roads were fine except where power lines were down. Crews were already hard at work, but it got more hazardous the farther north they went. The bridges across both the Waccamaw and Great Pee Dee Rivers were strewn with mud and debris and had water up to the bottom of the bridges. Only emergency vehicles were allowed across.

Tom kept his eyes on the road, highly aware of not only debris but also emergency workers clearing the highway. "It looked like he had weathered the storm in the new house, and then as he was leaving, one of those big palms came down on top of the SUV. Honestly, when I drove up on it, I thought it had been sitting there all night, and didn't expect to find a survivor, but his clothes were dry and the truck was clean. He must have pulled into the garage for the storm."

"Oh, Tom. Why did he go back to that house? It's just a house." Sarah stared at the road as closely as Tom, as if she could do anything to help from the passenger seat. She could watch for hazards. It was the least she could do.

"Because he's Jared, and he feels responsible. It was a freak thing. To survive a hurricane, and then get conked out by a tree." His eyes never left the road even as he shook his head in amazement.

"How much damage?"

"To the house? None that I could see. To his SUV? Totaled. Jared? Jury's still out. He was pinned in the driver's seat. Since the impact was from above, the airbags were no protection. The sunroof frame was what pinned him in. If he had been in the Jag . . ."

The tears had been flowing ever since she got into the vehicle. She was calm, she listened, and she was thankful Tom didn't ask those pesky "are you okay?" questions that would have infuriated her.

The lack of traffic on the highway entering Georgetown was

surreal. There were no traffic lights, only police and emergency first responders at intersections keeping things in order. They were ushered through with a simple wave and a grim nod.

The emergency room of the hospital was a different story. There was a variety of injuries from mild cuts and bruises to broken bones and a heart-attack victim. An elderly woman on oxygen lay on a gurney. Tom led her through to the desk where they waited as a nurse finished up with a young mother and her injured child.

"Detective, you're here about Mr. Benton, aren't you?" The nurse glanced up at them. "Dr. Garvey is with him now. If you could wait in the surgery waiting room, I'll have someone notify you when he has news." She looked over at Sarah. "Are you Sarah Crawford?"

"Yes. Has anyone called his parents?" She was a little puzzled the nurse knew her.

"No, ma'am. You were listed as his next of kin."

Tom looked at her grimly. "That's one of the reasons I came for you first."

Sarah nodded. She needed to sit down before she shook herself to death. His next of kin. Why did that have such a scary ring to it? You didn't need a next of kin on a daily basis, yet he had listed her, at some point in the last few weeks or months, as his next of kin. Not a wife yet, but acting as one on his behalf. Wow.

Tom led her to the small waiting room down the hall. It was quieter there. No crying children, no groaning injured. Normally she would be out there helping, but at this moment it was all she could do to walk down the hallway.

# CHAPTER SEVENTEEN

om and Sarah sat side-by-side in the waiting room, neither talking. Until they got word of Jared's condition, there wasn't much for them to do except pray and get lost in their own thoughts.

The door opened an hour later.

"Sarah Crawford?" The doctor looked down at the chart and then up at her above his reading glasses.

"Yes. How is he?" Her voice shook, and surprised herself as she realized how unrecognizable it was, even to her.

"We need to get him into surgery. His collar bone was broken. We've set that, but he has a small brain bleed. It isn't bad now, but we need to get it stopped before it does any damage. He still hasn't regained consciousness. We may be looking at a traumatic brain injury."

"Is it normal for him to still be out?" Tom's worried tone did little to alleviate Sarah's concern.

"It's better this way. Moving around is the worst thing he can do at this point, If he were awake, we would have him sedated. Right now, however, I need your signature, Sarah, allowing us to do the surgery."

Sarah's eyes grew round with shock. "M-My signature?"

"Yes, your signature. As his healthcare proxy, you have the right to make medical decisions if he is incapacitated. If not, we would be contacting his parents, but considering you are here, and they are not, well, I need your signature."

She reached over to take the clipboard and wrote her name on the paper next to the blue "x."

"Thank you. We're getting ready to prep him for surgery now. Would you like to see him before we take him back?"

"Can I?" She looked at Tom. Maybe he wanted to spend time with his friend. He smiled at her and shook his head.

"You go on. I'll be right here unless I get a call."

THE CUBICLE they had him in was small. There was room for the gurney with Jared lying on it, too still for her comfort, the necessary medical equipment, and one lone chair. She walked up to him and took his hand, trying not to exclaim in shock at his appearance. He was bruised and cut from the broken sun roof. Bandages swathed his shoulder where the collar bone was broken. There were tubes and electrodes everywhere. It was his poor hair that made the tears flow. They had shaved off about half of the thick, dark hair on top of his head, where the worst damage happened, and where the surgery would take place.

"Oh, God, please, please take care of him. He has so much more to do. I have so much more to do with him. I don't want to lose him now that I've found him."

She scrutinized him closely, looking for any sign of life outside of the steady breathing and beeping of his heart monitor. Did she imagine his hand tightened on hers? Probably.

The anesthesiologist and nurse came in, and she knew it was time to leave his side.

"Ma'am, we'll get you word in the waiting room as quick as

we can." The young African American nurse gave her a compassionate smile and a pat on her shoulder.

"Thank you. I'll be there. I . . . I need to call his parents. Let them know what's going on."

"You've got plenty of time. This kind of surgery takes a few hours. If there's one thing we don't want to rush, it's brain surgery."

Brain surgery. She knew it was his brain, but it was because he had been hit on the head by a . . . well, by a tree. She had thought of it as "head surgery." But it was his brain. It didn't get better. It got scarier.

She got to the waiting room in time to see Tom coming out the door.

"I'm sorry, Sarah. I don't want to leave you alone, but I've gotten a call, and I need to get across town to another accident scene. We're stretched pretty thin."

She lifted her chin and gave him a brave half-smile. "I'll be fine. They said it would be a few hours before we know anything." She shivered and looked him in the eye, searching for courage. "Oh, Tom. So many tubes and wires."

He pulled her into a brotherly hug and stood there while she sobbed. When she calmed, she stood back and gave him a watery smile. "I'll be okay. Will you be going close to the church?"

"Not for a while, but I'll check on things in a bit. Call me when you hear anything, and I'll let the folks know what's going on. When I get a chance, I'll bring Lucy."

"Thanks. I need to call the Colonel and Mrs. Benton." She tugged at her lip between her teeth. She had met them several times, including the surprise shower. They were very nice, but she had to admit being a little intimidated by the military bearing of the colonel, and keeping up with Mrs. Benton's switches in topics of conversation kept her on her toes.

"Don't worry. I have it on good authority they liked you very much."

"Well, let's hope being the bearer of bad news doesn't change their opinion."

Sarah reached up and hugged Tom again. "You go. You've got a whole county to take care of. I just have Jared."

"Remember, you're not alone." He pointed skyward and grinned at her.

"Believe me, that line of communication has been pretty much open all day."

When he left the room, she whispered to herself, "I just have Jared."

The nurse had given her the bag of Jared's personal effects, including his phone. She turned it on, thankful it still had charge and that he had shared with her his entry code. She scrolled through his contacts and found his parents' number in Silver Spring, Maryland, but called from her phone. She didn't want his number to come up and have his mother think it was Jared calling.

She heard the Benton's phone begin to ring, and Sarah's heart began to pound. What was she going to tell them?"

"Hello?"

It was the colonel.

"Colonel Benton? This is Sarah Crawford."

"Hello, Sarah, and please, call me Conrad. How is the weather down there? I heard it got pretty rough. Some weekend for the open house, huh?"

"Yes, sir. Um, it's been pretty bad." She paused.

"Sarah? Is something wrong?"

She took a deep breath. "I'm afraid there's been an accident. Jared has been hurt and is in surgery now."

She could hear him telling his wife what she was telling him.

"We'll be down there as soon as possible. If we can get a flight, we'll do that, but with this weather . . ."

"I know. And I know Jared would tell you not to rush. It's quite a madhouse around here at this point, as you can imagine."

"I know, we've been there. What happened? Are you all right?"

"Yes, I was at the shelter at the church during the storm. Jared had stopped at one of the properties and weathered the storm there. Tom said it seemed that it happened as he was leaving the property. A tree fell on his vehicle."

She heard his quick intake of breath. "How bad is it?"

"He has a head injury, and they're doing surgery now to alleviate the swelling and bleeding. The doctor was cautiously optimistic."

"Sarah, I'm sorry you have to deal with this. I'm sure Tom is close by."

"He left on a call, but he came to get me as soon as he knew Jared was hurt. He also knows I won't leave him until he's awake. I'll be here."

"Liz and I will be there as soon as we can. Call my cell if there are any changes or you need to talk. Wait a minute. Liz wants to talk to you."

"Sarah, have you seen him yet?"

Sarah took a deep breath to keep from breaking down. "I did. He's pretty banged up, and they had to shave part of his head where they'll be doing surgery."

"Bless his heart. And yours. It's hard to see someone we love in that shape."

"I know, Mrs. Benton. I can't believe he went back to check on a house instead of getting to shelter."

"Men, right? Sweetheart, please, call me Liz. We're family."

"Thank you. I'll be glad to see you both."

"You stay strong, and we'll be there before you know it. Take care, Sarah."

They ended the call, and Sarah collapsed into a chair in the corner of the waiting room. There were several families there, some looking beaten-up themselves, waiting on a loved one with bigger problems.

Mom and Dad. Sarah realized with all the confusion, she hadn't called her parents. She pulled her cell out and scrolled through her calls to find their number. When she heard it ringing on the other end, she started to relax.

"Sarah?" Mom answered on the first ring.

"Yeah, Mom, it's me." She was sure her loud sigh told the tale. She just couldn't keep it in any longer.

"Are you okay? You sound upset."

"Well, it's been a pretty upsetting day. First a hurricane and then an accident. Not me, Jared. He was leaving a property where he had stayed safe during the storm, and would you believe a tree fell on his truck?"

"Oh my goodness. How is he? Are you with him now? What vehicle was he in? I've heard there aren't any airbags to protect against something falling on a vehicle, and you never know, do you?"

"It was his SUV. He's in surgery, Mom." She could feel emotion welling up, wanting her to be there with her. She wanted a hug and assurance only a mother could give. She sniffed loudly and shook her head, trying to clear it.

"What did the doctor say?"

"He has a head injury and a broken collar bone. They're in surgery relieving the pressure and bleeding. Oh, Mom. What if he doesn't make it? What if he never wakes up?"

"Sweetie, glance at the problem, and gaze upon Jesus. He's got you both in the palm of His hand, you know."

"I know, Mom. I'm scared."

"He knows that too. Do you want us to come? What about the house? Was there any damage, or do you even know yet?"

"Not a clue. None of our houses were even on my mind. I called Jared's parents, and they're coming as soon as they can. It's about as far for them as it is for you. I'll ask Tom to check on Pilot Oaks and mine. Right now it's pretty chaotic. Pawley's Island was hit pretty hard. I remember hearing about Hurricane

Hugo literally cutting the island in half. I hope it wasn't as bad this time."

"I'm glad Lucy's there, and Jared's parents will be there with you. I'm looking forward to meeting them."

Sarah's lips curved in a smile. "I'm looking forward to that too. I wish it were under better circumstances. I'd better get off here. Cell reception is spotty."

"All right. Call me any time, Sarah. I mean that. Even after bedtime if you need me."

"What? After 9:00?" Her chuckle ended with a sigh. "I will, Mom. Love you."

"Love you, too, sweetie."

# CHAPTER EIGHTEEN

The storm surge had damaged homes to the second row off the ocean in some areas. Ground floor condos right on the beach would require massive cleanup, and power outages and downed trees were slowing emergency vehicles and residents trying to access their property. As the hurricane had stayed at or below a Category 1, those who had survived Hurricane Hugo in 1989 called this a mere thunderstorm in comparison. Still, for those unable to go home, it was difficult.

Tom was tired. He had been up most of the last two nights. The night of the storm he caught a catnap on the couch at the station at the insistence of the sheriff. After Jared was hurt, he had been called out to another accident scene that lasted into the wee hours. He drove back to the hospital and slept for twenty minutes in his car.

Heading into the hospital, he had two cups of coffee and a sausage biscuit in his hands. The Red Cross and a fast-food restaurant had partnered to provide breakfast for the emergency workers. He considered Sarah an emergency worker, too.

When he passed the ICU waiting room, he noticed it was empty. Sarah was probably still in Jared's room. As he entered, he waved at the nurse at the station as she put a finger to her lips. The only sound he heard was the steady beeping of monitors and the muffled sounds of the outside hallway. It was, for now, an oasis in chaos if ever there was one. Now if Jared would just wake up.

He looked into the window and smiled. Sarah sat in a chair pulled up to Jared's bed, her head lying on the mattress beside him, fast asleep. He was sure she didn't get much sleep the night before either.

A beep of equipment startled her awake, and she looked at Jared's face before looking for the origin of the sound. Tom opened the door and got her attention. "Hey. Sleep much?"

She raised an eyebrow. "What do you think?"

"Yeah. I figured you might need coffee."

She reached out for it with both hands. "Tom, you may be my favorite person right now. Present company excepted." She looked down at Jared. "He moved his hand a little last night."

"That's good, isn't it?"

"I don't know. Until I fell asleep, I couldn't take my eyes off of him. I was watching for anything. They did check his eyes and said they both reacted favorably to the light."

"You need to get some rest. Why don't you go lie down in the waiting room and I'll sit here?"

"I don't know."

"If you fall out, you'll do nobody any good. I'll come get you if anything changes."

"Pray for him?"

"I haven't stopped." He handed her a sandwich as she got up. He took her place by Jared's side, shaking his head at his friend lying there, unconscious.

"Here is his phone, in case his parents call." She pointed at the cell phones on the bedside table.

"Leave yours, too, so you'll sleep."

"Okay." She hesitated and looked down at her love. "I'll be right back, Jared."

She left the room, and Tom was left with the beeping monitors and his sleeping friend.

"Buddy, you've got to get well. You've got way too much to do in this life. I mean, that girl there, she's a keeper."

No movement, no answer from Jared.

Sarah's phone vibrated. He wondered if he should answer it or let it go to voicemail. It was Lucy. He hesitated. "This is Tom."

"Tom? Where's Sarah? Is she okay? Jared, how is he? I'm going nuts not hearing anything."

Tom grinned into the phone. It was good to hear her voice. "Lucy, calm down. Sarah's fine. She's in the waiting room trying to get a nap, and I'm sitting with Jared. I told her to leave her phone with me so she wouldn't be tempted to check it every few minutes. She's fine, and Jared's stable."

"Praise God."

"Yes."

There was a pause on the other end of the line. "How are you, Tom? And how is Jared?"

"I'm fine, and Jared is still unconscious, and his vitals are getting stronger. The doctor likes his chances." He heard a loud sniff. "Do you want me to have Sarah call you back?"

"If she needs to. When do you think I can get across the bridges to get to her?"

"It could be a few days before they're open to the public. I'll come over and get you, if you want. I'm in and out, but I can spare the time." I can do it for you. But he couldn't say it out loud.

"Thank you, Tom. I appreciate it. How does it look out there? Any word on Sarah's house? Jared's?"

"I haven't had a chance to talk to Sarah except about Jared, but I checked on the properties, and Jared's house was pretty much totaled. Her house was undamaged except for a few shingles and patio furniture blown away. The new house wasn't damaged, either."

"What about Pilot Oaks?"

"Mostly trees. I had a hard time getting back to the house because a couple of live oaks were down, but once I got back there, everything looked pretty good. A few gutters were loose, shingles, and one storm shutter had come loose. Not sure about the summer house."

"Oh, I hope it's not damaged. Sarah and Jared love that place."

Tom looked up to see Sarah in the doorway.

"Lucy, here's Sarah."

He handed the phone over to Sarah. "I'll stay with him. You talk to Luce."

SARAH SNICKERED. "HE CALLED YOU LUCE."

"Pssht. That means nothing. He hasn't called, texted, or emailed me since I left. Not even after the shower. I've moved on."

"Right. I guess he got you updated."

"He did. He's going to come over and retrieve me so you won't be alone as soon as he can get back."

"I'm glad. It's lonely here when Tom's not here. Jared's parents are coming as soon as they can, and when I can get an update on Pilot Oaks and my house, I'm sure Mom and Dad will be on their way."

"Tom said Jared's house was pretty much destroyed. Sorry. He said he hadn't had a chance to tell you yet."

"I guess we won't be moving in there after the wedding. Well, it wasn't his dream house, but it was nice, wasn't it? I wonder about mine. And the new house! Oh, I hope it's okay."

"He said yours was fine, and the new house. We were talking about Pilot Oaks when you walked in. It didn't sound too bad."

Lucy heard Sarah's sigh. "I don't even know what's going on in the outside world right now."

"A lot of cleanup, I'm sure. I'll be there as soon as I can. Wow. What an experience. If I were going back to school, I'd have a killer story for 'what I did on my summer vacation.'"

Sarah chuckled. "It would probably make the *Reader's Digest* 'Laughter, the Best Medicine' column."

"Maybe. Hindsight is always 20/20, isn't it? We're praying for Jared, Sarah. Mary Ann, Charly, and I."

"Thanks. See you later."

"Bye."

Lucy sighed and thought about Sarah, alone at the hospital waiting for a good sign. Maybe today would be the difference. The doctor said the sooner he came out of the coma, the better his prognosis. Please, God. Please.

# CHAPTER NINETEEN

Families and individuals were leaving the shelter as they got word of the condition of their homes. Some were devastated and would be coming back either to the shelter, or would be taken in by friends and relatives. Some would be able to start the cleanup process and sleep in their own beds that night.

Lucy was tired. So, so tired. By afternoon, Tom arrived to take her to the hospital to be with Sarah. She wasn't prepared for the leap in her heart and the lump in her throat when she realized how exhausted he was. Her hand involuntarily wanted to smooth his hair back out of his eyes, but she caught herself in time. She was glad his mother couldn't see it.

His face lit up in a tired half-grin when his eyes met hers. She could feel her face heat, but she simply smiled back. She patted Mary Ann's hand. "Tom's back."

"Oh, good. I wonder if he's been to the house." She shook her head. "Just because I want to sell it doesn't mean I want it to be destroyed."

Tom walked up to his mother. "I ran by the house before I came. There's roof damage, but that's about it. One of the live oaks out back is down, but it had some dead places in it anyway."

"Well, the house is one thing, but however is Jared? We've been waiting for word, son."

"Serious condition, but stable. They're observing him closely. The doctors don't think it's life-threatening, but they want to make sure."

Lucy let out the breath she had been holding. "Is Sarah okay?"

"She's fine. Just scared, lonely, and bored. I told her I'd bring you to the hospital as soon as I got Mom and Charly settled. Is that okay with you?" She thought he would never look at her. When he finally did, he swallowed thickly. She hadn't been able to hide the tears shimmering in her eyes. "It's gonna be okay, Luce."

When he squeezed her hand, she wanted him to pull her in for a hug so she could sob her heart out. To be this close to him, to be going through such a traumatic time with him and his family, and to not belong to him was driving her crazy. How could she stand this much longer?

She pulled her hand away and reached for her pocket. She looked down at the tissue in her hand and nodded. "I know. God's got this." His eyes were still on her. She could get lost in them.

He took a deep breath as Charly joined them. "Are you ladies ready? There's roof damage, but no reason not to be home. Power may be out for a while, but I'll fill up the generator. There may be a little cleanup on the porches and yard, but inside is fine except for the kitchen ell."

"Good. I'm ready to go home. I'm glad the church is here for those who need it, but I don't think I slept a wink last night."

Charly chuckled. "Mom, I heard you snore a few times. I think you did all right."

"Maybe, but I'll rest better in my own bed." Her eyebrow

lifted at the impertinence in her daughter's tone. "Just wait. You'll get old one day."

"I know. And I should have said a most genteel snore. Is that better?"

They all laughed, brightening the mood considerably.

Lucy looked over at their things. "Let me go touch base with Bro. Bill to see if I'll be needed tonight. I'll help you carry the stuff to the truck."

"Go ahead. I won't leave without you." He grinned. "Sarah would have my hide."

"And so would I, so you'd better not." Lucy gave him an absent-minded wink and turned before she could think about what she'd done.

I winked at him. I flirted like a teenager. As she walked across the fellowship hall, she shook her head in disgust. Way to put him on his toes, Luce.

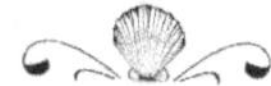

THEY SAY A SMILE CHANGES EVERYTHING. But a wink? Maybe. If he let it. But he wouldn't. Not now anyway. Too much to be done. Too much responsibility to be distracted by a leap of joy that shot through him when Lucy winked at him.

Tom mentally whacked himself in the back of the head as he loaded the air mattresses and bedding his mother and sister had brought with them. He helped his mother into the back seat, Charly next to her. When Lucy came out, she hesitated when the only seat left was in front. With him.

He didn't blame her. He'd been a grouch. He revealed too much at the shower. It had weakened his resolve, and now he didn't know how to talk to her.

She pulled open the door of the SUV and stepped up on the running board that helped her to get her slight frame into the large vehicle. He couldn't help but grin when she hoisted herself into the truck with a swift jump that landed her square into the seat.

She looked over at him. "What? You didn't think I could get up here? I'm from Kentucky, if you recall."

He held his hands up before he started the vehicle. "I never doubted you. I'm glad I had the one with running boards, or none of you would have gotten up here."

She quirked an eyebrow. "Bet we could."

"She's got you there, son. Now I might have had a hard time, but these young ladies are a little spryer than I." Mary Ann sighed. "And now, I want to get home."

"As you wish." He cut a glance to Lucy. Did she get the movie reference? She turned toward him when he said it. Her look was surprised, her face pink. She got it. He kept his face straight and merely raised his eyebrows.

"As you wish?" He really said that. Maybe the awkwardness from the scene at the shower was going to take a backseat to the situation at hand. Maybe he was rethinking his determination to keep himself away from all thoughts of romance. Maybe.

It was a quiet ride to the hospital after leaving Mary Ann and Charly at home. While they were with them, the conversation flowed with comments about this or that along the route between church and house.

Now they were alone. Did she dare bring up the shower? She looked over at him. He was concentrating on the road. There were still power lines out, flagmen making sure the utility workers as well as the drivers were safe. Since it was mostly emergency vehicles on the road, congestion was not a problem.

She could see the lines of worry and weariness in the crinkles around his eyes. Laugh lines. They spoke of days in the sun, a ready smile on his face. Her fingers itched to trace them. If only she had the courage.

He hadn't always had the weight of the world on his shoulders. How would that feel? Her father had made sure to prepare for any eventuality that might come up in her life, even his death. She hadn't known care and sorrow until he wasn't here anymore. And even then, who did she have to care for? Herself.

And now, who was she feeling sorry for? Uh, herself. She swallowed a lump in her throat.

"You okay? It's pretty rough out here, isn't it?" Tom glanced back and forth from the road to her face. He looked concerned.

"I'm fine." She sniffed loudly. "Doing a little self-inventory."

"Well, that's always fun, isn't it?" He sighed. "What's the verdict?"

"I'm a spoiled brat." She laughed and raised her hands, looking up at the ceiling of the truck.

He snorted. "I wouldn't go that far."

"I would. Remember the 'rich young ruler' in Matthew that Jesus encountered, asking what he must do to have eternal life? Jesus told him to sell everything he had, give it to the poor, and then come and follow him."

Tom nodded. "He went away sadly. I always wondered about that. He gave up the greatest gift of all, and for what?" Tom seemed to relax as they talked.

"Exactly. He went away sadly. He had a right to be sad. He didn't have eternal life. We don't have any right to be sad because we've accepted his free gift. And yet, in my case, anyway, when I don't get my way, I'm like that rich young ruler."

"In what way? I'm having a hard time following you."

"I'm used to everything going my way. When they don't, I wonder why God is not doing things the way I want them done."

He laughed.

"Exactly. It's laughable. I get bent out of shape because

rather than listening to what God wants me to do, in his time, I jump in with both feet and wonder why things don't go the way I want. I told you. I'm a spoiled brat. I've always wondered about that rich young ruler. Did he regret it? Did he change his mind and come back? Or did he simply take charge of his own life and forget that small incident that happened in his life?"

Tom pulled into the hospital parking lot and put the truck into gear. He hesitated, looking straight ahead, his hands still on the steering wheel.

"I never really thought about that. I guess we're all spoiled rotten in some way."

"Not you." Lucy looked down at her hands and knew her chin was quivering. Drat those emotions.

"Hey."

She felt his finger on her chin, tugging it so she had to look at him.

"Even me. Dad spoiled us in his own way. He made life fun. He kept us all distracted from the negative. I didn't know how to have fun after he was gone. I'd never had to before."

"I have a feeling our dads would have liked one another a lot." Her eyes filled with tears. "I'm sorry, Tom. I really am."

"For what?" He tilted his head and looked into her eyes.

A tap on the driver's side window caught them off guard. They both looked to see a young man next to the vehicle. Tom looked back at Lucy with a look of irritation, then turned back to roll down his window.

"Sam, how are you?"

The younger man seemed flustered. "I'm okay, now that I've found you. Are you aware there is still no word on the safety of the Highway 17 bridge over the PeeDee River?"

"Are you kidding? I've been over it three times in the last six hours. Did you call the transportation department in Columbia?

"SCDOT said they had people on the ground here, but they

haven't checked in with county yet. Thought maybe you'd seen some of them."

"Not to know who they were. I did notice a SCDOT truck over by the bridge crossing the Waccamaw." He seemed to forget Lucy was in the truck.

"Tom." She spoke his name, knowing he had more important things going on than discussing her spiritual life and her revelation that she was a spoiled brat. The fact that she thought of it made her feel a tiny bit better about herself.

He glanced at her. "Sorry, Lucy. Lucy, this is Sam Watson. He's the public information officer with the state police. Sam, Lucy Dixon. She's a friend of Sarah, Jared's fiancée."

She waved her fingers in his direction. "Hi, Sam." She reached over to unbuckle her seatbelt. "I can get in by myself, Tom. I know you've got things to do."

"I wanted to check on Jared." He looked a little annoyed.

She was annoyed too. One step forward, two steps back.

"It's okay. If there's anything to report, Sarah or I will let you know." She opened the passenger side door and stepped onto the running board.

"Talk later, Luce?" She turned back, and his eyes held her.

"Later." She smiled and walked around the vehicle. "Nice to meet you, Sam. Bye, Tom."

LUCY ENTERED the ICU about the time Sarah was coming out of the cubicle where Jared was still hooked up to several monitors and IVs. Nurses were there checking and changing the dressings on his incisions. No room for anyone else while they did that. When Lucy came in, she hugged her fiercely.

"I thought you'd never get here."

"Tom got me here as quickly as he could. He's got a lot on

him, hasn't he?" She swiped at an errant tear that threatened. "Stupid allergies."

Sarah was looking back at Jared and the busy nurses through the window. "Did you say something?"

"How's he doing?"

"His vitals are improving, and he's fluttered his eyelids a few times. Oh, Lucy. What if I lose him?"

"You won't, you hear?" Lucy's emotions were all over the place, but right now she needed to be strong for Sarah.

Sarah grinned. "I hear. Let's go to the waiting room. You'll have to fill me in on everything."

The waiting room was quiet. Only one other family had set up camp there. They nodded as they entered.

"We took Mary Ann and Charly home before we came here. I think Mary Ann was glad to think of sleeping in her own bed tonight."

"I'll bet. Had most of the people at the shelter gone home?"

"Most. There will be a few back to spend the night. Not all the roads are cleared for people to go home. Pastor's wife said she could take care of any kids that came back.

Sarah nodded. "Several of the people there were the folks in the immediate area. Except for power outages and buckets of rain, most of them will head home and stay."

Lucy took a deep breath. "They're predicting more rain. Tom said they were worried about flooding at this point." She stopped when Sarah closed her eyes in frustration. "Enough of that. Have you talked to your mom?"

"They're on their way. Jared's parents should be here in about an hour, and mine by tomorrow. I guess they can all stay at Pilot Oaks since Jared's house is damaged." She stopped and let a tear fall. "I can't believe we've lost his beach house. I need to get over there and salvage what I can."

"There will be time for that. You stay here and stay strong for Jared." A loud beep from the ICU cubicle got their attention, and

Sarah rushed into the room with the nurse, Lucy close behind, trying to stay out of the way.

"Nothing to worry about, sweetie. Just one of the IV bags getting low. Better get used to it, because our nurses are stretched pretty thin about now." The nurse gave them a tired smile as she changed the bag and checked all the other monitors attached to him.

Lucy had a sudden rush of sympathy for the young woman. "What's your name?"

"It's Jackie, ma'am."

"How long have you been on duty?"

"Luce, Jackie has been here since I got here. You've been here since yesterday, haven't you?"

"Yes ma'am, I have. It's not unusual, though. When we have an emergency, the doctors and nurses on duty expect to stay. The next shift can't always get here, so we try to nap in shifts when we can." Jackie gave them a warm smile. "We're glad we only have these two in ICU. It makes it easier to fill in for the ER nurses so they can rest from time to time."

Sarah hugged her. "You have no idea how much I appreciate it."

Lucy nodded. "What about your family? Do you have children?"

Jackie chuckled. "I do. I talked to them a few minutes ago. They said they had a ball at Calvary Church and didn't even notice the storm. My husband was on duty with the fire department, and my mother-in-law was with them at the shelter."

"Jolea and Tucker?" Lucy brightened right up. They were among her charges last night and were game for any lame activity she could come up with, and for that, she was grateful.

"Those are my rug rats." The young woman's broad smile showed pride in her offspring.

Lucy reached out and hugged Jackie. "They're great. And very helpful too. They took right up with us, and joined in every game and activity we did. Do y'all have a church home?"

"Lucy, you're not even a member of Calvary." Sarah laughed.

"Well, I feel like I am. And at this point, it's my closest 'home church' since you're in it."

"We've visited Calvary a few times. After this, I think we'll visit again."

"Oh, I hope you do. It's been great for Sarah, being new in the area, and I know I've always felt right at home there."

A beep sounded from Jackie's pager. "Gotta go. Lisa will be at the desk if you need her, and I'll check back when I can."

"Get some rest, Jackie. We're praying for you." Lucy smiled. She had made a new friend today.

"Don't worry. And thank you for taking care of my babies during the storm. It was good to know they were with people who loved them and were watching out for them." She looked down at her pager again. "Check with you later."

# CHAPTER TWENTY

Tom was back at his desk for the first time since yesterday. All communication had been via radio and cell phone. He was tired, he was irritated, and he was ready for a nap. That wasn't going to happen. Not for a while, anyway. When his mother mentioned sleeping in her own bed, he remembered he hadn't checked on his own house. That would have to wait. He knew it wasn't in the line of the surge, so he wasn't unduly worried. Now he was hearing rumblings about recovery efforts and collections starting already.

It was too soon. He knew, from past experience, that many people used the excuse of "collecting supplies for the needy" to clean out cabinets of old foodstuffs, clothing, and bedding that many times ended up in a storage unit and never distributed because it came before the definite needs were posted.

Disaster Relief coordinated with his office and Sam Watson with the state police. He needed to make sure Sam knew the policies and procedures. He was new, after all, even if he had some training. This was the real deal.

Sam seemed like a nice enough guy. He tried to refrain from judgment until he had reason to doubt a person, but he wasn't sure this time. Maybe it was the fatigue setting in. Maybe if he leaned his head on his desk for ten minutes . . .

"There you are, Tom. I was hoping you would get in before I left for the day." Sam was walking toward him, clearing all thoughts of rest.

Before he left for the day? He hadn't even begun to think of leaving for the day or for the week. As long as his people were safe and being cared for, he would work for the other fine folks of his county.

"Sam. What's up?" Tom took a deep breath and tried to erase the irritation from his face.

"I've got county Emergency Management on the phone. They want emergency feeding trailers on the ground by breakfast tomorrow. Where do we want them?"

"Good question. Have you, or they, talked to the FEMA folks? They're the ones to make that call, not us."

"Oh. Well, I thought it would be up to the locals."

"Not entirely. We call FEMA, they call disaster relief agencies and put them on standby, then all the coordination is done through FEMA and the county emergency services task force."

"Got it. I'll get on that." He walked away and turned at the door. "Thanks for introducing me to Lucy. She seems nice."

Tom twisted his mouth in a grimace where Sam couldn't see him. When he turned, he had his nonchalant mask back on. "She is nice."

"She dating anyone? Just curious." Sam smiled and quirked an eyebrow in question.

Tom coughed. Man, was this hard. It was one thing to think about Lucy dating someone back in Kentucky, but a guy he had to work with every day?

"She's here on a visit, helping Sarah with the wedding."

"Ah. Well, if I see her again, I might ask her. Never hurts to ask." He left the room to take a phone call without waiting for an answer.

"Never hurts." Tom mumbled the words as he looked, unsee-ing, at the papers and notes on his desk.

Lucy smiled as Sarah was caught in a huge bear hug by her future-father-in-law. Liz went straight to her son's bedside, tears falling as she smoothed back the hair that remained on one side of his head. "My baby boy."

Conrad joined her at Jared's side, keeping Sarah close by him. "Any improvement?"

"Some. He fluttered his eyelashes and squeezed my hand earlier." Her radiant smile said it all.

Lucy filled them in. "Not long after I had arrived at the hospital, we were sitting in the room, talking, when Sarah reached over to hold Jared's hand. When he squeezed her hand, she jumped up and looked at his face to see his lashes fluttering."

It wasn't much, but it was good to see Sarah lifted out of the mire of fear and doubt she had been in.

"Oh my goodness. Well, that's a good sign, isn't it? I mean, they said the sooner he wakes up, the better the prognosis, didn't they? Oh, and how is that sweet Mary Ann? I hate she's going through her vision problems. And Charlotte. Such a pretty girl. Is she still planning to go into broadcasting?"

The interchange between Sarah and Liz Benton was hilari-ous. Sarah went from radiant happiness to information overload, blinking her eyes in surprise as the topics changed with the wind.

"Lizzie, slow down. We've got plenty of time to talk about all those things. Right now I want to concentrate on our son." Conrad wasn't exactly using his military commander voice, but the authority in his tone seemed to calm his wife.

"I'm sorry. I'm so used to not having much time to talk, and I want to know everything." Liz hugged Sarah tightly. "I'm worried about Jared, excited about the wedding, and wondering about my dear friends. What a conundrum for this hurricane to come at this time."

Lucy intervened. "I think the doctor is supposed to come around 5:00 to check on him. Would it be okay if I swept Sarah off for lunch while you're here to watch over Jared?"

Sarah's look spoke volumes to Lucy.

"I think that's a grand idea. Conrad, go get me a cup of coffee, and I'm not moving from this spot until he wakes up." Liz sat next to her boy with determination.

"Yes, sweetheart." He turned to the girls. "You two go ahead, and we'll be here for the duration." He winked at Sarah and turned them toward the door as he followed to fetch the coffee. "Don't worry. At bedtime, we'll find a place to stay."

"Tom said Pilot Oaks is in good shape. Unfortunately, Jared's house sounds like a total loss." Sarah dipped her head.

"Well, I guess we could 'rough it' at Pilot Oaks." He chuckled and then waved them away. "Go. Eat. Rest."

Sarah smiled at him. "Thank you. I was glad when Lucy came, so I didn't have to be alone. Now I have family here. It helps tremendously."

# CHAPTER TWENTY-ONE

A week after the storm, Tom stood in the back yard of his mother's home, mentally calculating shingles, decking, and drywall. He'd taken pictures of the damage, inside and out. Neighbors had secured a tarp over the area of the affected roof, knowing Tom was tied up. Now to file the insurance claim and wait. They were the fortunate ones. One area was affected, the roof over the kitchen ell. No carpet, just soggy rugs and lost food from the rain and power outage. That meant the house was livable, and after getting the mess cleaned up, life could get back to normal.

He turned to see a car drive up. He grinned when Lucy got out of Sarah's car and walked toward him. "Hey, stranger."

"Hey, yourself. I didn't know the county let you off the leash long enough to come home." She grinned back at him, causing a flush to rise from his neck to his face. He'd missed her.

"Finally. Things are getting back to normal. I thought I'd better start thinking about fixing the roof. Well, as soon as we get the go-ahead from the insurance company. I could have it done in a few days if I didn't have to wait on them."

This was awkward. If they were supposed to be together, would he feel awkward around her? A voice, deep inside of him, reminded him he hadn't made any move in her direction after the shower and his revelation of what he considered his "best kiss." Now wasn't the time.

Lucy had changed the subject while his mind wandered. "– so I'll be helping Sam—"

"Wait. What? Helping Sam?"

"I said, I've been asked to help with the state/county police department relief effort. Sam is in charge, and he asked me to help since Sarah's tied up with Jared. I guess I seemed to be at loose ends." She shrugged and looked down at her toes.

Loose ends. Great. He'd rather her spare time be spent with him instead of Sam Watson. He didn't want to sound like a jealous boyfriend, because he wasn't. A boyfriend, anyway. Jealous, yes. Boyfriend? He wished. And yet, it sounded juvenile.

He brightened a bit. "I guess you'll have to come by the station a lot."

She grinned and cut her eyes up at him. "I suppose I will."

Lucy stood beside him, both of them contemplating the house with hands in pockets. "How long would it take you with a little help?" She pulled her right hand out of her pocket and up to shade her eyes as she looked up at him, squinting.

"For what?" Another change in topic. She reminded him of Jared's mother in some ways.

"The roof, silly."

"Depends on the help." He chuckled. "You offering?"

"I'll have you know, Mr. Macho Man, that I have served on construction teams on mission trips and with Habitat for Humanity, and I happen to have no fear of heights. So there."

A laugh burst from him. It felt good, if a little unfamiliar these days. The sight of her petite form, hands on hips, putting him in his place, was exactly what he needed. He held up his hands in surrender. "Forgive me for doubting you." He squinted back at her. "Can you provide references?"

"Very funny. What about Charly?"

"No heights for her. She turns into a puddle when she gets close to the edge of a balcony." He shook his head in disgust. "I'd rather not scrape her off the ground when she falls off the ladder."

Lucy's giggle tinkled through the air. "I understand. You've got my number, right? Let me know when you want to work on it, and I'll be here with my pink tool belt on."

"You're kidding, right?"

"Maybe I am, and maybe I'm not. You'll have to wait and see."

He wanted to reach out and hug her, but he didn't dare. He looked at her for a minute without saying anything. "I can't wait."

She coughed a little, blushing. "Okay. Well. Um, I think I'll go in and say hi to your mom."

He smiled. "She'd like that." As she turned away, he grabbed her hand. "Thanks, Lucy."

"You're welcome, Tom." Did he imagine it, or was there some reluctance in her pulling her hand from his?

LUCY FOUND it difficult to drag her eyes from his, much less her hand from his grasp. Stop it, Lucy. He's emotional about the house, Jared, etc. Any other time, Jared would be right here by his side, hammering nails and carrying shingles.

She sighed as she closed the front door behind her. There was a chill in the air, and the fact that dampness was everywhere didn't help.

"Lucy? Is that you?" Mary Ann came into the hallway with a

smile. "I thought I heard your voice outside with Tom. I hate to even ask him what the verdict is on the roof."

"Well, if staring at it could get it fixed, it would be right as rain by now." When Mary Ann chuckled, Lucy grimaced. "Sorry. Bad analogy."

"No, I'd say it was a pretty good one. Tom needs some encouragement. You may be the one to give it to him."

"I told him I'd help him with the roof. I'm sure he thinks I'm a poor substitute for Jared."

"If I know you, you'll surprise him. I think you do, quite often." Mary Ann squeezed her hand. "Now, would you like some coffee? I made my second pot. Seems like cleaning up hurricane mess calls for more fortitude than regular mess."

"That would be wonderful."

Lucy wondered what she meant by her surprising Tom. Her mind wandered as Mary Ann methodically and carefully pulled two mugs out of the cabinet and set them on the kitchen table, a large, sprawling affair in the middle of the room. It reminded her of the table on "The Waltons," where everyone gathered to eat, work, talk, and play. The center of the room and the center of the house. How long since this table had been filled with children? Generations, she was sure.

Her mind wandered back to Tom. Surprise? Him? Sure, there were some instances when he seemed a little off-kilter around her, but if so, why did he ignore her? Out-of-sight, out of mind? Ugh. Tom is unsurprisable. He's pragmatic. He's organized.

Her mind snapped-to. She was pragmatic. She was organized. But, she didn't take on the cares of the world like Tom.

Mary Ann smiled as she sat down across the table from Lucy. "Tom wasn't always so serious. Before his daddy died, he helped out around here, but he didn't have the responsibility and worry he seems to think he has to take on, now."

What could she say? "He's a good son."

"The best. But he's my son, not my husband, nor my father. Just because I can't see doesn't mean I'm less his mother."

"I'll drink to that." Lucy lifted the cup to her lips. "Do you think selling the house will make a difference?"

"I hope so." Mary Ann shrugged, her lips twisted in a slight grimace. "But I doubt it. He needs to think about himself and his future for a change."

"Maybe when things settle down."

"Thank you, dear, for looking for the bright side. That's something we've been lacking since Hayden died. He wouldn't rest until a body was smiling through her tears."

The familiar hurt in the region of her heart nudged the tears into her eyes. She was thankful Mary Ann couldn't see them. "Your Hayden sounds like my dad. When Mom died, it was the first time I had ever seen him at a loss. I was young, and he had a demanding job. Before long I would only see glimpses of sadness. Most of the time he was my fun, encouraging Dad. I learned a lot from him."

"I'd say you did. How old were you when your mother passed?"

"I was thirteen. We were living in Chicago at the time. When I was a freshman in high school, we moved to Summerville, and that's when I met Sarah. She is the best friend I ever had, and her mom took me under her wing from day one."

"Sounds like Tom and Jared." Mary Ann chuckled, and continued. "I'm glad Tom didn't let a little thing like Jared taking him out in football practice come between their friendship."

"Wait. Jared took Tom out?"

"Oh, yes. He was smaller than Tom but wiry and oh-so deter-mined. That boy can do anything he sets his mind to and make you feel like it was your idea all along."

"I can believe that. I think he's convinced Sarah she's the smart, beautiful girl she always has been." She paused to take a sip, hoping the lump in her throat would go away. "I hope he's okay."

"God's got plans for him, I know it. We have to pray. In fact, I think when we say we're going to pray, we should do it while we're thinking of it. Do you mind?" Mary Ann held her hand out across the table, and Lucy took it with a squeeze.

ucy heard a happy bark and saw Rainey Thompson of Lazy Acres Kennels laughing and walking with a quick step, trying to keep up with Oliver. He had been there since right after the hurricane when Sarah had decided to stay with Jared at the hospital. Lucy went to check on him every day, but today she was picking him up.

"Hey, Lucy! I hope there's good news about Jared." Rainey's wind-swept graying curls were tossed to and fro, and the smile on her face showed the love she had for her job.

"Hi, Rainey. He's in and out of consciousness, starting to talk more when he's at himself. They said it wouldn't be a quick turnaround."

"I know. Josh and I have been praying. This boy has been a perfect guest." She rubbed Oliver's ears and scruff as he leaned into her with enjoyment.

"He's a good boy. I don't know what we would have done without you." Lucy was receiving happy kisses from the dog, as well. She was one of his people.

"I'm happy to help. Now are Linda and Robert sure they

want to deal with him at Pilot Oaks? I don't mind keeping him a while longer."

"No, they arrived yesterday and said they would be glad to have him. He's their grand-dog, after all." Lucy laughed, and Rainey joined in.

"I know how that is." She opened the big canvas bag on her shoulder. "I've got his stuff all here. You might want to stop and get more dog food, although he's been a little off his feed. Perfectly natural under the circumstances. He'll pick right up once he gets back home."

Lucy reached out to hug the older woman. "Thank you so much, Rainey. You have no idea." She opened the door to let Oliver in and then strapped herself in. "See you soon."

"We'll keep praying. Tell Sarah and Jared hello, and tell Linda any time they need to bring Oliver by, or to come visit, my door's always open." Rainey raised her hand in farewell and walked back to the kennel, three other dogs trotting along behind her.

Lucy walked in the back door of Pilot Oaks to the wonderful scent of a beef roast in the oven and pies cooling on the table. "Prudie! I didn't know you were here!" She gave the elderly woman a squeeze and laughed as Oliver tried to get in on the action. "He's glad to see you too."

Prudie laughed as she scratched the dog's wiry head. "I've got contractors in and out of my house, so Robert came by and asked if I'd like to stay here in my old room until they get things buttoned up, and I said only if I could cook for him. He wasn't about to turn that down."

"Well, of course not." Lucy smiled, but she was concerned. "How bad was it at your house?"

"Not as bad as some folks, but roof damage and a window

blown in. Got lots of water damage. They're pulling carpets to make sure there's no mold. I was in the way, so it was a God-thing the way Robert showed up at my door."

"Lots of God-things going on these days."

Prudie nodded in agreement. "Um-hm. How's Jared? I still don't dare cross those bridges. All those emergency vehicles scare me to death."

"I know how you feel. He's getting better. He's talking some, sleeping a lot still. Sarah won't leave."

"I told him she was a keeper." She winked at Lucy as if it had been her idea all along to get Sarah and Jared together. "His mama and daddy are here too. When they were going to look for a hotel to stay in, Sarah insisted they stay here. No sense in that when there's plenty of room here."

"It's like circling the wagons, isn't it?" Lucy grinned. "Is Linda here? I brought Oliver with me to stay here since Sarah's tied up. I hope it won't be too much."

Prudie pointed to the corner of the kitchen. "I've already got his spot all fixed up. He'll be fine and good company for everybody. Linda's gone to the hospital with Liz Benton."

"All right, I'll catch her later. I've got a meeting at the police station."

Prudie's eyebrow went up. "Police station, you say?"

Lucy gave her a sideways look. "Yes, the police station. I'm helping with the Hurricane Relief fund."

"Oh. I thought maybe a certain detective was the draw." She smiled at the blush Lucy could feel rising on her face and shooed her toward the door. "Never you mind what I say. I'm old and tend to speak out of turn at times. Leave that boy here with me. I've missed him."

"Yes, ma'am." Lucy got out before she had a chance to see herself in the mirror. She knew saying she was going to the police station had made her blush. She really didn't want to know how deeply.

BETWEEN INSURANCE ADJUSTERS and the regular police work that wouldn't wait, Tom's desk had piled up in the few hours he had taken off to take care of his property. It seemed that contractor scams were already being reported, and he had several pieces of security-system films to watch to identify looters. Natural disasters brought out the best in some people–it brought out the worst in others.

He had his head down when he heard a familiar voice in the hallway. Lucy. What was she doing here? He looked up to see her through the glass, talking to Sam. Great. He put his head down. Maybe she didn't notice him. He glanced up again, only to see her walking toward him.

"Lucy." He stood up as she neared.

"Hi Tom. I was wondering if you knew when you wanted to start on your roof. I'm trying to plan relief fund stuff around that." She was very business-like. Organized and to the point.

"If you can't . . ." Tom began.

She arched an eyebrow as she interrupted him. "No way. You've got to see my pink tool belt. It was a deal, remember?"

"All right then, according to the weather, Friday and Saturday should be clear, and we can only hope nothing major happens so I can take off work."

She nodded. "Sounds good. I'll be there with tools on." Her grin belied the serious tone of her voice.

"Looking forward to it." Was that awkward, or what? Looking forward to what? Fixing a hurricane-damaged roof? Nope. Spending time with Lucy.

LUCY'S MEETING with Sam was awkward. Was he hitting on her? He hadn't come right out and asked her for a date, but she could tell he was feeling her out. He was good looking, in his own way, but he wasn't her type.

Okay Luce, what is your type?

Hmm, local police officer with a roof that needs to be repaired and is so stubborn it makes you crazy? Bingo.

As for Sam, there was something she couldn't put her finger on. Oh, well. She hoped he would take the hint and not ask her out and that she could let him down easy if he did. He didn't deserve to be hurt.

She wheeled in to the parking lot of the hardware store. The lumberyard was busy, but the tool belt aisle was empty. She perused the offerings, almost in despair of finding a pink tool belt, and lo and behold, there it was. She giggled when she pulled it off the rack. Not only was it a full-blown leather tool belt, it was pink, and it had shiny silver rivets both decorative and functional. Perfect.

She picked up a hammer and a pry bar to add to her collection.

If only she had her own tools here. All her stuff was in storage, including her personal cloth tool belt. But this one was better. It was pink. She smelled the brand-new leather and smiled. She couldn't wait to see his face when she showed up.

She paid for her items, laughing along with the check-out clerk at the pink tool belt. He told her she wouldn't have to worry about anyone stealing it from her.

Her phone vibrated as she made her way to the car. She didn't recognize the number on the screen. It was local, though, so she picked up. "Hello?"

"Lucy, it's Sam. Sam Watson?"

"Hi Sam. Was there something you forgot to tell me earlier?" She remembered now. She had given him her number, and she had written his down but neglected to put it in her phone.

"No, we're still on to meet with the Emergency Management director at nine in the morning, aren't we?"

She frowned, glad he couldn't see her face. "Yes, I've got it in my calendar. Do you need me to get there before that?"

"Maybe a few minutes. I thought we could get our stories straight by then." There was a pause. "Um, I need to talk to Tom about some things I've been hearing about. Well, it's about misuse of funds."

"What? Why is this the first time I've heard about this? What misuse of funds?" She could feel her blood pressure going up.

"I'm sure it's nothing serious. I'll try to get to the bottom of it so we won't be caught short at the meeting. Don't worry. We'll talk about it tomorrow. Unless . . ."

"Unless what, Sam?" She was starting to get irritated. His words were measured, and she sensed nervousness in his speech patterns. She worked with high school students. Of course she could sense when someone wasn't telling the whole truth.

"Unless you'd like to discuss it over dinner tonight?"

There it was. He knew she wouldn't be able to stand not knowing what was happening. *Am I so easy to read?*

She paused, much like he did, earlier, but for different reasons. If something was wrong, she needed to know about it. If Tom was involved, she wanted to know about it. If the only way to find out the details was to go to dinner with Sam, was she willing to take that chance?

She sighed. "Fine. I can meet you. Gilligan's Seafood?"

"I can pick you up. Say around 6:30?"

"No, I'll meet you. I'm going to the hospital to check on Jared and Sarah, so I won't be home. 6:30 is fine. It shouldn't be crowded on a Wednesday."

He seemed a little irritated. "Fine. I'll see you at the restaurant. Maybe I'll have it all worked out by the time I see you."

"I hope so. See you at dinner."

"Looking forward to our date."

She frowned into the phone as she changed his contact information to show his name when he called. It would make it easier to not take his calls.

When she got to the hospital, she was feeling more and more cranky. By the time she got to Jared's room, she was kicking herself for agreeing to meet Sam.

"Why am I such a dingbat?"

Sarah laughed. "Who said you were?"

"I did. I agreed to go out with Sam Watson."

"Really?" Sarah looked surprised. "Why?"

"Because he tempted me with information. You know I can't wait a day to get info if I can get it today." She shook her head. "And right before he called, I was thinking how glad I was he hadn't asked me out."

"You jinxed it, Lucy."

"I know." She looked over at the sleeping patient, and back to Sarah. "I'm sorry. I'm all het up about my issues and almost forgot why I came. How's the patient?"

Sarah looked at Jared and shook her head, a small crease forming between her brows. "This morning the doctor said his vitals seemed better. He's been sleeping more today."

"Maybe that's a good thing." Her heart hurt to see Sarah so concerned.

"Maybe. I don't know. I get these feelings."

"What feelings?"

"Like it's not over. So, I pray."

"That's the best you can do, friend." Lucy squeezed Sarah's hand in support. "How are the folks doing?"

"His parents come every day, and his mom has stayed with me quite a bit. You just missed Mom and Liz. When the doctor gave us a good report this morning, they decided to go to Pilot Oaks for a while, and they'll bring me supper later. Mom and Dad are dealing with cleanup on the grounds and some trim that was damaged."

"I'm glad they're nearby. All of them."

Sarah shook her head as if to clear it. "Change the subject. Please. Tell me about this date you have tonight."

"I am not calling it a date." Lucy huffed. "I'm working with Sam on the relief fund at the police department. Apparently there are rumors of mismanagement of funds, and we have a meeting with Emergency Management tomorrow. He actually said we needed to 'get our story straight.' Now what can he mean by that?"

Sarah looked startled. "Has someone been dipping into the till?"

"That's why I agreed to meet him. If something wonky is going on, I want to know about it. He said he needed to talk to Tom. Is he insinuating Tom is involved?" She put her hands to her face and pushed her fingers through her blonde locks in frustration.

"I can't imagine Tom having anything to do with this. Listen to what he has to say and work it out from there."

A beep from one of the machines monitoring Jared's vitals began to beep.

Sarah jerked up, her eyes going first to Jared's face and then to the equipment. "That's a different one." She pushed the button to call the nurse, but they were already at the door.

"Ladies, you need to wait outside." The nurse ushered them outside as three other nurses began to check Jared out. "We've called the doctor, and he's in the building. We'll let you know as soon as we find anything out from him."

Silent tears streamed down Sarah's face. "But they said he was better?"

Lucy pulled her friend to her and held her as she sobbed. "Shh. Pray. Just pray."

# CHAPTER TWENTY-THREE

"Sam, I'm sorry, I can't leave the hospital now. I need to be here with Sarah while Jared's in surgery." She paused to listen to his objections.

"How long will the surgery last?" Sam sounded a little put out.

"They don't know. He came very close to coding. They found another small brain bleed, and more swelling came up today." Lucy was trying to talk, listen, and watch the comings and goings all at the same time. Sarah's and Jared's parents had all arrived, so she had taken the opportunity to call Sam and cancel. He had arrived at the restaurant to find her a no-show.

"I'm sorry about your friend, and I'll keep you posted about the other issue. It's not looking good, but I don't want to get into it on the phone."

"I understand. I'll be here at the hospital if you need any information on my end, although I can't imagine what that would be." At this point, she wanted to get off the phone.

"Thanks, Lucy. And tell Sarah I hope things go well."

"I will. Thanks, Sam."

Lucy turned the ringer off on her phone. She didn't want any other interruptions. A pang of unwanted jealousy swamped her as she observed the family group huddled around Sarah. Not because she wanted to be in Sarah's situation but because her support system had dwindled down to nothing. When things happened in her life, who could she count on to be there? Grandmommy? Yes, if she could, but she's not getting any younger. Sarah. Always. But no parents. No future in-laws at this point. She wasn't sure she had ever been quite this alone.

TOM STEPPED out of the elevator of the surgical floor and strode out and down the hall. He looked for Lucy first. There was a tear rolling down her face. Had something happened? Had Jared . . . No, he wouldn't even think that. He glanced at Sarah, surrounded by her parents and Jared's, and they didn't seem distraught, only worried. He started walking toward Lucy. She looked so alone.

"Are you okay?" He wanted to pull her into a bear hug and hold her until she didn't have breath or worry, but he didn't. He didn't have the right. He had heard through the grapevine that she was going on a date with Sam. What grapevine? It was Sam who told him.

Lucy sniffed loudly. "I'm fine. A little overwhelmed but fine. Sarah and I were talking and all the sudden things started beeping and nurses came in and started talking about coding and made us go out in the hall and the doctor came and they rushed him to surgery and he's got another bleed and swelling on his brain and it's so scary!" After the stream of accelerating words, she caught her breath in a sob.

Tom didn't hesitate this time but pulled her to him and let her cry. "It'll be okay. Doc knows what he's doing, and do you think God's going to let us miss the chance to be maid of honor and best man at their wedding?" He handed her a freshly-pressed handkerchief.

She mopped up with the white cloth and shook her head. "No, I don't think He would do that to us." She looked up at him, tears still swimming in her eyes, but a smile on her face. "You carry a hankie?"

He let her go, reluctantly. "What can I say? My mama taught me right, and she even taught me how to press them." He could feel his face flush. There were times when his neatness was plain embarrassing.

"A true southern gentleman." She laughed the sound like a balm on his worried soul. "Thanks, Tom. I needed a hug."

"You're welcome." He looked down at her and gestured toward the family group. "Let's see what's going on."

"ALL THOSE YEARS riding a bike without a helmet. I should have been more careful." Liz Benton kept shaking her head in worry as she sat in the waiting room of the hospital. "My poor baby boy."

"Now, Lizzie, I don't think a bicycle helmet would have been much protection against a falling twenty-foot palm tree." Conrad put his arm around his wife. "And you sitting here worrying about it isn't going to help matters any."

Tom and Lucy walked over to the group and found seats. "Conrad's right, Liz. Jared's been in more dangerous situations than this."

Jared's mother shivered. "Don't remind me. I remember when he was in the accident with Annabelle. It was a nightmare. I guess I've gotten soft in my old age." She smiled, tears dotting her lashes, up at her husband, patting him on the knee as she wiped her face with the tissues available in the waiting room.

Tom spoke directly to Sarah. "How long has he been in surgery?"

She looked at the clock on the wall. "Two hours and thirteen minutes." She swiped tears from her eyes. "I wish they would tell us something. Anything."

The group fell silent. Tom wanted to say something encouraging but was at a loss. His best friend was facing surgery twice in a week's time. That couldn't be good. *God, it's up to You. It always has been, but there's not a thing any of us could do or could have done.*

A small hand reached into his and squeezed. He opened his eyes to see Lucy's head bowed and her eyes closed as his had been. A smile reached his lips as emotion welled in his chest. He squeezed her hand back.

Footsteps coming down the hallway made them all look up. It was the surgeon. Everyone stood, and the doctor waved them back down and pulled an extra chair over so he could sit.

"Have a seat. Jared's good. The surgery went well. It was a tiny bleed we missed. We've drained off the excess blood, and there doesn't seem to be any inflammation. That's what we were worried about. We took our time, and he should be waking up in an hour or so. We'll keep him in recovery for a while for observation. He should be back in ICU tonight and maybe to a regular room by tomorrow, depending on how alert he is."

Tom observed Sarah through the explanation. She visibly relaxed, as did he and the rest of the group.

Sarah spoke up. "Is there . . . any sign of brain damage?"

"Shouldn't be, but until he's awake for an extended amount of time, we won't know for sure. Any kind of brain injury, even mild traumatic brain injury, can cause damage, but not necessarily permanent. Considering this is at least his second TBI, not counting football injuries." The doctor grinned up at Tom. "Memory loss, trouble finding words, being emotional at weird times; those kinds of things are common even a year after the injury." He chuckled. "Or, as my wife would say, being a man could also have something to do with that."

Sarah smiled. "I've already noticed that."

Tom raised his hand. "I do want to say, when Jared took me out in a tackle the first time I met him, he did have a helmet on."

Conrad Benton guffawed at that. "Son, I have a feeling you've kept him alive a lot of times and not only on the football field."

"You're probably right." Tom was glad that he and the doctor were able to lessen the serious mood. "There are only two things we can do now. Wait, and pray."

The doctor nodded. "Yes. Time is a healer in all things, and God's time is always better than ours." He stood up and shook Sarah's hand, squeezing it between both of his. "I'll keep you posted." He nodded and turned back toward the surgical suite.

They heard the elevator ding, and out came the pastor and his wife. As they approached, Tom greeted them and left them to Sarah and the parents. He looked at Lucy, much calmer than she had been earlier, and gestured with his head to follow him, which she did.

"Are we still on for roofing 101 on Friday?" He absent-mindedly reached for her hand, and when she squeezed his, he realized what he had done. Being on a roof with her was going to be murder. For one thing, he would worry about her falling and getting hurt. For another thing, he couldn't reach out and touch her any time he wanted. That would be difficult. He smiled at the thought.

"Lord willing and the creek don't rise. Or in this case, the ocean." Lucy's tear-streaked face grinned up at him. She was flushed as well. Maybe she didn't mind him taking her hand.

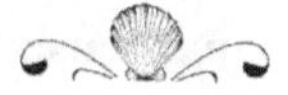

Lucy and Tom both turned when they heard the elevator again. It was getting past visiting hours, so there hadn't been much elevator activity in the last hour except for hospital staff and the pastor and his wife.

She closed her eyes in frustration. "I forgot to call Sam." She looked up at Tom when she felt him squeeze her hand tightly and then let it go. "What's wrong?" She was confused. Did he not want Sam to know about . . . well, about what?

"Sam." Tom's unsmiling face greeted him.

This wasn't like Tom. She had never seen him antagonistic toward a fellow officer. She kept looking from one man to the other. They both seemed to stand up straighter. Was this a competition? Why did the thought of Tom being jealous make her want to smile? *Because you love him, you silly girl.* She straightened her face and waved a greeting to Sam.

"Hi, Sam. Sorry I didn't call you. The doctor was here, and right after that, the pastor came. It's been pretty crazy." She had to be careful or she would start babbling with nervousness.

"What do you need, Sam?" Tom seemed to be working under the assumption that Sam wouldn't be here unless it were official business.

"I was checking on Lucy. We had a date tonight, and she had to cancel to come and be with Sarah." He looked over toward Sarah, as if measuring the distance between Tom and Lucy, and Lucy and Sarah. "I'm assuming she's fine?"

"No, she's worried and scared. Thanks for understanding, Sam." Lucy looked at him and then anxiously at Tom. She had a bad feeling.

"And Jared made it through surgery. He'll be in recovery for a few hours." Tom was staring a hole through Sam, underlining the fact that he hadn't asked about the patient.

"I'm glad to hear it." Sam focused on Lucy. "Could we talk for a minute?" He glanced at Tom. "In private?"

She glanced back and forth between the men once more.

"Sure. How about I walk you down to the lobby?" Anything to get rid of him. She didn't want Sarah to know there was anything going on.

"Fine."

He held his arm out for her to take, but she smiled and clasped her hands in front of her. No need leading him to think there might be something between them. And no need for Tom to think that, either.

When they reached the elevator and entered the cubicle, Lucy broached the question. "What was so important that couldn't wait until tomorrow?" Business. All business.

"I didn't want to bring this up. Me working for state and Tom working for county has made this a little uncomfortable."

"Uncomfortable, how?" What was he insinuating?

"I had a buddy to look up the account for the relief fund."

"And? Is there a problem?"

"There is money missing."

"What? It can't be! I made most of those deposits myself." What in the world was going on?

"I know, and I know you couldn't have done anything wrong. Do you have the checkbook and ledger?"

"Not here. They're at Sarah's house. I've been going over them to get ready for the meeting with the mayor and county judge tomorrow."

"Okay. Bring them and come a little early tomorrow, and I'll show you what we found. Have you looked at the online statement?" His face was flushed. Odd.

"No, I haven't been on the online account." Not that she couldn't. She hadn't had a reason to before now.

"Don't worry about it. I'll explain it all tomorrow." They had arrived at the lobby. "Don't mention this to Tom, okay?"

"Are you accusing him of something?" She narrowed her eyes but tried to look vague. It wasn't easy. Vague wasn't in her DNA.

"No, not at all. I'll . . . I'll show you tomorrow." He kept looking at the elevator, as if he thought Tom would follow them down. "I've got to go. I know you want to get back upstairs . . . to Sarah."

She would not blush. She was starting to get angry, but she would not let him see it. "Yes, I need to get back to the family." There. She underscored that Tom was part of her family, and he was not. "See you in the morning, 8:30 sharp."

Sam nodded. He reached out for her hand, but she was already turning back toward the elevator. When she reached the metal doors, she looked back to see him exiting through the automatic doors. Good riddance.

What in the world?

# CHAPTER TWENTY-FOUR

Tom got to his desk by 7:30 the next morning, still divided between being angry at Sam for showing up at the hospital, and worrying about Jared. All he could do for Jared was pray, but Sam? He would get to the bottom of it.

They didn't know each other well. Sam was a few years younger than he, and they hadn't gone to high school together. He and Jared went to Waccamaw High, and Sam went to Georgetown High. Two schools in close proximity were bound to have rivalries. He pulled up the database of state and county employees. Wait a minute. Sam transferred to Waccamaw his senior year. He didn't go to the police academy with Sam, but maybe he was behind him and he missed him.

There he was. Graduated from Waccamaw High in 2006. No wonder he didn't know him from sports. Sam was a freshman when he was a senior. Graduated from Clemson in 2010. Go Tigers. What was his degree? There it was. Computer technology. Really? He was a computer guy? Minor in counseling. Interesting.

He was so intent on his research that he was startled to hear a familiar voice in the hallway. Was that Lucy? He looked at the clock. He had burned a good hour on his research-slash-stalking session. It wasn't stalking if you were a police officer. At least that's what he told himself.

He couldn't understand everything she was saying, but when he walked to the door of the squad room and looked down the hall, there she was. She looked angry, but her voice was well-modulated. Sam didn't look as if he noticed anything amiss. She glanced at Tom in the doorway. Her eyes widened, and she nodded. What was that about? He tilted his head in question, and she looked back at Sam with a sweet smile.

"Sam, if you'll excuse me for a few minutes, I need to touch base with Tom about a project we're working on for his mother. I'll meet you in the conference room, okay?"

Sam glanced over at Tom with a raised eyebrow. "Fine. I'll meet you in the conference room." He walked away.

"Lucy, what's going on?" She was upset. When Lucy came back last night after walking Sam out, he could tell something wasn't right. She was quiet, and that was not like Lucy. Now there was a sparkle in her eyes that wasn't there when she was talking to Sam. That was a nice thought. He smiled at her, and she smiled back then frowned.

"Oh, don't do that. Don't smile at me, because when you do, I lose all the thoughts in my head." She closed her eyes and flushed bright red. "Did I say that out loud?" She slowly opened her eyes and grimaced at the huge grin on his face.

"Yep. You did. I'll try to contain myself."

"Thank you. Because I need your level, organized head for a few minutes before I have to meet Sam, the mayor, and the judge." She glanced up at the ceiling. "Oh, Lord, why did this have to come up now?"

He walked her over to his desk and offered her a seat. "You are every bit as organized as I, so what's the problem?" He was beginning to get concerned.

"Someone has been fiddling with the relief effort money." She sat there, staring at him.

"How? I thought everything was locked tight with security?"

"I thought so, too, until I looked at the online bank activity. According to that, there have been several withdrawals from the account with a police department debit card." Her pointed look said it all. "Yours."

"That's impossible. I don't even use the department card for cash advances." He got his wallet out and started looking through the cards. "I haven't even had it out in over a month." He dumped the ones in the larger part of his wallet on the desk. He looked up at her. "It's gone."

"What is?" Lucy looked confused.

"My debit card. Also my personal debit card isn't in the right slot. Who could have done this?" He had his suspicions, but he wouldn't say until he had more proof.

"The only other person with access is Sam. Why would he implicate you? You're not even on the signature card."

"I don't know, but I will find out." He looked up into Lucy's worried face. "Don't worry. We'll figure this out. Are you up for a little investigative work?"

"You'd better believe it. Try to keep me away. According to this, about ten thousand dollars has gone missing. That's too much not to miss, which I'm sure is why Sam pointed it out before this meeting."

"Go to your meeting. When you're done, send me a text. I'll leave, and you can meet me at the bank. I'd like to see those signature cards and the online account info."

"And, we won't be seen leaving together. What can I say at the meeting? What if he brings it up?"

"If he does, go along with whatever he says. Say it's being looked into, and that you have no idea how this could have happened." He took her hand. "Are you okay?"

She nodded. "I'll be fine. He doesn't know how much I know. Last night I hadn't looked at the online account."

"Huh. He was a computer major in college." Tom twisted his lips.

Lucy's mouth dropped open. "Really? How do you know that?"

"I may have looked at his employment records after last night." His sheepish look made her smile.

"I was that transparent, huh?"

"I knew something wasn't right, so I wanted to look a little deeper." He looked at the clock. She would be late if she weren't careful, and that wouldn't look good. "You go on to your meeting, and I'll keep digging."

"Yes, sir." She gave him a salute. "See you in a bit."

"Looking forward to it." He leaned back in his chair and watched as she walked out of his office and down the hall. She was well worth watching.

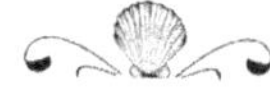

**DONE.**

That was the text she sent. It didn't seem like enough, but it was unobtrusive, and Sam never saw her send it.

"Uh, Lucy?"

"Sam?"

"Would you like to grab lunch, since we missed our date last night?" Sam was smiling like the cat that swallowed the canary.

She swallowed the bile rising in her throat and smiled. "I'm sorry, I've got errands to run, and then I'm heading to the hospital to check on Jared."

"How's he doing?"

"Much better. He's still in and out, but a lot of that is medication." At least he asked about Jared. It was odd how he very seldom did.

He nodded. "Thanks for not bringing up the discrepancy in the account. I'd rather have more evidence before we bring it to light."

"I agree." She scrutinized his expression, looking for a "tell." "I'll check on it this afternoon. I didn't have time to do all I wanted to last night." Should she play the dumb blonde card? This one time, maybe?

"It can be pretty complicated. Online stuff, you know." He was still looking pretty satisfied.

"Oh, I know. I get on the Internet and get lost sometimes. It's difficult to navigate – especially the bank site. I'm no computer expert." What would he say to that?

"It's not hard once you get used to it, but I was a computer major in college."

Did she imagine it, or did his chest puff out a little bit?

"Really? Wow. I don't think I could have done that. Elementary Ed was difficult enough." Lord, please forgive me for lying.

He laughed. "I'll walk you out."

"Thanks, Sam. I'll talk to you tomorrow."

They reached the door, and he held it for her to pass in front of him. "I'll look forward to hearing from you."

She waved her fingers and hurried to her car, wondering if she could walk a little faster to get away from him.

TOM GOT out of his unmarked car when Lucy pulled up beside him in the bank parking lot.

"Sorry. Sam was chatty on the walk out the door." She grimaced a little. "I was glad he didn't bring up the discrepancy. Said he wanted 'more evidence' before he brought it up." She cut her eyes up at him.

"More evidence, huh? Let's see if we can get more

evidence." He put his hand to the small of her back and ushered her into the bank.

"How can I help you today?" The teller gave them each a friendly smile.

Tom pulled out his badge and laid it on the counter. "I'm hoping you can help us."

"Is this a police matter?" The young woman looked nervous.

"Yes, I'm afraid so. I need to see the signature cards for the police relief fund account."

He nodded at Lucy.

She pulled out the checkbook for the account as well as her I.D. "I'm one of the signatories on the account, and I noticed a few debits on the online statement that I do not have in my records."

"Oh my. Let me get an accounts manager." She looked across the lobby and waved at a middle-aged man in a bank-issue polo shirt. As soon as he saw her, he made his way to them.

"Tom! How are you? Something we can help you with?"

"Hey, Mason. Good to see you." He shook hands and looked at Lucy, who was standing there beside him. "Mason Beckman and I go way back. His dad was my little league football coach. Mason, Lucy Dixon. Lucy is Sarah's best friend, staying with her until the wedding."

"You must be the maid of honor. Better watch out hanging out with Jared's best man, unless you need help with a speeding ticket."

"Nice to meet you, Mason. I forget that Tom seems to know people everywhere he goes." She grinned, but still looked apprehensive.

"Mason, we may have a problem, and I'd like to keep it on the down-low if you don't mind."

Now it was Mason's turn to look worried. "No problem, Tom. Tell me what you need, and we'll take care of it in my office."

The teller spoke up. "Mr. Beckman, they asked for the signature card for an account. Would you like me to bring it to your office?"

"Thank you, Nadine. I would appreciate it. Now, follow me and let's see if we can get this figured out." He led them across the shiny lobby to a glass-enclosed area where he invited them to sit down.

"It's like this, Mason. Lucy checked the station's relief fund account last night after someone tipped her off that there were funds missing. She checked, and sure enough, there are."

"Let me pull up the account." He took the card Nadine had brought to him and keyed in the numbers.

"Can I see that card?" Tom reached out to take the card Mason held in his hand. It had three names: Lucy Dixon, Sam Watson, and Tom Livingston, but with no signature under his name.

"I was never supposed to be on this signature card." Tom looked at his banker friend and noted the surprise on his face.

"According to this note on the account, Officer Watson opened the account with his name and Lucy's, and came back and added yours later." He took the card back and inspected it. "When a teller fills out info on an account, they initial it in the top corner. This looks like Carol's initials. Let me call her in here." He picked up his phone and pushed a button. "Carol, could you come to my office for a second? I need to ask you about an account you worked on."

He hung up the phone. "She'll be right in. We'll get to the bottom of this."

There was a light tap on the glass door, to which Mason answered, "Come in."

"Can I help you, Mr. Beckman? Hi, Tom, Lucy!"

"Carol, do you remember Sam Watson coming back in and adding Tom to this signature card on the relief fund?"

"I do. It was last week. I remember thinking he could have

sent a letter with Tom to come and take care of it. He said he would have Tom come in and sign it. He added his department card to the account for access that day."

"Was anything said about adding my personal debit card to that account?"

She looked horrified. "Goodness, no. That would send up too many red flags. Has something happened?"

Mason answered her question grimly. "Maybe. Thank you, Carol. I'll keep you posted."

"Thanks. Because I wouldn't want to think I had done something that would get anyone in trouble. I was following the rules, I hope." She wrung her hands before going back to her station. "If I can do anything . . ."

"I appreciate it." Mason paused. "Carol, you did the right thing."

"Mr. Beckman," Lucy began.

"Call me Mason. Any friend of Jared and Tom's is a friend of mine."

"Thank you, Mason. Would it be possible to add another card to an account through the online portal?"

If Lucy had used the blonde card earlier, she certainly wasn't, now.

He stopped to think. "It wouldn't be easy. You would have to get into the employee portal to do that. Everything can be done online, within limits." He stared at the computer screen that had come to life with the account information. "Here we go."

Tom frowned, wishing he could see the screen. "Can you print out the activity for the past week? Also any activity on my department card and personal debit card?"

"Sure. Let me pull up those other accounts on other windows."

Lucy looked over the banker's shoulder. "This is interesting." She pointed to one specific transaction. "According to this, you made a withdrawal at an ATM at the time you and I were looking at your mom's roof the other day."

"That's impossible." He stood up behind her to see. "That was three days ago. Wait, which card was it?"

"The department one." Lucy turned to look at him, nodding. "The one that's missing."

"That shows how crazy it's been. I didn't even notice it wasn't in my wallet. See if there are any withdrawals using my personal debit card."

Mason clicked on another window to pull up Tom's personal account.

"Looks like there was an attempted transfer early this morning, but it didn't go through." Mason turned and regarded both Tom and Lucy. "Tom, this is looking like bank fraud. You might want to think about getting a warrant so we can print up these records for you to use."

"I will, Mason. Thanks for your help. We'll include in the warrant any video surveillance tapes you might have at the ATM." He paused. "So there hasn't been any money directly put into my personal account?"

"No. Not yet, anyway. Anybody that could get into our system enough to put your info in there is a person to keep an eye on. Do you have any ideas who it might be?"

Tom and Lucy looked at one another again. "I'm afraid we do. I'll let you know when we get the warrant."

Mason closed out the windows and rose. "I'm glad you brought this to our attention. I put a block on the account. If anyone wants to make a deposit into the fund, I'll take care of it myself. I put a note for the tellers to signal me if there's any activity."

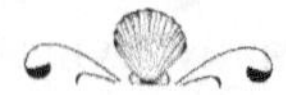

"Hungry?" Tom hesitated when they got to their cars.

"Starved." Lucy was so relieved she couldn't stand it. And when she was relieved, she ate. "I need to move my car, though. I wouldn't want Sam to see it parked here at the bank."

"Good idea. How about we drive over to the real estate office and leave your car there. Maybe we could find some crab cakes somewhere?"

Her smile blossomed. "Harrelson's? I'm feeling the need for the Crab Cake Lady."

"Harrelson's it is. See you in a minute."

They turned onto Highway 17 and made their way to Crawford and Benton Real Estate. Lucy was talking to herself. Talking to God. "Thank you, Lord, for not letting Tom be a crook." She laughed at herself, and then sobered. "Lord, if Sam has done this, help him to see what he's done and be repentant. He'll never be able to be a cop again. Show him Yourself. Help us to be You, to him."

When they stopped at the office, Lucy grabbed her purse and went to Tom's car, wiping a quick tear.

"What's wrong?" He leaned over.

"I was praying."

"Okay. Can I ask what about?"

She could tell he was concerned. She smiled and touched his arm. "Well, first I thanked God that you weren't a crook."

He threw his head back and laughed. "I can't tell you how relieved that makes me."

"Hey, me too. That's why I need crab cakes." She sobered. "I prayed for Sam. If he's done what we think he's done, he's ruined his career and maybe his life. I don't know where he stands with God."

Tom turned his hand to grasp hers. "You're a good woman, Lucy Dixon."

"Not really, just constantly trying." She squeezed his hand. "Now I'm hungry, and you know once you've eaten Crab Cake Lady's crab cakes, you are ruined for anything else."

"Noted." He let go of her hand and prepared to leave the parking lot. He paused. "Did you really think I was a crook?"

"No, and may I add that I was relieved it was so evident you're not a crook." She arched an eyebrow. "I watch television. I know how hard these cases are to prove. Be glad me and my pink tool belt are your alibi."

"Oh, believe me, I am!" He laughed and drove her to the seafood market.

# CHAPTER TWENTY-FIVE

Friday dawned clear and dry, for which Tom was thankful. The roofing project could be completed in a day, if Lucy was as good as she said she was. He caught himself whistling. With everything going on, he'd been too preoccupied to do much but keep his head down and put one foot in front of the other.

He drove to the family home with shingles and nails weighing down the pickup truck. It would be nice to have a day outside, especially if it included Miss Lucy Dixon.

As he unloaded the materials on the back porch, close to where they would be working, he heard the screen door squeak.

"Is that you, Tom?"

"It is, unless there's another man bringing you shingles and nails." Teasing his mother was his dad's way of keeping her from getting too serious. It usually worked.

"You silly boy. Would you like breakfast before you get started? Charly's fixing waffle batter and bacon."

The smell of bacon wafted out and awakened his taste buds. "Still no classes today, huh?"

"No school. There are still too many people out of pocket."

He nodded in agreement. "I'm not surprised. I had a bite, but I could be convinced. Is there enough for one more?"

Mary Ann laughed. "Of course there is. When Lucy gets here, y'all come on in and get some food. I'll make extra coffee. It's sunny, but it sure hasn't warmed up much, has it?" She rubbed her arms.

"I daresay if you were going to be working on a roof, you'd be glad it was a little cooler this morning." Tom clapped the dust and grime off his hands. "You feeling okay this morning?" After his dad's sudden heart attack and subsequent death, he tried to stay aware of his mother's health.

She waved her hand in dismissal. "I'm fine. I just don't work hard enough anymore. It's a good thing I don't live any further north."

"Amen to that." Ah, there was Lucy. He heard her car door slam and called out. "Come on around back."

After a few minutes, he was worried. He started around the house to see if she was all right. "Lucy?"

She met him, fully armed, and instantly struck a pose. Laughter built up in him, along with another feeling that had nothing to do with the pink tool belt and hammer she wore or even the pink high-top sneakers. It was the spring in her step and the grin on her face that made his heart leap.

"So? Pink tool belt?"

"I give up. You even found a pink hammer to match." His head shook in disbelief.

"I have a confession to make." She twisted her lips. Guilty? "I did have to buy the tool belt."

"Aha!"

She put her finger in his face. "Only because my own tool belt is in storage in Kentucky. I do own my own tool belt and hammer. Oh, and this hammer didn't come pink. I bought a can of spray paint while I was at the hardware store."

"The shoes?"

She looked at him in amazement. "How could you even doubt I would own pink sneakers? Do you even know me?"

"I bow in apology. You look like you're ready to work. I wish Mom could see your get-up." He smiled down at her pink cap completing the picture.

She tilted her head and gave him a sad little grin. "I do, too. I think she would enjoy it."

And he knew she meant it. He took a deep breath before he spoke. "Before we get started, would you like waffles?"

"Are you kidding? I overslept this morning, so I had to call Sarah on the way here, and I didn't have time to eat anything. Please tell me there's coffee?"

"You know it."

Lucy sighed with pleasure. "My motto is 'a day without coffee is like a day without sunshine.' Don't you agree?"

"Most definitely. Come on in. Charly's got it ready to pour on the waffle iron."

"Oh yum. I haven't had waffles since . . . well, since Daddy died. They were his favorite, and he passed down the waffle gene to me." A shadow passed over her face, but she brightened as they entered the kitchen.

"Lucy! I'm glad you're here, child." Mary Ann hugged her. Tom noticed the tears in her eyes as she hugged his mother back even tighter.

"Thank you so much. Charly, it smells wonderful in here."

"Have a seat. I've got one coming off the waffle iron, and it's got your name on it." Charly put a mug of hot coffee in front of her as the steam stopped billowing from the iron, indicating the waffle was done.

"Hey. What about big brother?" He winked at Lucy as Charly handed her the plate of the golden-brown delicacy.

"Ladies first, right Mama?"

Mary Ann smiled. "Yes, sweetheart, ladies first."

Lucy laughed as she reached for the butter. "You've done a good job with one of your children, at least."

"Don't forget the handkerchief."

"True. I appreciate that you taught your son about real hankies. I didn't know they still made them."

"There. See? I'm not totally incorrigible." He crossed his arms on the table, waiting for his food. This was fun.

"I'm glad to know you're keeping up your training. Tissues have their place, but a good hankie? Now that shows breeding. At least it did, according to my mama. Now she was a trip. Had to have everything just-so, and she expected to be treated as the matriarch she would have been, had the old ways of her mother's era continued."

"My Grandmommy is a little like that, but she's very independent. My grandfather died before I was born, and she carried on, running his business like he did, and even better." Lucy cut a piece of her waffle and sighed. "This is wonderful."

"It's right to adjust to change instead of fighting against it. Don't you think so, Tom?"

Did he? For him, change had meant losing something. He grew up hearing his granny talk about how good things used to be. But were they, really? When he found out about his parents' call to missions, he realized they lost something by not letting their circumstances change. There was regret in not accepting change. Was that waffle done yet?

"I won't argue with you, Mama."

"See you don't." Mom grinned and pushed herself up from the table. "If y'all will excuse me, I have an appointment."

Tom straightened up. "What appointment? Do you need a ride?" Charly looked as confused as he.

"Relax. I'm going to my homemaker's meeting. I'm going to teach them some basic crochet stitches. I can do that with my eyes closed. Good thing, huh?" She laughed at her own joke, and they joined in. "Prudie is coming over to give me a ride."

"Sounds like fun. One day I want to learn how to crochet. I've tried, but it's not for me, I guess." Lucy shrugged her shoulders.

"Never say never. There was a time when I couldn't crochet for the life of me. Oh, I could do the stitches, but they weren't even. I could tell what kind of mood I was in according to the tightness of the stitches. Tense? Extra-tight. Relaxed? Extra-loose. Didn't seem to be an in-between for me. Once the kids got older and I wasn't rushed, it got better. Oddly enough, I think it's been better since my sight started going. As long as someone gets the yarn for me, I can do the rest." She smiled. "One of these days I'll teach you."

"I'd like that."

"You all enjoy your breakfast and be careful out there on that roof, you hear?"

"Yes, ma'am." All three said it at the same time and laughed when she left the room.

They heard her voice drift from the area of the front door. "I heard that."

"WELL, Mr. Foreman, are you ready to get started?" Tom drained his cup, and Lucy wondered what it would be like to share a breakfast table with him every morning. Was he a morning person?

"Let's hit it." He got up and thanked his sister for breakfast. "What's for lunch?"

"I'll let you know when I know." Charly shook her head in disgust. "He always wants to plan ahead and know exactly what's going to happen next."

"Hey, I like to know what to look forward to. And food is important."

"Tom, it's healthier if you eat to live instead of living to eat."

Having grown up an only child, Lucy was enjoying ganging up on Tom with his sister.

"Whatever. Let's go break in that tool belt and hammer."

Lucy followed him out the door. "How many bundles will we need?"

He looked up the ladder, shading his eyes. "I bought four bundles of shingles and a roll of felt paper. I hope we don't find more damage when we get up there." He glanced at her. "Did you bring your sunscreen?"

"Already applied, thank you." He cared.

"Let's get up there with the pry bars and see what we've got. There was some bare decking showing, but I don't think we'll have to replace any of that. It leaked where the felt came off in the seams." He gestured to the ladder. "Ladies first."

"Always. Plus, if I fall, I hope you'll catch me."

"Or at least break your fall."

She started up the ladder. The front part of the house had a steeper roof than this side, but it was still pretty high off the ground. Thank goodness she didn't suffer from fear of heights. Another good gene she received from Grandmommy.

"Oh, Tom. The view from up here is spectacular." She could see over some of the trees straight to the marsh. It seemed to go on forever. "Wouldn't it be neat to have a crow's nest up here, where you could just come up and look out over the trees?"

"This plantation went that far at one time. We were one of the first rice plantations before the Revolutionary War." He began prying up the shingles on the edges of the damaged part. "The Carolinas were the largest rice producers in North America for over two hundred years."

"Wow." She started following his lead on the other edge of the damage. "And your family has lived here that long?" To have that kind of legacy, that kind of family, was unheard of for her. Today's mobile society had hit her family hard.

"Since before the Civil War, we have. A blessing and a curse, you could say."

"How can it be a curse? It's a legacy."

"It is until the place owns you instead of you owning the place." He rested his arm on his knee for a minute. "It all depends on how you look at it, I guess."

Lucy concentrated on the broken shingles and torn felt she was removing. The thought of a place "owning you" never occurred to her. She loved the home where she lived in Kentucky, but she didn't have any qualms about selling it. It was a house. Her grandmother's house was the place that spelled "stability" in her life but not as much as the people in her life.

"Do you think about this place as a legacy or an albatross?"

"Mama looks on it as an albatross. She and Dad wanted to leave, but her mother was set on staying here."

"I take it your grandmother wasn't willing to let them go?"

He stopped. "I think she didn't know how to let them go or how to let this place go. They were living here, and she had her chicks in her nest like she always had. And it stayed that way. She got her way. She saw her grandchildren raised here as well as her own children."

"What about you?"

"I can see it both ways, but I don't have the say-so." He smiled at her. It was a sad smile. "When I got out of college and got the job at the police department, I had a pretty tidy sum in the bank. Mama encouraged me to buy a house and get out on my own. I'm glad I did, but I'd come back here in a heartbeat if I could afford it."

"Legacy means a lot to you. I can tell." She paused in her work. "I know our legacy is in Heaven, but I wish I knew more about my family. My mother's family is scattered all over. I never knew her parents. Grandmommy is the only grandparent I ever knew, and Dad was an only child. What did they do? What did they stand for?"

Tom laughed. "Sometimes you're better off not knowing. Every family has its secrets and its black sheep."

She waved her hand in dismissal. "Oh, I know that, but I don't even have cousins to turn to in times of need. How many cousins do you have?"

He stopped and looked up into the sky. "Hang on. I'm counting."

"See? I have two cousins. Two. And they live in California. I've seen them maybe three times in my life."

"I'll give you a good deal on some slightly-used cousins of mine."

She laughed out loud. "I may take you up on that."

"Thirty-five."

"Thirty-five what?" She stared at him incredulously. "Cousins?"

"Yep."

How can anyone have thirty-five cousins?

"Dad was one of ten kids, and Mama was one of five. They were a prolific bunch. Our branch was the smallest."

"Do they all live around here?" She still couldn't wrap her head around thirty-five cousins.

"No. They're spread all over, but a lot of them do."

"I'd better not bad-mouth you around the community, huh?" She grinned as she finished pushing the old shingles and felt off the side of the house. She wiped her hands together and put her hammer in her tool belt.

"Better not. They're probably related." He stood and surveyed their work. "Good job. Now we get to do the easy part."

"Not until you do the heavy lifting." She looked down at the shingles and felt to be brought up. "Are you sure you can climb a ladder and carry one of those bundles?"

"It's not my first rodeo. Don't worry. I'll carry them one at a time. They're only seventy-five pounds each."

She raised her eyebrows. "Is that all? I'm surprised you don't carry them all."

"I may be strong, but I ain't stupid. I'll get the felt so we can get it nailed down before lunch." He started down the ladder as she stretched her arms up in the warm sunshine.

"Sounds like a plan. In the meantime, I'll be up here enjoying the view." She looked back over the panoramic view not visible from the ground. "So, so beautiful."

Before continuing down, Tom stopped at the top of the ladder, looked at Lucy, and smiled. "Totally." When she looked down at him in surprise, he winked and went on his way.

"Slow down, Sarah, I can't understand what you're saying." When Tom came up the ladder with the roofing felt, Lucy was still standing on the roof, her finger in one ear and her phone at the other.

He laid down the felt and whispered to her. His gut began to churn with worry. "What's happening?"

Lucy put her hand up to stop his talking. He was familiar with that signal. She couldn't hear what Sarah was saying if she was listening to him.

"He's awake? Oh, Sarah! That's wonderful!" She looked up at Tom with a happy smile. "Okay. We'll wait until later to come. Love you too! Bye!" She pushed the "end' button on her phone and reached up to hug Tom.

He squeezed her extra-tight. Probably tighter than she had intended, but it felt good. "I'm assuming Jared is awake?"

She pulled away, red-faced, and began fiddling with the clasp on her overalls. "Yes. He's awake, clear-headed, and has already told her that the wedding would not under any circumstances be postponed." She grinned. "He said he wasn't waiting one more moment for her than he had to."

"That's my boy." He laughed, having an idea of what Jared was thinking. If he spent much more time alone with Lucy, he would have no hope of sticking to his plan of not burdening her with his family.

"They're running tests this afternoon, and Sarah said no visitors until this evening." She lifted her shoulders, shaking with happiness. "Sarah couldn't talk for laughing and crying at the same time."

"I can only imagine. Did the doctor say anything about long-term?"

"No, that's why they're running tests. They hope to know something by tonight or tomorrow." She paused in thought. "Hmm. You know what this means."

"It means Jared is okay?" He looked at her in confusion.

"No, Mister Best Man, it means we've got to get on the stick. Neither of them will be in any shape to finish planning a wedding. That means it's up to you and me."

He laughed at her hands-on-hips stance, even as she balanced on the roof. She was in brigadier general mode now. He saluted her and said, "I'm ready for my orders, sir, er, ma'am."

Her gaze softened. "Thank you, soldier. I'll keep you posted."

He nodded. "I think, for now, if we're not going to the hospital until later, we can get this felt down and the shingles on within the next two hours. What do you think?"

"I think we have motivation now, don't you?"

He grabbed her hand and squeezed. Such a small hand. Was that a blister forming on the inside of her palm? He rubbed the tender spot.

"Definitely." The relief rushing through him made him feel lightheaded. Or was it Lucy? He didn't care. Jared was going to be okay. Lucy was by his side. The sun was shining, God was in His Heaven, and all was right with the world. For now anyway.

AFTER A QUICK CLEANUP, Lucy was ready and waiting to go to the hospital. Tom had offered to pick her up. "With the extra patients in the hospital, there's no reason to clog up the parking lot with our two vehicles." She smiled. Yeah. That was why he insisted on picking her up.

Was he softening toward her? She caught glimpses of the Tom she had met last summer; a little more carefree, even though the world around them was falling apart. A few more smiles, even though he was worried like crazy about his best friend. And when she spontaneously hugged him on the roof? She sighed. He definitely hugged back. That had to be a little bit of Heaven.

After picking him up at Lazy Acres, Oliver stuck to her like glue and was beside himself to see one of "his people." He wouldn't let her out of his sight. The kitchen at Pilot Oaks was getting a slight face-lift, and Lucy had agreed with Linda Crawford that Lazy Acres might be a better place for Oliver for a few days.

After the hurricane scare, Lucy preferred staying alone at Sarah's with Oliver there at night. She was getting attached, and so was he. He would have showered with her if she'd let him. When she left the bathroom, he was waiting right there at the door and followed her every step of the way. She sat down in Sarah's easy-chair, patted her lap for Oliver to join her, and began to pray.

"God? Are you there? I know You are. Anybody that is the Alpha and the Omega, the Beginning and the End, is everywhere. I tend to forget, and I'm sorry. Sometimes I only come to You when I'm sad or upset about something, but not today. Today, I thank You for a happy day. Forgive me for not thanking You earlier."

Tears began to fall from her eyes, and the familiar pressure in her chest from trying hard not to cry began to release. She had been angry with God, and she had avoided Him. It wasn't right, and her remorse was right up there with that niggling feeling of irritation that things hadn't gone exactly as she had planned.

"I know You love me and anything You allow can be used for good. I love him, You know? I can't imagine being happy with anyone else. If Tom isn't who You have for me, would You take this away? And if he is who You have for me, would You please tell him that?"

She giggled through her tears. "I know I can be capricious, but You made me, remember?"

She hugged the fluffy dog and wiped away her tears before scooting him off her lap and heading to the mirror. The damage to her makeup was repaired in time to hear Tom drive up into Sarah's driveway. She put Oliver in his crate with his toy, double-checked herself in the mirror, and was at the door before the bell rang.

TOM OPENED the door to Jared's room to let Lucy pass, smiling at his friend over her head. "So you decided to join the rest of the world, huh?"

Jared grinned back. "I did it to get out of picking out curtains and silverware." He gave a fake flinch when Sarah swatted his arm. After the swat, she hung on to his arm for dear life, and his other hand covered hers with a squeeze.

This was what he needed to see. Sarah and Jared had been through it, nevertheless the teasing and the flirting? It was still there.

"Do they have you hooked up to enough monitors?" It worried Tom a little to still see the many tubes and wires.

"Humph. They want to know if I burp around here. Not that I've had much to burp. They did let me have broth a couple of hours ago. I don't suppose you snuck me in a burger?" Jared's brown eyes beseeched him.

"I'm afraid not. Sarah here would kill me if I did."

Sarah nodded. "Yes, I would. I want you in tip-top shape for October sixth. That means you do exactly what the doctor tells you."

Jared chuckled. "And what Sarah tells me too."

"Well, yes. We only have your best interest at heart, dear." Sarah arched her eyebrow.

"I'm sunk."

"I'm thankful he knew his name, knew my name, knew the date of our wedding, and remembered that his house was no longer there." Sarah gazed on her fiancé.

"That was rough, even though we didn't plan to live there forever. It's a shame to lose a valuable piece of property like that." Jared shook his head. "But you know, the important thing is we're all alive, and nobody lost anything that couldn't be replaced."

"Amen, brother. What is your recovery looking like?"

Jared cut his eyes to Sarah, who nodded at him.

"Recovery can last anywhere from six months to two years, but the fastest will be the first few months. Doc told me I'll suffer from some anxiety and irritability and will probably have a hard time concentrating."

"Sometimes he forgets words, but the doctor said this was common, and may continue." Sarah smiled at Jared. "I'm glad to have him back. It's up to me to keep the anxiety and stress down."

Jared squeezed her hand. "As long as it doesn't double it for you."

Lucy nodded. "I thought as much. I told Tom since you're both tied up with this whole recovery thing, we would have to pick up the slack on the wedding front." She looked up at him. "Right, Tom."

"Was that a question?" Tom gave her a sideways look.

She focused her glare on his face. "No, it wasn't."

"What she said, then. I'm sure she'll let me know what I need to do and when I need to do it." This time Tom flinched when Lucy not-so-gently elbowed him in the ribs.

Sarah snorted. "Lucy is a task-master. Don't cross her."

"You're telling me. We completed a two-day roof repair in less than a day. She's stronger than she looks."

Lucy looked up at the ceiling. "It wasn't that big a job."

"It would have been for me by myself. Hey, if you stay around here, I may start flipping houses again and hire you for a flunky." He loved to see her blush. Could he maintain that level of camaraderie with her? Nope. Couldn't be done. He'd have to hug her every once in a while, and that would slow down construction work.

Sarah spoke up. "Watch it, Tom. Lucy would end up being your boss. She organizes everybody."

"It would be interesting to see who is the best organizer, Tom or Lucy." Jared tilted his head to one side. "Tom is the most organized person I know, but Lucy?"

"She's a drill sergeant, a taskmaster, a slave driver." Sarah grinned. "But she's also my best friend."

"I'm beginning to feel like a cross between Attila the Hun and Martha Stewart." Lucy looked back and forth at the group.

Tom whispered in her ear, loud enough for everyone to hear. "They're just jealous."

"Well, of course they are, but really? Slave driver?"

"Okay, I'll take that one back. However, you are a taskmaster and a drill sergeant. Admit it." Sarah laughed at Lucy's shaking head.

"Fine. I guess I'll have to live up to my name. And do we have a contest, Tom, between me and you?" She gave him her Cheshire-cat grin. "I'd be interested to hear about your ideas about wedding planning and organizing."

He held his hands up in mock-surrender. "I concede already. Consider me your flunky for wedding planning." Or anything else, for that matter.

She reddened slightly and nodded. "Very well. We'll get started tomorrow. We have an appointment with Emmaline at 10:00 in the morning."

Sarah laughed. "Don't leave me out completely!"

"Don't worry. You've already done the hard part. Well, for the most part." Lucy wrinkled her nose. "What about your venue?"

Sarah looked down at Jared. "What do you think? Atalaya is closed until November. We could always get married on the beach, I guess. Or at Pilot Oaks?"

Jared was quiet, thinking, then his smile grew. "How about the church for the ceremony?"

Tom could tell Sarah liked the idea. Calvary Church had a beautiful sanctuary: white wood paneling, white walls, white pew ends with wooden pew backs, and deep burgundy carpeting and upholstery. The stained-glass windows had every color in the rainbow. "I love it."

"Pilot Oaks for the reception? After all, that's where I fell in love with you."

Sarah leaned down to kiss him. "Pilot Oaks, it is. I happen to know we can get a deal on the venue."

"I'll tell Emmaline, and we'll get on it. Right, Tom?" Lucy poked him.

He clicked his heels and stood at attention. "Yes, ma'am."

Jared's laugh was the best thing Tom had heard in a long time.

om sat at his desk in the squad room, chin in hand, thinking about Jared, weddings, Lucy, Sam, and missing funds.

He heard footsteps in the hallway and looked up. Sam came to the squad room door and halted when he noticed Tom at his desk. He looked surprised.

"I thought you were out for the weekend, working on your roof?" Sam didn't greet him, just started talking.

"We were able to get it done yesterday. Did you need something?" The last thing he wanted was for Sam to know he and Lucy were on to him. The information he had received from the bank yesterday was enough to end Sam's career. He was anxious to find out why he did it. Why steal money from the fund, and beyond that, why try to frame him?

"Uh, no, thought I'd stop and speak when I saw you here. How's Jared Benton doing?" Sam didn't seem to want to meet his eyes.

"Better. He came out of the induced coma fine, and the prognosis is good." Why the sudden interest?

"That's great. He's getting married soon, isn't he? Lucy mentioned a wedding."

"Yes, in October."

"Lucky guy. Maybe someday." His laugh sounded forced.

Tom kept his expression neutral. His first instinct was to avoid him, but maybe finding out more about him would help him understand what his motivation was.

He leaned back in his chair, feigning a relaxation he didn't feel. "Yeah, me too. I've never even been close. You?"

Sam cleared his throat nervously. "A long time ago. A girl I dated in high school. We were young and dumb."

"What happened, if you don't mind my asking? I mean, you're not married now."

"She was killed in an accident." He stared at Tom. It was a little disconcerting.

What was going on? "That's tough. It's hard to get over stuff like that."

"Yeah. Well, it probably wouldn't have worked out. I guess we'll never know, will we?"

There was an edge to Sam's voice he hadn't noticed before. "I guess not." Tom was relieved when his phone notified him of a text message. **Emmaline @10, remember?** Thank you, Lucy Dixon.

"Hey, that was a reminder about an appointment. I'll talk to you later." He texted back a "thumbs up" to Lucy.

Sam seemed to come back to his usual affable self. "Sure. Hey, have a good rest of the weekend."

"You too. See you Monday."

Monday was the next meeting of the relief fund committee. He wasn't on it, but wild horses couldn't keep him away.

LUCY TAPPED her fingers against the steering wheel as she sat in front of the station in Georgetown. What was taking Tom so long to get out here? She didn't want to be late for the meeting with Sarah's wedding planner. She rolled down her window a bit and glanced around, glad it was a pretty day. The majority of the storm debris had been cleared away. You could still see evidence in broken trees and washed-out yards, but this was a community that prided itself on keeping things neat and tidy. It wasn't only a tourist area, it was a charming place where people lived their lives.

People like Tom, Jared, and now Sarah. Could she think of it as home? Maybe. The breeze felt good. Her nose picked up the signature scent of salt and earth from the marsh. She was about ten blocks from the ocean, and even here the marshes and tidal rivers brought the ocean inland. She had seen Sam enter the building as she was coming down the street and was glad he didn't see her car. There was something strange about the whole thing. Every time Jared's or Sarah's name came up, he seemed to tense. He was friendly to Tom, but . . .

Tom opened the car door on the passenger side. "Mornin'. Are you sure you need me for this?" He folded his tall frame into the Mustang.

Lucy laughed at the anxious look on his face. He was dreading this, she could tell. "Fear not. I'll make the big decisions. It only needs to look like Jared is being represented." She gave him a cheesy grin and pulled out into traffic.

"So that's how this works." He arched his eyebrow at her. "I always wondered."

"Today we're deciding on tablescapes."

"What on earth is a tablescape? I mean, I have an idea based on the words, but, really? Tablescapes?" He released a sigh. "Why not say, 'we're picking out tablecloths and centerpieces?'"

"Because it's much more than that. You'll see. Emmaline is going to have three or four to choose from, or we can mix and match.

We had just started talking about centerpieces when the hurricane happened and everything went nuts." She glanced over at him while waiting at a stoplight in the downtown area of Georgetown. "What have you been up to this morning? I was surprised when you wanted me to meet you at the station. Any news on the relief fund?"

"No, but I did have an interesting conversation with Sam this morning."

Tom seemed thoughtful. Preoccupied. "What was it about?" She hoped it wasn't about her.

"He came in and asked about Jared. It was odd."

"What's odd about that? He was there the night he had surgery."

"Yes, and then he mentioned the wedding and how lucky Jared was to have found Sarah." The crease between his brows deepened. "He mentioned he had come close once."

"Okay, that is a little strange. Maybe he was looking for sympathy. He's not married now." She pulled into a parking spot in front of Quince Wedding Designs. Before she got out of the car, she turned to look at him full in the face. She could tell he was troubled. "Is there something I'm missing?"

"I think it's rather that I'm missing something." He unbuckled his seatbelt and opened the car door. "It'll come to me. For now, let's see how many layers of tulle we think is appropriate for an outdoor wedding in hurricane season."

"Funny guy." As he opened the elegant establishment door to usher her in, she turned and winked. "I'm surprised you know what tulle is."

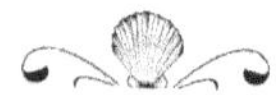

WHILE TOM and Jared watched the football game on television, Lucy sat next to Sarah in the hospital room, showing her pictures of the table decorations for the reception.

"What do you think of the runner on the wooden tables instead of the tablecloth?" Lucy was worried about this decision. Tom had convinced her that if the wind got up, tablecloths could be a nuisance, but runners were nice and tailored.

"I love it. The distressed wood table gives enough rustic to be casual, and the brass and white make it formal enough to go with Pilot Oaks." Sarah smiled as she looked through the pictures. "You two did a good job. I don't think I would have thought of all this by myself or with Jared."

"Emmaline is a wonder. She had stuff put together, and when we got there, we all started mixing and matching until we found a combination we all liked. Even Tom had good input." She swiped through more pictures, laughing as she got to one particular image.

Sarah chuckled. "Is that Tom?"

Lucy laughed and looked over at the guys, engrossed in the game. "Shh. He doesn't know I took that one." It was a picture of Tom fingering different grades of tulle fabric, a frown on his handsome face.

"You could definitely use that one for blackmail someday." Sarah laughed louder as the guys looked over at them, a quizzical look on both faces. She dismissed them with a wave. "Sorry to interrupt the game, boys."

Lucy snorted quietly. "They don't have a clue, do they?"

"No, they're in their own little world."

They looked at each other, saying in unison, "Football world."

"I guess the World Series will start soon after we get back from our honeymoon." Sarah sighed and shook her head. "What are your plans after the wedding? Beyond taking care of Oliver and house-sitting, I mean. You know you're welcome to stay after we get back."

Lucy arched an eyebrow at her friend. "Now I can't think of

anything more awkward than being 'the roommate' with two newlyweds."

Sarah sighed. "I know. I can't either." She giggled. "I imagine come game day, I'll wish for a roommate that doesn't yell at the television."

"I hear ya. I don't know. With the house being sold and all, I guess you could say I'm homeless. Grandmommy wants me to come and live in Atlanta, preferably with her, but I'm not sure I want to do that. With you here, and the rest of you migrating here eventually, I thought about moving here. And then I thought to myself, 'I can't depend on my friends or family for my happiness.' That being said, I'm waiting for a sign. God knows what He wants me to do. After the hurricane and everything else, I knew I was supposed to be here at this time."

Sarah leaned over and hugged Lucy. "I don't know what I would have done without you, Lucy. Would you believe I'm not even worried about the wedding anymore? Yeah, we still have around two hundred people coming to the wedding, had to change the venue, and the groom will have a very short haircut, but the details are falling into place."

"Speaking of details, the flower girl dresses came in, and they are adorable! The blush tulle and pearls are perfect. When will the girls be here? I don't think there will be many alterations, but just in case . . . ." Lucy had pulled up the calendar app on her phone and was looking over appointments for various wedding activities.

"They'll be here next weekend and won't go home until after the wedding. Since the ceremony will be at the church and the reception at Pilot Oaks, Susan wanted to be here to help Mom and Dad get the house ready." Sarah paused. "Wow. It's coming fast, isn't it?"

Emotion welled up in Lucy's chest. Why in the world did she feel teary-eyed all of the sudden? "My buddy's getting married."

"Hey, you two." Jared raised his voice. "It's half-time and I want pizza."

Sarah looked at Lucy. "Is it me, or is the patient getting a little demanding?"

"It's not you. I think boredom has set in now that he's graduated to real-people food." Lucy tilted her head to look at Tom. What kind of patient would Tom be? Even worse, she was sure. She grinned at him. With a surprised expression, he grinned back.

"Luce, I'm going to get this man some pizza. Want to come with me?" His expression was tender.

She wondered at that but wasn't going to question it. Not now anyway. She was simply going to enjoy every minute she could get when he was in this kind of mood. "Sure. What can I bring you, Sarah?"

"Cheese sticks and marinara. And a large sweet tea."

Jared chuckled. "Only in the South does someone order sweet tea with pizza. Make it two, please."

# CHAPTER TWENTY-EIGHT

Monday dawned dreary and gray. Tom's mood matched the sky.

It had been a great weekend. Jared's rehab was moving along, and the doctor assured them he would be walking alone by the wedding. He might have to rest more than he planned, but other than that, he would make a full recovery, hopefully within six months.

It was an answer to prayer. Tom had prayed, and just about every believer he knew in the county had prayed for Jared Benton. Who knew there were so many prayers going back and forth? It seemed everyone he ran into had seen his name on a prayer list.

As he drove down Highway 17 toward Georgetown, the gray skies seemed to tamp him down. The thought of what was coming that day had weighed on him, even during the good times. This couldn't continue. God was in control, so why was he trying to pick up the reins?

"Thank you, God, for the healing You've done in Jared's life. How could I even doubt You're in control, seeing the miracles You've performed? Thank You, Lord." He thought a minute about the meeting coming up this afternoon with Sam, the mayor, and the county judge. "Lord, bring something good out of this meeting with Sam. I don't know why he's done this, but You know his heart, and You love him. Help me to love him too."

He crossed the bridges into town, still in a prayerful mood, still thinking about Sam, Jared, and Lucy.

Jared. He sat up straighter in his seat. Sam said his girlfriend had been killed in a car accident.

It couldn't be. Surely not.

He turned right to go to the hospital instead of left to go to City Hall and the station. When he parked, he pulled out his phone and called the receptionist to let her know he would be late. He started to pull up Lucy's number, and thought again. He'd wait until he had talked to Jared.

It was still early for visiting, but this was business. He made his way to the fourth floor, dodging breakfast carts and nurses intent on their morning routine. He paused at Jared's door, knocked, and entered at Jared's request.

"Hey, you're early." Jared smiled and winced as the nurse struck a vein to draw blood. "The vampires come every morning to relieve me of my blood."

The nurse grinned. "You should be thankful the real vampire didn't come. He likes to draw blood at 5:00 in the morning. I don't believe in this before sunrise stuff."

"I've seen him a few times." He glanced down as the fourth vial filled with blood.

She finished, removed the rubber tourniquet and needle, and put a bandage on his arm. "Now you be good, you hear?" She patted him on the arm and left the room.

"Every morning?" Tom shook his head.

"Yep. Every morning. I'm surprised I have any left." Jared reached for his coffee cup and settled into his bed. "What's up?"

"Does something have to be 'up' for me to come see you early?" Man. He dreaded bringing this up. At the moment when

Jared seems to be recovered from the tragedy that changed his life eleven years ago, it has to come up again.

"You're pensive." Jared's dark brown eyes were boring a hole in him.

Tom chuckled. "Pensive? Okay, that's a Sarah word if I ever heard one."

"Maybe so, but it's accurate."

Tom took a deep breath. "I told you about the relief fund?"

"What about it?"

"What I didn't tell you, and what you can't tell anybody, is that money is missing from the fund. I've been working on figuring out who it is, and Lucy's been helping me."

"Lucy? What's she got to do with this?" Jared was shifting himself into a more upright position in his bed.

"Relax, she's not in any danger. She's the one who caught it. She had volunteered to manage the account since everyone else in the office was tied up with post-hurricane events." He cleared his throat. "Do you know Sam Watson?" Tom watched Jared. His face was a blank as he shook his head.

"Name sounds familiar." He frowned. "No, it's not coming to me."

"He was a couple of years younger than you. Went to Georgetown High, transferred to Waccamaw his senior year. I didn't know him, either. He knew you."

"How?"

"I can't be positive, but I think he knew of you through Annabelle."

Jared turned pale. "Annabelle. Sam Watson. I got nothing."

Nothing but confusion. "Did you ever know who Annabelle was dating?"

"I don't think so. The concussion blocked out some of the details, and I think I hoped she would tell somebody, maybe her friend in Charleston." He looked at Tom in horror. "Do you think?"

"What do you remember about that night? The night of the accident?"

Jared closed his eyes and shook his head, as if trying to alternately remember and wipe the images from his head. "I remember getting to her house." He looked up, shaking his head. "Tom, I was going to break up with her that night."

"I know it's hard. What else do you remember?"

"I remember her face. She had a bruise on her right eye and cheek."

Tom thought a minute. "You're sure it was her right eye?"

"Yes. When I went into her living room, the fireplace was to the left, and she was sitting on the couch, facing it, to my right. Her right side was away from me, and she had her elbow resting on the arm and her hand covering it." He closed his eyes for a second. "Until she turned to look at me. That image is burned into my mind."

"That means whoever hit her was left-handed." Tom thought about writing down that bit of information then realized he would never forget it.

# CHAPTER TWENTY-NINE

*L*ucy was waiting in the hallway, wondering what was keeping Tom. He knew what time the meeting was, and he knew how nervous she was. She knew tapping her size-6 high heels wouldn't help, either, but still she tapped.

She had ducked seeing Sam, wanting to touch base with Tom before the meeting. And now the meeting was about to start, and if Tom didn't get here in time, she would have to go in there and face the music without him. Maybe instead of tapping, she would pace.

She made one round of the hallway, and on her way back toward the door, she saw him. "Where have you been? I've been going nuts."

He held her off by raising both hands. She could see the lines of stress and worry on his face, and her heart softened. "What's happened? Is it Jared?" Her eyes widened, and her heart constricted. "Is he okay?" She covered her mouth with her hand, dreading what he might say.

"Jared's fine. I went to see him. Something came up in a conversation I had with Sam that brought up a few questions I needed to ask Jared." He looked at his phone. "I'll explain it all later. Let's get this over with, shall we?"

She narrowed her eyes. "You promise you'll tell me." It was a statement, not a question.

Tom sighed. "I promise."

She nodded. "All right, I've got the statements from the bank." She walked by his side toward the conference room, hurrying to keep up with his long stride. She stopped at the door and leaned closer to whisper. "Did you know that the bank contacted the SCBI?"

"I heard. It may not be enough to prosecute, but it will start a file on him, and they'll keep an eye on his activities from now on." He reached for the door handle. "Ready?"

She nodded. "Prayed up."

"Even better."

"Glad you both could join us." Sam's raised eyebrow made Lucy's hackles rise.

How dare he?

Tom, gentleman that he was, held her chair and waited until she was seated to sit in his own chair.

"Sorry we're running late. I had a last-minute stop to make, questioning a witness on a case."

The mayor and judge smiled and nodded their forgiveness. Only Sam looked peeved.

Tom glanced at Sam then back at Lucy. "Mayor Hynes, Judge Simpson, you've both met Lucy Dixon?"

Judge Simpson smiled. "Yes, and I must say, you've been a delight to work with."

Sam spoke up, starting the meeting without another word. "Now that the pleasantries and explanations have been voiced, may I say I appreciate you all being here today. As you know, the relief fund has taken in over one hundred thousand dollars in the last few weeks. We're getting checks and electronic deposits from all over."

"It's been a God-send, I have to say. Those folks need all the help they can get." The mayor turned to Lucy. "Miss Dixon, having your help has been invaluable. Everyone else has been tied up taking care of their own trauma, having someone slightly removed from the fray has been a blessing."

Lucy blushed. "Everyone here has been wonderful to me and to my friend Sarah, and I was happy to help in any way I could. I hope the money gets to the places it needs to be." Sam's eyes narrowed when she mentioned the fund. She looked away.

Sam straightened the papers in his stack and cleared his throat. "And that's why we're meeting today. I've been checking on the account, and I've noticed a few discrepancies in the debits from the fund."

The judge looked surprised. "Should we even have any debits yet?"

Lucy understood his concern. Disbursements weren't to begin until the following week. People in need were instructed either to come to the county government building or to go online and fill out the application form applying for aid. After that, a committee would distribute the funds until it was gone.

Tom spoke up. "No, there shouldn't be. That's what was disturbing." He looked at Sam and back to the two elected officials. "There are a few things that are disturbing."

"I agree." Sam interjected. "According to the online account, there have been several ATM debits made with one particular credit card."

"And which card was this? I wouldn't think a relief fund would have a debit card attached to it." The mayor was beginning to get agitated.

Tom held up his hand. "I think I can help you there. You see, the account, unbeknownst to me, was attached to my department debit card. The card that is missing from my wallet."

Judge Simpson's face was getting redder and redder. "When did this happen?"

"My missing card or the debits?"

"Both."

"I didn't realize the card was missing until Lucy found the missing funds that were tied to the card. We went to the bank to check it out, and found some pretty interesting information." He smiled over at Lucy. "Would you like to share with the gentlemen what we found out?"

She smiled at Tom and then looked at Sam with a withering expression. Would that he would actually wither. Hmm. Looking over at him, he did have a little bit of a "withered" look about him. A little pale. A little green around the gills?

"I would be happy to." She handed packets of copied evidence she had gathered. The bank statements, the signature card, and the record of debits from Tom's card prior to the incident.

"As you can see, prior to the debits from the relief fund, there have not been any types of debits on Tom's card. He has a spending limit on the department card of one thousand five hundred dollars."

Sam shifted in his chair. He looked uncomfortable with the line of discussion. "That doesn't mean he didn't skim from the relief fund account."

"There's also the signature card on the account. There is my name and signature and Sam's name and signature. When I signed it, Tom's name was not on the account." Lucy made sure the gentlemen saw the addition of his name.

"Tom, were you aware that you were on this account?" Mayor Hynes focused on Tom.

"No, sir, I was not. The first time I knew of it was when I went to the bank and asked to see the signature card." He looked at Sam. "Can you shed light on why the teller told the manager that you had come back alone and added my name, saying I would come by to sign it?"

"Without your signature, how did they allow your card to be used?" Judge Simpson leaned forward in his chair.

"It was all done electronically. A security check found that their employee portal had been entered outside of their computer network. Only a person with excellent computer skills would be able to do this."

The mayor and judge were silent. "Watson, what do you have to say?"

Sam cleared his throat. "I think this is all a huge misunderstanding. I will definitely look into this matter, and hopefully we can rectify the situation."

Tom shook his head. "I think it's a little late for that. Lucy, would you share the other information we were able to retrieve?"

Heart in her throat, she pulled out the images from the security cameras at the ATM machines. She laid them out, one by one. In each photo, was a man, wearing a Georgetown County Sheriff's Department cap. It was difficult to see the face, until the last one. He had been distracted, or maybe a little over-confident, and looked to the side, allowing the camera to get a perfect profile of his face.

Sam stood up. "This is insane. Those could have been taken at any time."

Lucy spoke up. "No. No, they couldn't." She pointed to the bottom margin of the photos. "Look at the timestamp on the bottom of the image. Look at the time of the withdrawals." Lucy shook her head. "How did you think you could get away with this?"

"You're smarter than I thought." Sam fisted his hands and looked at her with what looked like hatred in his eyes.

"Yes, she is." Tom stood up and pulled out his handcuffs. "She's the one that spotted the details." He walked up to Sam. "Sam Watson, I'm placing you under arrest."

Before he got the words out, Sam threw a punch that landed Tom on the conference table. At that moment the door opened, and the sheriff and a state trooper entered the room and subdued him. Tom slid off the table, putting a hand to his right jaw. "That was some left hook, Sam. I didn't even know you were a lefty."

What did the fact Sam was left-handed have to do with anything? "Tom? Are you okay?"

"I'm fine. I wish the statute of limitations on assault and battery wasn't up on an incident from eleven years ago."

"What incident?" Lucy was confused. This made no sense. They were arresting Sam for fraud and also assault and battery against a police officer now. What happened eleven years ago?

"Sam knows what I'm talking about." He looked at the angry young man. "Don't you?" He shifted his jaw and straightened to his full height. "You told me you had a girlfriend years ago that died in a car accident."

"So?"

"Tell me her name." Tom stood nose-to-nose with Sam.

"You already figured it out. Why should I?" He smiled at Tom. "You people are so perfect, living your perfect little lives, acting like nothing ever goes wrong. Some of us had to claw and scrape to ever get ahead. But you know what? I didn't kill Annabelle. Jared Benton did."

Tom rubbed his jaw angrily. "Get him out of here."

The trooper led Sam out into the hall and to a waiting car.

"Tom? What is going on?" Lucy went to Tom's side and pulled his hand away from his jaw and grimaced. "Ouch. You need an ice pack. Sit. I'll be right back." She looked at the other two men, obviously shaken. "Don't talk until I get back. Please."

She ran out of the room, straight to the kitchenette area where she had drunk coffee with both Tom and Sam. And to think she considered dating Sam. She looked in the freezer of the small refrigerator and was relieved to see a box of ice packs for times such as this. She wrapped it in a threadbare dishcloth and took it into the conference room, glad to miss the main squad room.

"Thanks, Lucy." Tom took the ice pack and put it to his face. "That was a real left hook. Who knew a computer guy could do that?"

"Computer guy? What's that got to do with Jared? What has any of this got to do with Jared?" Frustration raised the decibels of her voice another level. Fear made it shake. Were there things she didn't know about Jared? Were there things Sarah didn't know about Jared?

# CHAPTER THIRTY

He couldn't be the one to tell Lucy about Jared and the tragedy that killed Annabelle, his high school girlfriend. It wasn't his story to tell. Sarah knew, and she understood. As far as he knew, beyond Jared's parents and Prudie, he and Sarah were the only ones alive who knew what really happened that rainy night.

Tom looked across the table at the judge and the mayor. "Gentlemen, I'm sorry we had to bring you into this."

Judge Simpson held up a hand. "Tom, I'm glad I was here to see it all first-hand. You can be sure I'll be in touch with Watson's supervisor. I am curious, though. What does Jared Benton have to do with all this?"

"This? Nothing. An old grudge dating back several years. As I said, unfortunately, any wrong-doing by Sam back then is protected by the statute of limitations."

"There's no statute of limitations on murder." Mayor Hynes narrowed his eyes. "I've always had a lot of respect for Mr. Benton, and I know Alex Crawford did, but an allegation of murder is tantamount to libel."

"Yes, sir, it is. You can be sure I'll talk to Jared. If he wants to press charges, I'll be glad to serve the arrest warrant." He looked over at Lucy. There were tears in her eyes. They hadn't fallen. She was holding it together, but they were brimming.

Help me out, Lord.

Tom stood, as did the other two men. "I'll keep you posted, gentlemen."

"I'll expect a full audit of the relief fund to see how much we've lost." Judge Simpson shook Tom's hand and Lucy's.

Mayor Hynes did the same. "You can be assured that nothing that happened in this room will leave it until the proper time. This investigation isn't over, I'm certain."

Tom nodded approval and looked over at Lucy as the men exited the room. "Let's get out of here for a little while."

"Yes, please." She gathered the papers and began to place them in her binder. "Will you need these?"

"I'm afraid so. I can take them if you'd like."

"I never want to see them again." She handed him the sheaf of papers. As she picked up her purse and phone, she paused. "Why did Sam accuse Jared of murder?"

Tom sighed. It was going to come up. "Jared didn't murder anybody."

"Why did Sam say that?" Confusion was etched on her face.

He held the door for her and ushered her into the hallway. Sheriff Oakley came to them. "Had a little excitement?"

"Yes, sir, and I will be back to write up my report."

"Don't wait too long. Details get fuzzy after you leave the scene." The older gentleman nodded. "See you after a while."

"Thank you, sir." He took Lucy's hand and led her to the door. "We need to talk."

LUCY DIDN'T SAY a word as she got in the car and Tom started driving. She didn't know where they were going. It was the last thing on her mind. Lucy's thoughts were a scramble of images: the many moods of Sam Watson, Jared and murder, statutes of limitation, Sarah, the wedding, Tom. And who in the world was Annabelle? She was old enough to know life was messy, and not everyone has a pristine past. But did a less-than-perfect past have to affect her best friend?

God, there's a reason I'm here. I'm going to wait and see what it is.

When she realized they had stopped, she looked up to find the car parked close to the walkway to the beach at Pilot Oaks. They were far enough away from the house that they didn't need to stop in and talk, but Lucy waved at Robert Crawford. He was trimming a crepe myrtle bush that had been damaged in the storm.

"Let's go for a walk."

She nodded. High heeled pumps weren't the best footwear for walking on the beach. As soon as she got to the bench next to the head of the boardwalk, she pulled them off and walked barefoot, leaving her shoes next to Tom's.

Tom reached for her hand, and they walked in silence for a few minutes. She didn't dare interrupt his thoughts. Hers were a scramble, and she didn't know what was going on. How crazy must the thoughts be in his head?

The salty breeze and lower humidity had a calming effect on her nerves. When Tom squeezed her hand and stopped, she faced him. At least she tried to. She faced his shirt buttons, which made her smile when she looked up in his face. "Thank you."

"For what?"

"For bringing me here." She tilted her head, trying to relax, knowing the worry line was still between her brows. She could feel the tension. "The beach always helps."

He looked around at the peaceful scene. "It does, doesn't it?" His half-smile was tender and a little sad.

"You said we need to talk."

"Yes. There are things I'm not at liberty to tell you. Some things happened eleven years ago that pretty much crushed Jared for a while. It wasn't until last year, when he met Sarah, that he seemed to put it behind him." He narrowed his eyes. "Do you understand?"

"No, but I do understand the trust of a friend. I don't need to know everything, unless Jared wants me to." She wanted, terribly, to know what had happened, but this was where faith came in, wasn't it?

"Eleven years ago, Jared and his girlfriend, Annabelle, were in a car accident. They were both injured, and Annabelle didn't make it. Jared's memories of that night are sketchy."

She pondered this information for a minute. She looked up at Tom's shuttered eyes. There was more. "And where does Sam Watson come into this?"

"We think he may have been dating Annabelle while Jared was away at college." He looked away. He drew in a deep breath and exhaled slowly. "That's really all I can say."

"Let me get this straight. Annabelle was cheating on Jared, with Sam, and now he's accusing Jared of murdering Annabelle?" This didn't make sense. There had to be more to it than that.

"There are a few details that are Jared's to tell. I'm sorry."

"Does Sarah know? I mean, she's going to marry the man, and she's my best friend." Her nerves were beginning to rev up again, along with the tears.

"Sarah knows the whole story." He pulled her to him in a hug. "It'll be all right, Luce. It will. Jared isn't a murderer. He's a guy who got caught in a situation not of his choosing. A situation that, if anything, drew him closer to God."

She relaxed into his arms and began to sob. She could hear that still, small voice. "Trust me." God was on the move. Could it be possible that her merciful Father could even save Sam?

Jared had lived through this trauma and was still, to some

extent, living through it. But he was humble. He was merciful. He walked justly. Could she do the same, trusting God not only with herself, but also with her best friend? She was so used to organizing and micro-managing her life and the lives of everyone around her that she had only used faith when it was convenient. Times when she couldn't understand why things like this would happen.

She knew her dad was with God, in Heaven. She knew her mother was too. Those were the big, complex things she couldn't, in her humanity, understand, so she left it up to God. But things like this? Things that could be avoided, like someone with a past? That's where she tended to use her own sensibilities and stick to the high road. She was all about pulling people up to where she was, but was she willing to get down in the dirt with them and work alongside them?

Her tears were spent, soaking the front of Tom's dress shirt. "I'm sorry. Your shirt may never be the same."

Tom laughed and tightened his grip on her. "That's all right. I didn't like this one that much anyway."

She pulled away and wiped her face with the hankie he pulled from his pocket. When she finished her face, she tried to wipe his shirt. "It's a good thing. It has mascara and eyeliner on it." She gave him a twisted grin.

"Do you think you need to go talk to Jared?" She narrowed her eyes with sympathy. It couldn't be a pleasant conversation.

"I do. Go with me? Sarah may need support too." His pleading expression tugged at her heart.

"Of course I will. And if you need to talk without me there, don't you dare hesitate to ask me to leave. Promise?" She gave him her most teacher-like glare.

He smiled, and the sun came out in her heart. "I promise."

# CHAPTER THIRTY-ONE

man in a dark suit was coming out of Jared's hospital room when Tom and Lucy arrived.

"Nate?" Annabelle's brother?

The man turned at the mention of his name and flinched slightly at the sight of Tom.

"Livingston."

Tom felt his blood pumping. Had Nate come back to harass Jared and Sarah again? Last year's encounter at a park in Charleston had almost scared Sarah to death.

"What brings you here?"

Jernigan cleared his throat and faced Tom, hands on his hips. "I came to see Jared."

When he did, Tom saw a badge and a holster.

"In what capacity?"

Nate brushed his hand across his nose and looked away for a second, his throat moving with emotion. "I saw Sam Watson earlier."

"And?"

"And he spilled it all. He was one angry young man." He

pulled out his ID and showed it to Tom. "I work for the state police, Critical Response Team, couple of years now."

This was the first he'd heard of this. "Why'd you come all the way over here to see Jared?" Tom wanted to hear him say he was wrong. Nate Jernigan had spread rumors and filth about Jared ever since his sister died. He glanced over at Lucy, whose eyes were as big as saucers. Poor girl, she didn't have a clue.

"I came to make things right."

"For eleven years of bashing his reputation and threatening him?" Tom's hands balled up into fists, but he relaxed when Lucy reached out and grabbed his arm.

"Tom." Did God send Lucy's still, small voice because he wasn't listening to His?

Nate bowed his head. "Last year, when I met Jared and his girlfriend in Charleston, I was in a bad place. I was drinking too much, I was in trouble on the job, and my girlfriend had broken up with me. She'd had enough. When I saw Jared, I remembered what Annabelle looked like in that hospital bed. It was like every bruise on her came from him, and every bitter thought was his fault." He raked his hand over his face. "Sam Watson was raving like a lunatic. He saw me in the hallway and started yelling Annabelle's name, so I asked to talk to him."

"What did he tell you?"

"Everything. He was angry at Annabelle for going out with Jared that night yet thought hitting her and asking her to get an abortion was okay. He said he was going to go back and make up with her, but he wanted her to realize how much she missed him first. He blamed Jared for her death, when he caused it, if you want to look at it that way. He blamed Annabelle for every bit of unhappiness he experienced." He shook his head. "It was sickening."

Lucy spoke up. "So Jared didn't—"

"Jared didn't do anything except be the Boy Scout he always was." Nate gave her a bitter smile. "He was being a friend, helping her in a bad situation. When we found out Annabelle was pregnant, we assumed the worst, that it was his. Mom and Dad had relaxed their rules with Annabelle because they had trusted Jared. They had no idea she was sneaking out to see Sam. They didn't know him, and I was already grown and gone into the military. I've worked in the same building as he for two years and didn't know there was any connection between him and my family."

Tom held out his hand. "Thank you, Nate."

He snorted and took Tom's hand, shaking it. "Nothing to thank me for. I've learned a lot in the last year, and in the last few hours I think I've learned even more. Life's too short to hold a grudge."

SARAH WAS WIPING tears from her eyes when Lucy and Tom entered the room. Jared looked like he had seen a ghost.

"Are you two okay?" Lucy looked from one to the other.

Jared spoke first. "For me, I feel like a ton of weight has been lifted." He squeezed Sarah's hand. "I think Sarah's more emotional than I am."

"I remember how scared I was when we met up with him at Battery Park. Do you think he had been drinking that night?"

Jared nodded. "I smelled it on him." He scooted over in his bed and pulled on her hand to sit beside him. "And now his family will know what really happened." He sobered. "I hate they have to know all that."

Tom shook his head. "When I met him in the hallway, I felt sick."

Jared smiled. "Me too. I thought he was here for round-whatever." He sobered. "Sounds like he's getting his life back together."

"Yeah, about the time Sam Watson's is falling apart." Tom shook his head. "He needs our prayers."

Lucy observed the two men. Their lives had been in upheaval because of these two men, and here they were, talking about praying for them. She smiled and wiped away tears all at the same time. Sarah had found herself quite a man.

Jared looked up at Tom. "Nate told me Sam tested positive for drugs."

Lucy perked up. "That explains the cash withdrawals from the relief fund."

Tom nodded. "I'm sure it does. It didn't make any sense to me, but drugs do things to your brain that are pretty unexplainable."

"He'll never do police work again, will he?" Her quiet voice amplified her concern.

Tom shook his head. "No, he's burned that bridge. The best he could hope for would be security in the private sector. He's got some recovery to go through first."

"And does he even realize he needs it?" Sarah asked, more comment than question.

They were all quiet. While a load had been lifted off Jared's shoulders, Lucy still sensed a sadness in the room. Sadness for a girl she'd never heard of until today. Sadness for the wasted, bitter years in Nate's life. Sadness for the choices Sam had made.

"But why you?" Lucy walked over to Tom, hands on her hips. "Why did he try to frame you?"

"Probably for the same reason Nate blamed Jared for Annabelle's death. Bitterness, jealousy, and anger."

"It's that verse." Lucy was struggling to remember all the pieces of the verse in Micah. *"He has shown you, O man, what is good; And what does the Lord require of you but to do justly, to love mercy, and to walk humbly with your God?"* She looked from the tall, handsome man beside her to the one in the hospital bed. "That verse describes you both."

Tom put his arm around her shoulders. "I think you're giving us way too much credit."

"No, I'm not. I'm giving God credit." She smiled up at Tom. "And maybe the two of you a little bit."

Sarah turned and kissed Jared on the cheek. "I for one am proud to be marrying you, Jared Benton."

Lucy tilted her head up and whispered to Tom. "I think it's time those wedding plans got finished up, don't you?"

# CHAPTER THIRTY-TWO

"Knock-knock." Lucy called through the kitchen screen door at Pilot Oaks.

"Lucy-girl, you get on in here. You know you don't have to knock. You're family." Prudie was taking pies out of the larger of the dual ovens in the large commercial range.

Lucy took in a deep breath and sighed with delight. "It smells wonderful in here."

"Pecans from our own trees, and this new whiz-bang stove doesn't hurt, either. Mercy, I don't want to think about how much this thing cost." Prudie laid down her potholder and turned to Lucy. "It wasn't a necessity, but I surely am glad the Crawfords decided to spring for it."

"I, for one, am happy you have it. I keep thinking about all the good stuff we can cook on this beauty. I drool a little bit every time I see it."

"What brings you out here?"

"Sarah and I have an appointment at the bridal shop for a final fitting. The wedding dress is ready, and mine is too. We'll need to go back in a few days when Susan and the girls get here, and again when John and Allie get here with Jared's niece and nephew. Do you think it's crazy to have a four-year-old and two three-year-old girls as flower girls?" Lucy's giggle was infectious.

"Maybe you should tie their wrists together to go down the aisle. That way it'll be easier to catch them if they're stuck together!" Prudie laughed along with Lucy. "Is little Alex in the wedding?"

"Yes, he's an honorary usher. Since he's eight, and not so little, he convinced them he was too old to be a ring-bearer. He'll usher in his great-grandparents and grandparents."

Prudie nodded. "He's a good boy. Looks for all the world like his Uncle Jared." She smiled then pointed a finger at her. "I'm glad you're here. I've been sketching out ideas for the groom's cake." Prudie bustled over to the small desk in the corner of the kitchen. "Get yourself some coffee and have a seat. I made a fresh pot."

"Good timing. I was thinking a cuppa would taste pretty good right now. You know I would have been glad to have the bakery doing the wedding cake do the groom's cake too. I know it will mean a lot to Jared that you're making his cake."

Prudie brought the notepad over to the table and sat down. She didn't say a word but simply pushed it across the table.

Lucy was speechless. This woman wasn't only a good cook, she was an artist. The drawing was of a scale-replica of the house Jared had bought Sarah. It was his childhood home and was just down the road from Pilot Oaks.

"Prudie. What can I even say?" She couldn't get her head to stop shaking in disbelief. "This is amazing. You drew this? And you can make a cake that looks like this?"

"I believe I can. I've been online studying up on some techniques." She adjusted her glasses. "See what looks like tabby there on the foundation and the porch columns? Mixed nuts and toffee. The basic structure is cake, and the rest is more like decorating a gingerbread cake. Do you think it'll do? Will he like it?"

Prudie's self-confidence seemed to waver now that she had shared her creation.

"Like it? I think they'll both love it." Lucy grinned. "Can we keep it a secret?"

"I hope to. It's not going to be easy with Jared staying here and both of them making themselves at home in the kitchen." The older woman smiled, wiping a tear from her eye. "I'm glad I get the chance to do this for them. Jared's a blessed young man to come out of not one, but two accidents that could have killed him."

"I guess God's not done with him yet, you think?" Lucy squeezed Prudie's hand. "This is going to be the prettiest wedding yet. Do you think Mr. Crawford would have liked it?"

"Alex? I think he would have been over the moon. Oh, he'd have grouched a bit about all the people around, but deep down? He would have had the time of his life. Jared made life bearable for him. Having family around would have been the icing on the cake." Prudie laughed. "Speaking of icing, I need to drive over to Jared's house and get a better idea what color to make that icing!"

Lucy got up from the table. "I can't thank you enough. You know, this place would be a great wedding venue for anyone. The double parlor is nice and open, the dining room is amazing, and the patio? Oh my. Anyone would love to get married here. I don't know why they didn't think of it before the hurricane."

Prudie pondered as she pushed herself up from the table. "I've lived through several hurricanes in my lifetime. A few have been scary, some have been run-of-the-mill and not much punkin', but I think this one has made those two even more aware of appreciatin' what they have."

"I think you're right. This place is a touchstone."

"Yep, it's where it all started. I think Alex's prayers over this place have made it pretty special."

"I think yours had something to do with it too."

"Maybe so, maybe so." She caught sight of the clock as she hugged the young woman. "What time is your appointment?"

"Not for another hour. I thought I'd stop in and visit the invalid for a few minutes."

Prudie harrumphed. "That boy is so excited to be out of the hospital, you can hardly hold him down."

"The fact that his wedding is less than three weeks away might have something to do with it." Lucy arched an eyebrow and grinned. "I don't blame him. He was still way too long."

"Amen to that. Now you scoot out of here so's I can work on my secret plans some more. I'm thinkin' about putting a bell on Jared in case I need time to hide the evidence if he's coming close."

"Good idea."

THE DRIVE HOME from Blythewood gave Tom plenty of time to think. Sam Watson was being held there, at the state police headquarters. His deposition would be enough to put him away for a while. He hoped Lucy wouldn't have to testify.

As upside-down as life had been the last few weeks, he knew he hadn't spent enough time reading the Bible or praying. He had quite a list of things to think about and to pray about, and in no particular order.

His personal life was spinning out of control, and control was what he wanted. Or at least he thought he did.

"Of course I want a family, Lord. Someday. But until I get Mom and Sis settled, I can't think about that. And this whole deal with Sam. Wow, God, where did that even come from? Was Sam that desperate, or did he see getting me in trouble as a way to get back at Jared?" His mind wandered as the landscape passed by in a blur. Focus, Tom. "Jared. Lord, You outdid Yourself there. You've got a lot left for him. I hope his wedding, and his marriage is all You could ever want for him. Sarah too. She's a peach."

Tom prayed out loud in his car, which was the norm for him. If anybody saw him, they would think he was talking on his phone. Making his way south, away from the scrub of sandy lawns and flat farmland to sand and surf, he tried to empty his mind. He knew he couldn't hear God through all the clutter.

Lucy.

He almost jumped when her name popped into his head. "Uh, Lord, did I do that?"

Lucy.

"I know, Lucy's been on my mind a lot. I'm ready to listen now. What do You have for me? How can I help Mom? What about Jared? How can You use me to help him, the way he's always helped me? And Sam—Lord, I want to be someone he's not angry with. If I can say anything, do anything, let me know what it is."

Lucy.

He began thinking about her. Here he was, in his thirties, and had never had a serious relationship. He had thought maybe he was destined for bachelorhood, but that wasn't what he wanted, deep-down. When he met Lucy, he didn't want to think he fell for her because Jared had fallen for Sarah. That would be too easy. Life wasn't supposed to be easy. You worked hard, and you settled for what you thought God had for you.

Then again, maybe God didn't want him to settle. Maybe He did want the absolute best for him. Maybe Lucy wasn't the distraction. Maybe everything else was. It was easier to summon up anxiety and worry about his mother and his sister than to summon up contentment and peace.

The concept hit him. Hard. He wasn't supposed to manufacture contentment and peace.

*He has shown you, O man, what is good; And what does the*

*Lord require of you but to do justly, to love mercy, and to walk humbly with your God?* Micah 6:8

Three things: do justly, love mercy, and walk humbly with God. In other words, as Jared always said, "do the next right thing."

He drove a few miles in silence then expelled the breath he seemed to be holding.

"Forgive me, Lord, for not listening. Forgive me for trying to put on Your shoes, and for trying to 'fix' everything for everyone. It's not my job, but if You want to use me, I'm available. Thank You for loving me, for giving all for me, and for wanting the absolute best for me. And I can't imagine any more 'best' than Lucy Dixon."

His smile broadened at the thought of the blonde pixie on top of the roof, holding her hands up in the glorious sunshine. That was a girl to spend the rest of your life with. A humble thought hit him. Had he pushed her away one too many times? Shaking his head, he banished the thought. That was the 'fixer' within him trying to work it out. This was a job for God.

As he drove into the parking lot of the Georgetown County Sheriff's office, he thought about his former dream of working for the FBI and what his life would have been like. He wouldn't have been close to home for his family when his dad died. He wouldn't have been there to help Jared.

Tom parked the car and laughed out loud. And he wouldn't have been there to meet Lucy. "Thank you, Lord, for Romans 8:28. *We know that all things work together for the good of those who love God: those who are called according to His purpose.* You knew what was going to happen before I was born. Thank you for reminding me, and keep on reminding me."

# CHAPTER THIRTY-THREE

When Lucy tried on her bridesmaid dress, she realized she had lost a little weight in the last few weeks, and her roofing tan line did not go with her dress. She had to laugh.

"Okay, Miss Perfect, your wedding dress fit you perfectly. What's going on here?"

Sarah chuckled. "Well, you've been running all over the place doing my wedding planning for me, as well as catching criminals, and I've been sitting at the hospital. Note the fact that I have no tan lines at all." She held her arm up and scrunched her nose. The time spent indoors had made her creamy complexion that much creamier.

"I'm going to have to give in and get a spray-on tan to even this up." Lucy sighed. She turned this way and that, looking at herself in the dusty pink dress. "Oh well, I hope they've improved since the last time I had one. I rubbed orange on everything I touched for a week."

"You could do that, or we could spend a day at the beach sometime before the big day." Sarah raised her eyebrows.

"I could go for that." The seamstress unzipped her dress and held it up while Lucy stepped out of it. After getting dressed in her shorts, shirt, and sandals, she sat down next to Sarah and hugged her. "It's good to see you smiling again."

"It's been pretty rough." An involuntary shiver ran through her. "When I think about how close I came to losing Jared . . ."

"But you didn't." Lucy was in staunch-friend mode today.

"No, I didn't. I kept repeating that verse, *Delight yourself in the Lord, and He will give you the desires of your heart.*" She smiled. "It was tough to 'delight' when Jared was in surgery or lying there unconscious, but you know what?"

"What?"

"I learned to listen a lot while I sat there by his bedside."

"You mean, listen to God?" Lucy was pretty sure that's what she meant, but there was something that made her ask.

"Partly." Sarah tilted her head. "It's hard to explain. I learned to listen to the sounds of the hospital, the inflection of the doctors' and nurses' voices, to Jared's breathing, and then, I started hearing God's voice coming through. Honestly? He speaks through everything."

"Amen, sister." Lucy stood and stared at her face in the mirror. "Sometimes He speaks through mirrors too. I think I'm being led to get a facial before the wedding. What do you think?"

Sarah quirked an eyebrow. "I think that sounds fabulous. In fact, so fabulous that I've made appointments for us, Susan, Allie, and Jessica to have the works. Mani-pedi, facial, and massage on Saturday, before the bachelorette party, because I love you all." She grinned. "I also figure we'll need the relaxation after taking the kiddos to their fittings."

Lucy nodded and laughed. "You are the best friend a girl could have. And when did you learn to be spontaneous? I thought that was my department?"

"You, girlfriend, have been spending way too much time

with Tom Livingston. Jared and I have decided that organization is winning out over spontaneity." Sarah cut her a sideways look.

Lucy put her hands on her hips and stretched her full height. "No way. I've always been able to do both. Very organized people have time to be spontaneous."

Sarah laughed at her diminutive friend. "Hmm. It looks like you need to work on Detective Livingston. When he does something spontaneous, I'll declare you the winner."

Lucy shook her head in dismay. "I'm doomed."

THE YARD and barnyard area around Tom's ancestral home was cleared of hurricane debris. There would be enough limbs and fallen branches in the pile for a great bonfire later in the fall. That is, if his mother still owned the property.

Tom put the mower away in the barn and walked up to the house in the fading sunlight. The shadows were getting longer, earlier, with each passing day.

He was trying to drink it all in. A few people had come to look at the house. It seemed like people were more curious than interested in buying an almost-three-hundred-year-old house. The historical society had expressed an interest, but they wanted a better deal than they could give them. They seemed surprised that his mother wanted enough to buy herself another place to live.

He opened the front screen door and noticed his mother sitting on the swing on the front porch, keeping the swing going with one foot.

"Hey." Tom walked over to her and sat on the swing, his arm around her shoulders.

"Hey, yourself." She seemed quiet.

"Everything okay?"

She gave her son a sad smile. "Pretty much. Smellin' the fresh-cut grass and missin' your daddy."

"Me too."

They sat this way, swinging and thinking of days gone by. The crickets had started, as had the frogs, bringing the sounds of his childhood to the present. The mosquitoes would be out any minute now. He was thankful his mother always insisted on planting marigolds and lemongrass close to the porch to repel the unwanted pests. It occurred to him that summertime lasted much longer here than in a lot of places. The trees hadn't even started turning yet.

"I went to see Jared today and visited with the folks too. How does he look? He was always such a good-lookin' boy."

"They had to shave off part of his hair, but it's growing back. He looks like he got a crew cut for the wedding." He laughed, hoping his mother would perk up.

She smiled. "I'm glad. He seemed in good spirits, excited about the wedding. It was good to visit with Liz and Conrad, and with Sarah's folks. That wedding is right around the corner, isn't it?"

"It is."

"They said you'd been helping Lucy with some of the plans. You haven't said a word." She swatted him on the knee.

"Not much to tell. She picks stuff, and I agree. Isn't that how it's supposed to be?" He grinned when she started laughing.

"I did train you right, didn't I? Oh, Tommy, I wanted to see you and Charly get married." She heaved a sigh and shook her head.

"Mama?"

"Oh, I'm not dyin' or anything. I just can't see. Don't worry. I get a little maudlin and a little lonesome."

Did she regret trying to sell the house? Or was this a case of the blues? He was trying hard to listen, to find out what God was trying to tell him in all situations.

"Mama, I need to ask you something."

"Anything I can help you with?"

"I don't know. Maybe."

"Well, go on, then." She had perked up a little. Her impatience amused him.

Where did this idea come from? God, is that You talking again? There was nothing for it but to say it out loud.

"What would you think about trading houses with me?" There. He'd said it. He had voiced the idea that had come to him not two minutes ago.

She sat there for a moment, pondering. "Are you serious, Tom?"

"I am. I don't want to see the house go out of the family if it doesn't have to. I love this place."

"I love it too, but Tom, I don't want to burden you with this place. It's too much. You've got your whole life ahead of you. Don't waste it working on an old house. It's just a house."

"Relax, Mama. Number one, it's not a burden. I want to raise my kids here. And don't worry, I won't waste my life doing anything I don't want to. I want to help you, and I want to help me too."

"Are you sure? I don't want to be like my mama. She wouldn't even consider losing this place, and look what it did to me and your daddy." Her voice grew rough with emotion.

"Mama, you are not your mama, and I'm not you or Daddy. I'm me."

She put her hand on his cheek and looked, as best she could, at his face. He knew she could see shapes, and sometimes glimpses, close-up. "Sweet boy. You are your own man, aren't you?"

"If I'm not now, I won't ever be." He laughed and kissed her on the cheek. "To be honest, I'd be happy if you let me sell my house and you stay here with me."

"Absolutely not. If I do that, you'll never get married."

"All right, then, shall we make a deal?" He spit in his hand and put it out for a shake.

"Thomas Sumter Livingston, did you spit on your hand and expect me to shake it?"

"Mama, you changed my diapers and washed my face with your spit. What's the difference?"

"The difference is you're a grown man and I'm a grown woman and we're doing a business deal. How about we hug on it?" She leaned into his hug and squeezed him back. "Good doin' business with you, son." She patted his face again and smiled. "Now somebody needs to call that realtor and take this house off the market."

"Yes, ma'am."

She got up from the swing and started into the house. When she entered the front room, she shouted up the stairs. "Charlotte Anne, we have a change of plans."

"You didn't?" Jared laughed with Tom, reliving the business deal he made with his mother. "I thought you were all for modern, neat, and, more than anything, clean?"

"Aw, the old house is clean. As for neat, I guess when you start thinking long-term about your life, you realize life is pretty messy anyway. May as well learn to live with it."

Tom knew he was sounding out of character, for him. "Let's keep it on the down-low for now."

Jared narrowed his eyes. "Any particular reason?"

Tom looked out at the back lawn of Pilot Oaks. "Maybe. Nothing I'm ready to talk about yet." He smiled. "I'm glad to have you back."

"Me too."

They sat in companionable silence on the patio, Tom in a rocker and Jared comfortable in a chaise lounge. It was everyone's job to keep Jared as immobile as possible, and Tom took this mission seriously. "You want me to bring pizza for the game tomorrow?"

"That would be awesome. Prudie's making wings, and teaching Sarah how to do it."

Tom grinned. "Sounds like a good skill for her to have."

"You bet. For a self-proclaimed non-cook, she's good at it."

"Better watch the waistline." Tom stretched and patted his flat stomach.

"I'll leave that to you guys on the most-eligible-bachelor list."

Tom chuckled. "Yeah."

His mind went to the lady that was most likely to challenge his status in that category. Lucy. He had never had a "type" of girl he went for. It was always what they were like. Not that he didn't notice a pretty girl. He wasn't that virtuous. Lucy bowled him over the first time he met her, which had made him suspicious. It wasn't like him to be entranced, and that's what it was like when he was with her. He was entranced by everything about her, from her looks to her high-pitched giggle, to her love of everything organized.

And there was that pink tool belt. His face relaxed into a smile that went all the way from head to toe.

"Tom?"

He looked at Jared and knew his face was red. It wasn't from the sun. "Did you say something?"

"I did, and you were totally out to lunch." Jared's laugh deepened his embarrassment.

"Sorry, I got sidetracked."

"Derailed, more likely. I was asking about the relief fund case. Any word?"

Tom sobered. "I recorded my deposition the other day, and Lucy won't have to testify. His arraignment was this morning." He shook his head sadly. "He pled guilty."

"I guess that's a good thing?"

Tom weighed his words. "I suppose. Since it's not a big dollar amount, he may only get probation. Sentencing is scheduled for early November."

"Is he still in jail?"

"Yes. The fact that he was a cop has made it a little dicey for him."

"They're not making it easy on him. That's good." Jared looked down for a minute. When he looked at Tom, his eyes looked tired. "He admitted to hitting Annabelle?"

Tom noted the hurt in Jared's eyes. Time heals wounds, but it doesn't always reduce the trauma. He knew Jared had forgiven Annabelle years ago, not only for cheating with another man, but also for lying to him. Jared kept her secret out of respect for her family. Now that the secret was no longer hidden, it was like reliving it all over again.

"He did. And he had the gall to accuse you of murdering her in that accident. You know you have grounds for a libel case against him." It was a statement, not a question.

"I know." Jared shrugged his shoulders and shook his head. "I think we've all been through enough. Half the town thought I was the cause of her death anyway, and the people who know me, know it was an accident. Now more people will know there was more to it without me having to drag the family through more tragedy."

Tom looked him in the eye. "I would do the same."

"One of these days, though, I'd like to talk to Sam. He may not want to talk to me, but I'd like to meet him face-to-face."

# CHAPTER THIRTY-FOUR

The weather report for the week of Jared and Sarah's wedding was wide-open sunshine and warmth, something that didn't always happen in October, considering they were still officially in hurricane season.

Lucy stretched as she woke in the guest room of Sarah's beach house. Today she and Tom were helping move in Jared's things, most of it new, because his house had been destroyed in the hurricane. There were also shower gifts, until now stored at Pilot Oaks, to un-box and put away.

The original plan had been for them to move to Jared's beach house until the remodel of their dream house on Pilot Oaks Road was finished. The hurricane changed that plan in an instant. Now they would stay here at Sarah's beach bungalow.

Lucy still wasn't sure what she should do. Post-hurricane activities had kept her busy, and she hadn't spent much time planning for "after."

That was unlike her. In normal circumstances, she would have had her life planned out months in advance, but this had been an unusual year. Without a school year to focus on, she was adrift. The most she knew was that after the wedding, she was going to visit her grandmother for a few weeks. After that? Only God knew, and she was okay with that.

She smelled fresh coffee brewing. Sarah wasn't organized, but she was a creature of habit. And one of the best habits, in her opinion, was her love of coffee in the morning. The smell of java and the sound of the surf pulled her out of bed. Her robe lay across the chair in her room, and she put it on and slipped into her mules. It was wonderful to be where it was actually around sixty degrees first thing in the morning, in October. No fuzzy slippers here.

"Good morning, sleepyhead." Sarah smiled as she poured scrambled eggs into the skillet.

"Who are you, and what have you done with my best friend?" Lucy gave her a mock-glare and sat at the counter, chin in hand.

Sarah smiled. "I hope Jared doesn't think I do this every morning. I couldn't stay in bed any longer. I woke up at six-thirty raring to get things unpacked and in the cabinets."

"Good. I didn't want to have to recant all the warnings I've given him about how to treat you early in the morning."

"Please don't. I don't think I could sustain this."

Both young women laughed and startled when the timer went off.

"My biscuits are done. You get to be the judge for my first solo attempt."

"What? Remember our biscuits in freshman Home Ec?"

Sarah pulled the sheet out of the oven. "I do. I think these look a little better, don't you?" She turned and showed Lucy the light, fluffy, very tall biscuits. "Please take a picture and send it to my mother." When Lucy just looked at her quizzically, she said, "No, really. She's got to see these."

Lucy laughed and complied. "They're beautiful. Didn't you say she tried to teach you how to make biscuits once?"

"More than once. It didn't take. I asked Prudie to teach me, and I guess I needed incentive. Jared's pretty good incentive, don't you think?"

Lucy smiled at her friend. "He is. Oh, Sarah, this time next week, you'll be married. You'll be Mrs. Jared Stuart Benton!" She squealed, and then clapped her hand over her mouth. "Did I just squeal like a schoolgirl?"

Sarah giggled. "Yes, you did, and I hope you do it for every event in my life. Promise?"

She arched a brow and tilted her head. "Sounds like I do it naturally, so I don't think it'll be a problem."

"Speaking of squealing, how are things with Tom?" She dished scrambled eggs onto a plate, along with crisp bacon. "Want some jelly? Or honey?"

"Honey, please." Lucy busied herself putting butter on her biscuits. After that, she poured a dab of honey on her plate to spoon onto the biscuits one bite at a time. "I'm not sure. About Tom, I mean."

"Okay. Would you like to elaborate? And would you like to eat this on the patio?"

"I'll try, and yes, definitely, on the patio. Let's pray first."

"Yes." Sarah said a prayer of blessing and thanks. They picked up plates and cups of steaming coffee and went out the French doors to enjoy the sunshine. Balancing her plate on her mug, Sarah grabbed the extra biscuits, and Lucy did the same with the butter and honey. "We might need more."

"I'll say."

When they got settled into their seats and began eating, Lucy took a swig of coffee. "About Tom. It's hard to pin it down. One day he seems like he's very interested in me. The next day he acts like a big brother. I know he's a friend I can count on but anything more? I would say the ball is in his court."

"How do you feel, Lucy?" Sarah's hazel eyes bore into Lucy's blue ones.

"Me?" She hadn't talked about her feelings, except to God.

Was she brave enough to voice her innermost thoughts when they might not work out?

"Yes, you." Sarah gave her a withering look.

She put her mug down and played with the eggs and bacon on her plate. "Do you want the grown-up Lucy version I would give to my grandmother, or the ever-an-adolescent version I would give to my best friend in a note folded like a paper football?"

"Um, the latter, please."

Lucy spooned up a bit of honey and used her biscuit to clean it off before taking a bite and closing her eyes in pleasure. "Oh, Sarah. This is amazing."

"It's lard."

"What?" Lucy's eyes flew open in confusion. "Lard?"

"I put lard in the biscuits instead of shortening. Makes a world of difference." She waited for Lucy to finish chewing and swallowing. "You were saying?"

"I was saying. Yes." She had a hard time meeting Sarah's eyes, and she came to the conclusion Sarah was going to wrangle it out of her if she didn't spill her guts. "I can't think of anyone I'd rather spend my time with."

"Or your life?" Sarah's eyes grew wider by the moment.

"That would be up to him."

"Oh, come on. I want to know about you. How do you feel?" Sarah narrowed her eyes as if trying to draw the information out of her.

Lucy scrunched up her face, considering what to say. She tilted her head as her gamine grin came out, one-sided. She couldn't keep it in. "When I think about Tom, I get tingly all over, and I want to giggle. Satisfied?"

"Very much so." Sarah folded her napkin and placed her elbows on the table. She leaned toward Lucy with a conniving grin. "What are we going to do about it?"

Lucy drank the last of her coffee, folded her napkin, and

stood up. "We are going to do nothing but wash new dishes and put them in cabinets, and then we're going to that last fitting for my dress and meet up with the sisters and kids for their final fittings." She felt more light-hearted than she had in days. She grinned at her best friend. "After all that, maybe we'll talk about it."

TOM WALKED in the door of the bridal salon in time to see the prettiest bridesmaid in the world. The dusty rose chiffon swirled around her as she twirled on the riser in front of the mirror. For a moment, there were no other people in the room, and she hadn't seen him yet. When the flower girls, also dressed in their tulle-and-chiffon dresses, began to twirl and giggle along with Lucy, he couldn't help but laugh along with them.

"Tom!" Sarah walked across the room to greet him, but his eyes were still on Lucy.

He looked down when Sarah crossed his sight-line. "Oh, hi, Sarah. Emmaline wanted me to come in to have the hem on my pants and sleeves checked."

"Awesome. We're finishing up. Lucy had to have her dress taken in, and the little girls had their final fitting. We're good to go!" She leaned in with a whisper. "Can you believe the wedding is this weekend?"

"Crazy, isn't it?" He tilted his head to see around Sarah's head. Lucy was looking right at him, smiling. "How was the bachelorette party Saturday night?"

Sarah sighed. "Amazing. The pampering was just what we needed. After the spa, we went to Captain Dan's for a seafood feast and watched a romantic comedy at my house. Total relaxation." She smiled, following Tom's gaze. "Doesn't Lucy look great?" Sarah's arched eyebrow was not lost on him.

He looked down and grinned. "She does." When he looked

back up, she was gone, and Jessica and Susan were out. He was sure his disappointment was showing on his face because Sarah patted his arm and laughed.

"Have a seat. I'm sure the alterations lady will be calling on you soon. Too many girls back there right now."

"I'll wait until the estrogen level goes down a bit." He smiled at the radiant bride-to-be. "Everything going okay with the wedding preparations?"

She smiled through a mist of happy tears. "It couldn't be any better. I wouldn't care if there was nothing but Jared, me, our family and friends, and the preacher, but Lucy has gone out of her way to make this the wedding of my dreams. Thank you for all your help too. We're blessed."

Tom hugged Sarah and handed her his handkerchief, which made her smile. "Anything I can do for you and Jared, ask. I'm available."

"I know you are. Everybody has been great. Now if you could get Jared's hair to grow a little faster." She laughed.

"Sorry, can't help you there. We'll just have to be glad he's here, crew-cut and all."

"Oh, believe me, I am."

Lucy walked up to them, hearing their conversation. "Isn't it amazing how much Jared looks like his dad with the shorter hair?" She grinned. "At least you know what he'll look like when he gets old."

"Tom's here." Sarah pointed out the obvious.

"No kidding?" Lucy arched a brow at her friend. She turned to Tom. "Hi, Tom. Here to get your sleeves and pants checked one last time?"

"Yes. Does Emmaline think I've grown or something?" He was enjoying seeing her face flush when she turned to him.

"No, it's only that the extra tall like you and the extra small like me are more prone to have something either too long or too short. It never hurts to double-check."

"I understand. You had to have more alterations? Been on a diet?" Maybe if he teased her a little, she would loosen up.

It was working. She gave him a mock-glare. "No, Detective Livingston, I have not been dieting. I've been a tad busy, if you will recall, roofing houses, chasing outlaws, and planning a wedding." She poked him in the stomach. "I could say the same thing for you."

"No dieting here." He sucked in his gut and took a deep breath. "Real men don't have to diet."

"Oh really?" She raked her gaze up and down his lean frame. When she looked back into his eyes, she blushed furiously.

"No, we drink extra water and do extra runs, and the pounds come right off." He raised his eyebrows. It was fun baiting her, and she took the bait so easily.

"Ugh. Men. If I never hear about the famous 'water diet' again, I'll be perfectly happy."

"Mr. Livingston?" The seamstress came from the back. When he held up his hand, she continued. "We're ready for you now, if you'd like to try on your pants and jacket?"

"I guess we'll see if I need any alterations now. You girls have fun." He made his way to the curtained-off hallway, and turned when he heard Lucy.

"No high-water pants, Tom, you hear?" She batted her eyelashes.

He gave her a slow smile and winked. "If they're too short, I'll be sure to wear me some great socks."

# CHAPTER THIRTY-FIVE

*L*ucy walked around Pilot Oaks. Everything was ready for Sarah's wedding. The wedding dress hung in her parents' bedroom, where Jared wouldn't get a glimpse of it. Extra furniture had been moved out of the double-parlor or rearranged into small conversation areas. The patio was being strung with café lights, and on Friday the extra tables and chairs would be delivered. The final decorations wouldn't go out until Saturday morning, the day of the wedding.

Linda Crawford and Liz Benton were sitting on the patio cutting lengths of satin ribbon for the simple pew-end decorations. It was something that could have been done by the wedding planner, but with the change in venue, this was added at the last minute, and the mothers of the bride and groom wanted to have a part in decorating for the wedding.

Susan and Mike, Sarah's sister and brother-in-law, had taken their two girls to the beach down the path, along with Jared's brother, sister-in-law, and their son and daughter. The families had clicked, and the children had a ball together. Jared's niece, Lily, at four, had taken her role as "head flower girl" very seriously, having had experience being the flower girl at her aunt

Jessie's wedding. Sarah's three-year-old twin nieces looked up to her as if she were a queen.

Everyone was busy. Sarah was at the office, trying to get things done before leaving for her honeymoon, and Lucy was at loose ends. Tom was at work, and Robert and Conrad, the dads, had taken Jared to his physical therapy appointment.

She paused at the door to the kitchen and knocked. She knew Prudie was hard at work on the groom's cake. "Prudie, it's me," she whispered.

"Come in, Lucy." She pushed a hair out of her face with the back of her wrist to keep the icing out of her hair. "Your timing is perfect."

"Good! I needed to be useful, and Linda and Liz have ribbon-cutting underway. What can I do?" She looked at the beautiful structure. "Oh my goodness. Prudie, you're almost done."

The older woman looked up over the top of her bifocals. "Almost only counts in horseshoes." She looked back down at the last piece of "shingle" she put on the roof, made of wafer-thin pieces of chocolate. "I'll have quite a bit more to do once we get it transferred to the grass."

Lucy looked at the table to see a large silver platter covered in toasted and colored coconut. No wonder it smelled like summertime in the house.

"The coconut grass has cooled now, and I hope we can get this cake transferred to the center without it falling apart."

"Tell me what to do, and I'm on it." The confectionary house looked as sturdy as its brick-and-mortar model down the road.

"I've got some extra toasted coconut if any of it rubs off." Prudie washed the chocolate off her hands and faced the task, hands on her hips. "Let me think a minute. I don't want to compromise the porch structure."

"It's for sure it's too much for one person." Lucy laughed.

"At least we're the same size. Can you imagine trying to do this with Tom?"

Prudie laughed along with her. "That boy." She shook her head. "He's handier in the kitchen than Jared, that's for sure, but you're right, he's one tall drink o' water."

Lucy smiled. "That's what my grandmother said about him. He does stand out in a crowd."

"'Specially when you're lookin' for him, isn't that right?" Prudie arched an eyebrow at her.

"I suppose." She shrugged. "But that's neither here nor there. We need to get this cake on its lot." An unexpected sigh came out as she looked down at the cake for the wedding.

"Your day will come, girl, have no fear of that."

"I know. It seems to be taking a long time, doesn't it?"

"It'll come all at once, heed my words." She turned and grabbed a pizza board and came toward Lucy. "I think this will work. It may crush the grass, but I can fix that."

"All right. Do you want me to take the handle and you pick up the cake?" Lucy didn't trust herself not to drop this creation. Her eyes went round at the thought.

"That sounds good. I'll pull up from the back first, then I'll work my way around as you push in the paddle."

Slowly but surely, inch by inch, the cake, on its cardboard foundation, made its way onto the paddle. The cake and candy bungalow eased onto the yard made of green toasted coconut with minimal damage.

"Oh, Prudie. I'm glad that's done." Lucy tore off a paper towel to blot the sweat beaded on her forehead. "That was nerve-wracking."

Prudie sat in the chair with a thump. "I declare, I think I've put in a day's work in the last ten minutes."

"Let me get you something to drink. Coffee?"

"Goodness, no. I'm burnin' up. There's sweet tea in the refrigerator, and I thank you."

Lucy filled two glasses with ice and poured the sweet elixir to within a half-inch of the rim. She took a swig as she handed Prudie her glass. "We deserve it."

After resting for five minutes, Prudie started bustling around, checking for damage. "Do you see anything that needs fixin'?"

Lucy inspected it carefully. "Nothing but a little grass that got mashed by the paddle."

"No big deal, there. I can rough it up and put some more on top of it." She went to work sprucing up the landscape of the cake creation. "Now I need to pipe the mullions in the windows and put the dentil molding on the trim. I was afraid, since they're more delicate, they would be crooked if we tried to move it after they were on there."

Lucy was still stunned at the craftsmanship of the cake. Standing over two feet tall and two feet deep and wide, it was smaller than the wedding cake, although not by much. "How have you kept this hidden?"

"I've been workin' on it on this rolling cart." She pointed to the stainless-steel cart pushed up to the table, wheels locked. "I work on it a while, and then push it into the pantry. Thank the Lord for a walk-in pantry that stays cool. Let's get the platter put on the cart so's I can get it out of the way. Jared is getting more mobile by the day."

"Good idea."

Lucy began to lift on the tray opposite Prudie when she heard a knock on the back door. They both startled and looked at one another in horror. What if it were Jared or Sarah? In tandem, they looked toward the back door, where the split Dutch door was open on the top to expose the screen door. They both heaved a sigh of relief.

"What are you ladies up to?"

It was Tom.

Lucy and Prudie looked at one another and laughed in relief. Speak of the devil.

"Can I help?"

This made them laugh harder. Lucy recovered first. "I think we've got it. You're too tall." This spun them into even more laughter.

"You can come in as long as you don't distract us." Prudie winked at Lucy, and Lucy's face warmed. "Are you ready?"

She felt clumsy now with Tom in the room. "In a second." She took a deep breath. She couldn't let Tom see he was affecting her. "Okay, let's do this."

"Are you sure you don't want me to help? That's huge."

"You're too tall, remember?" Lucy squelched him with a look.

"First time anybody has ever complained that I was too tall." He looked a little pouty. When he noticed their tea, he asked, "Mind if I get myself something to drink?"

"Go right ahead, and don't talk for a few minutes."

He raised his hands in surrender and reached for a glass in the cupboard next to the sink.

"Is there--"

"Shush." Lucy gave him the glare again.

Tom halted.

On the count of three, Prudie and Lucy lifted the cake and set it gently on the cart without incident.

Prudie looked over at Tom. "All right, you can talk now."

"Are you sure?" He looked at Lucy with a sheepish grin.

Lucy smiled. "You were about to ask a question?"

He brightened. "Oh yeah. Is there any more tea?"

# CHAPTER THIRTY-SIX

*I*t was here. Jared and Sarah's day. The day that almost wasn't. Tom patted his breast pocket and felt the packet that held two rings: Jared's bulky band, and Sarah's tiny, to him, wedding band.

He couldn't help but smile. The weather had been cloudy that morning, which had the women in an uproar, fearful of rain. He'd always heard rain on a wedding day was good luck. He didn't know who for. Not for anyone who got in the way of wedding-planning females.

He got to Pilot Oaks in time to help set up tables and chairs for the reception. The ladies were at the church putting the last touches on the pews and around the altar, and Emmaline, the wedding planner, was in full-force at Pilot Oaks preparing for the festivities after the ceremony. Prudie gave up her kitchen to the catering company, and she was flitting around finding antique linens and serving pieces for them.

Tom drove down the road, noting the departing clouds, and it seemed things were settling down so everyone could get ready for the real event. Since the church was close to Pilot Oaks, Jared had rented an antique car to carry Sarah and her parents to the church. Tom was en route to pick it up.

His phone buzzed, and Lucy's face came up on the screen. He pushed the speaker button and said, "Hey, Luce."

"Hi Tom. Where are you?" He could tell the time crunch was starting to wear on the maid of honor.

He chuckled. Probably a mistake. "I'm on a mission for the groom. What do you need?"

"Aspirin . . . no, she said ibuprofen."

"Are you serious?" She called, and all she needs is something for a headache?

"Yes, I'm serious. This is absolutely no time to be asking a person if they're serious. Can you please stop at the pharmacy and pick up ibuprofen? She doesn't care what brand, as long as it's ibuprofen."

"I see Walgreens up ahead. Consider it done."

"Thank you, thank you, and thank you. I would have gone myself, but I just got my nails touched up and the manicurist threatened me with my life if I messed them up."

"No worries. See you later. Bye, Lucy."

"Bye, Tom. You're a lifesaver."

His phone beeped, signaling the end of the call. He shook his head and laughed as he got out of the car at the pharmacy. His laugh faded when he stood in front of the myriad of pain-relief agents. He didn't have time for this. He scanned the rows and found what he wanted.

If it made the day go smoother for any of the ladies in the wedding party, it would be worth it.

He jogged back to his car and headed toward the car-rental lot.

When he pulled up, there she was, a white 1936 Rolls Royce "Wraith." It was the perfect car for a perfect day. He walked around it, freshly washed, towel-dried, and waxed, looking forward to driving it.

The attendant came out with the keys, and a smile. "You here to pick up the Rolls?"

"I am. Anything I should know about driving it?" He looked inside, seeing the supple brown leather interior and shiny wood and chrome trim.

"Naw, it's been rejigged to an automatic transmission and air conditioning. It even has power windows and locks." He showed him the panel on the door handle. "It's an easy one to drive if you're used to big vehicles."

Tom grinned. He pointed to the chauffeur's hat on the seat next to the driver's seat. "Does the hat come with the car?"

"Sure does. Most brides like to think they're a princess for a day, and that chauffeur hat seems to do the trick."

"I'll be happy to wear it." Tom shook the man's hand. "My best friend is getting married today, and I can't wait."

"Hey, tell Jared that Rob said congratulations. He sold me and the wife our house a few years ago."

"I'll do it." He got into the car, donned the hat, and saluted. "Off we go." Tom laughed when he looked at the text on his phone. From Lucy, no less. "Never mind. Found meds."

ALL THE WEDDING party except for Lucy, Sarah, and Sarah's parents had left for the church. Lucy was getting dressed and touching up her makeup while Sarah and her mother spent a quiet moment alone. She was trying hard not to think about what her own wedding day would be like, without her mother.

She wasn't jealous of Sarah. She loved her too much for that. She did have a touch of sadness in her heart that tempered her joy a little bit.

Better grab extra tissues. She didn't usually cry at weddings, but how often did her best friend in the whole world get married?

She could sit down and cry right now if she wasn't afraid of messing up her makeup.

She put the tissues in her tiny beaded purse large enough for lipstick, phone, and tissues and stopped by the master bedroom where Sarah was getting dressed.

"Come in, Lucy. One more selfie before we leave for the wedding?" Sarah had calmed down once she got rid of the tension headache that had plagued her since yesterday. "Mom, you get in this one."

"Oh, you don't want me in there. My bifocals make it hard to see what to look at."

Linda got in the huddle anyway.

Sarah looked at her phone and turned it around to show them the picture. "That was a good one! Last picture as a single woman." She looked back and forth at her mother and her friend. "Wow."

Lucy blinked away the tears that threatened. Thank goodness for waterproof mascara. "Well, you'll stay single if we don't get out of here. Jared sent a car to pick us up. I'll go on down and be ready to help you in."

"I'm going to get your dad. He wanted to see you before we left." Linda scurried down the hallway, leaving the two girls alone.

"This is it."

Sarah nodded, her eyes pooling with tears.

"Don't do it." Lucy gave her a tear-filled glare. "Stop it."

"I'm okay." She daubed her eyes with care. "And Dad hasn't even come in here yet. Oh Luce, I'm a wreck."

"No, you're not. You're getting ready to marry your best friend. Not me, your other best friend." Lucy gave her a cheesy smile to lighten the mood.

"He is, you know." Sarah took a deep breath, and let it out. "I don't simply love him enough to marry him, I love him enough to spend the rest of my life with him, through good and bad times.”

Lucy smiled with compassion. “This is a milestone of telling everyone in the world the two of you are together, no more or no less after the wedding than before.”

“Wow. That’s it, isn’t it?” Sarah looked up and smiled. Robert Crawford was standing in the doorway gazing at his youngest daughter.

“How did I get blessed to have three of the prettiest ladies in my family?” He grinned at her, his eyes a little misty.

Sarah walked over to him and into his bear hug.

Linda objected. “Sarah Jane, you’ll crush your dress!”

“I don’t care. I’m going to hug my daddy whenever I want to.” She looked in the mirror to check for damage. “See? Nothing out of place. I didn’t even get any lipstick on him.” She chuckled. “This time anyway. I can’t promise for later.”

Lucy looked at the clock on the bureau. “We’ve got to get out of here if we’re going to be on time.”

Robert nodded to Lucy. “You go on down and tell the driver we’re coming. I want to pray with my wife and daughter before we go.”

“Aye, aye, sir. See you downstairs.”

She rushed, carefully, down the stairs. Thank goodness the wedding was indoors. They were able to wear spectacular heels with their dresses and have pretty flats to put on for the reception.

She opened the front door and laughed. There was Tom, hat in hand, swooping into a bow as he opened the car door.

“Oh, I thought you were Sarah.” He closed the door and took his place once again.

“This was your errand? Oh my goodness, Sarah will be ecstatic. This is such a cool car!” Lucy walked around the gleaming white vehicle. She never thought to ride in a beauty like this. Her dad had liked antique cars, but never got around to buying one, so she trailed behind him at car shows and auctions as a spectator.

"Pretty sweet, isn't it?" Tom grinned and stood straight in his spot, not wanting to miss Sarah.

"Sweet is one of many words I would use to describe this beauty." She opened the passenger-side door and looked inside the vehicle. "Polished walnut dash and trim, tan leather interior. Oh my goodness." She looked up at Tom. "Did you know they only made 1,201 of these cars?"

"I did not know that. I also did not know that you knew cars."

She smiled at the surprise on his face. It was nice to keep him guessing.

"This comes of being a motherless child with a gear-head dad. I traipsed all over with him to car shows."

"He schooled you well." The door opening signaled Tom to get back in position and Lucy to close the car door.

Sarah gasped as she came out the door. "Dad!"

"Don't look at me, sweetie. This was all Jared, with a little help from Tom, your driver for the day." Robert took her hand and helped her down the steps, her mother holding up her dress and veil to keep them off the ground.

Tom smiled and repeated his low bow. "Hello, I'm Tom, and I'll be your driver today."

"This is amazing. And exciting." Sarah looked over at Lucy. "Your dad would have loved this."

"Pretty cool, huh? And I get to ride in it too!" Lucy willed the wistful tears away.

Sarah settled into the wide backseat with her parents, and Lucy rode in the front seat with Tom.

"AUTOMATIC TRANSMISSION? WOW." Lucy was taking it all in.

Tom shrugged as he maneuvered the car around the circle drive and down the winding driveway to the road. "Yeah, a little part of me wishes it were original."

"It's still amazing. Makes me miss my dad, though. He would have insisted on driving this baby."

Tom smiled as she caressed the leather seats and wood trim. His dad would have loved her. Car enthusiast notwithstanding, she would have been a girl after his own heart.

He caught the mist of tears in her eyes when she glanced his way. He took her hand and squeezed it. "Are you okay?" He kept his voice low, not wanting to disturb the family unit behind him.

She squeezed back. "I'm okay. I realized, this morning, my best friend has a new best friend." She gazed at him as he turned his head to the front to drive. "You too."

"Yeah. It hit me too." He glanced out the window and cleared his throat. "I'm happy for them. They found the other part of themselves." He paused. "God has a plan for them all right."

"He has a plan for all of us." Lucy's quiet voice touched his heart.

"Amen."

Did God's plan for him include Lucy? He let go of her hand to feel his breast pocket, where the wedding rings were resting. They were still there. He had to remember to give Jared's to Lucy. When he was sure the wedding rings were in place, he patted his pants pocket, where another box resided. It was there too. He smiled, and prayed silently. *Thank you, God.*

# CHAPTER THIRTY-SEVEN

The harpist, a friend of Sarah's from her days as a music student at Murray State University in Kentucky, played a variety of hymns and love songs for the gathering congregation. As the car pulled up to the front of the church, Tom and Lucy both jumped out to help Sarah disembark. Her dad, however, beat them both to the punch.

"I'll help my daughter out this one last time, if you don't mind." He smiled at Tom, who was prepared to do his best imitation of a chauffeur.

"Listen, Mom, Dad." Sarah paused. "Do you remember what they were playing for a prelude the first Sunday we came to church here?"

Linda Crawford laughed. "I've slept since last summer."

"'Great Is Thy Faithfulness.'" Sarah smiled.

"It's a special song, isn't it?" Robert put his arm around her shoulders. "Hymns glorify God, and they also remind us to give Him the glory."

"I miss Granny." Sarah daubed at her eyes. It was like she was willing the tears to go away.

Robert smiled. "I do too. She would be so proud to be here."

Lucy touched Sarah's arm. "Are you ready?"

Sarah took a deep breath. "I'm ready. I've never been so ready." She grinned at Lucy, and they laughed together.

"All right, Linda, you go on ahead, and Tom, you go around to the side door and meet up with the guys. Nothing can happen until you two are in there!" Lucy put everyone in the correct order and looked at Tom's hair. "Stand still"

He had thrown the hat into the car and was raking his hair back with his fingers, but when Lucy said "stand still," he froze.

He winked at her as she straightened his hair back into place.

"Stop it. You'll have my face the same color as my dress." She couldn't hide her smile even as she tried to stay stern. This was no time for shenanigans.

"Will I do?" He put his hands on her upper arms and looked into her eyes.

She tilted her head, unable to break away from his gaze, and then realized she was the one holding up the process. She took a breath, released it, and swatted his arm. "You'll do. Now get in there!"

He laughed as he jogged down the sidewalk to the side door of the church.

"All right folks. This is it. Where's Emmaline?"

They made their way up the stairs to the small vestibule where the wedding party waited their turn to process down the aisle.

Emmaline Quincy, armed with stylish glasses, an up-do, and a white clipboard, made her way to the bride. "Everything is going as scheduled. Is Tom with the other men?"

Lucy nodded. "Yes. He should be there now."

Emmaline smiled. "Good. Let's get in line, people, like at the rehearsal, remember?" She shook her head and whispered to Lucy. "They never remember."

Lucy giggled.

Emmaline clapped her hands softly. "Okay, people, grandparents of the groom, grandparents of the bride; parents of the groom, mother of the bride. The mothers will light the unity candle, and when they are seated, the gentlemen will come out. As soon as they are in place, the bridesmaids Jessica, Susan, and Lucy; flower girls Lily, Trudy, and Abby; then the pièce de résistance, the bride and her father. Got it?"

Everyone nodded. Things were going like the well-oiled wheel they hoped for. Lucy wished she could be behind the flower girls to watch their entire walk down the aisle, but she would be up front by that time.

"I Will Be Here," by Steven Curtis Chapman was being played by the harpist as the mothers lighted the unity candle together. The symbol of two families being united threatened tears of loneliness, but looking down the aisle, she caught a glimpse of her grandmother halfway up the aisle on the end. She kept glancing back, hoping, Lucy was sure, to get a glimpse of her granddaughter. She smiled and waved, bolstering up her internal fortitude, and Grandmommy winked back. She wasn't alone. Even if Grandmommy hadn't been here, she wouldn't be alone.

She stood behind Sarah's sister, Susan, as she waited for her cue to proceed down the aisle. Her mind was a swirl of emotions, reminiscences, and checklists. Was there anything she had forgotten? Of course not. Would the little girls balk at making their way down the aisle? Lily was sure she could get Abby and Trudy down the aisle, but three-year-old babies could be stubborn. What if they simply refused to do it? No, she couldn't think that way.

Susan made her way down, and she waited until she reached the middle pew before she began to walk. She put a smile on her face and walked in time to the music, her steps slow and measured, but natural. Up front, the gentlemen looked spiffy in their dark gray tuxedos. Jared's had a white vest, while the groomsmen had darker vests a few shades lighter than their tux.

She raised an eyebrow when she saw Tom, and her smile turned into a silly grin. The audacity of the man, winking at her now. Her face warmed with a deliciousness that unsettled her and calmed her all at once.

When she reached her spot, she turned, getting in position to view the children and Sarah coming down the aisle. This was what they had been planning since ninth grade, and it was happening. The little girls started their trip down the aisle, and Lucy had a fleeting thought of how nice it would have been to have a ring-bearer.

Ring.

Wasn't she supposed to be carrying Jared's wedding band?

She had been so caught up in making sure everyone else was doing what they were supposed to do that she had forgotten the ring. When she threatened to "conveniently" forget the ring back in the summer, she was joking. She would never do it. She felt the color drain from her face.

TOM'S main concern today was making sure Jared stayed upright. He had gained a lot of his strength back, but he still tired easily. He and Sarah agreed their first dance would be their last at the reception. Jared looked good. His color was good, and his hair had grown in enough to cover his incisions. He would have scars there, but as thick as his hair was, nobody would ever know.

Lucy coming down the aisle toward them was a sight to behold. Her dress swirled around her feet, and the sparkling shoes on her tiny feet peeked out with each step. She was as beautiful as the bride, in his opinion. After giving her a wink, he smiled as she blushed. It was like having a super power, to be able to make a woman blush like that.

Walking past the flower-laden pews, the three little girls

strewed flower petals along the aisle. Yeah, somebody would have to clean that up, but he wouldn't think about that, now. Jared's nephew, Alex, named after Alex Crawford, had done a good job of ushering in the greats and grands.

As the girls got to the altar, finishing up their task and taking their places next to their mothers, Tom turned to smile at Lucy before Sarah came in.

What he saw scared him to death.

She was staring at him, her face looking like she'd seen a ghost. What was wrong? Had he forgotten his tie? He reached up to his hair. Had he messed it up after she'd fixed it?

As the music changed to the Bridal Chorus, Linda stood to signal for all to rise for the bride. While everyone was turned toward Sarah, Tom looked at Lucy again, shaking his head. She was mouthing something. Sing? He wasn't supposed to sing. No, it couldn't be that. Wing?

Lucy rolled her eyes in disgust, turned back to Susan, and whispered something to her. Susan's eyes grew wide with fright. She looked past him at Sarah's brother-in-law, Mike. Tom turned to him with a stiff whisper. "What's Lucy trying to say? Wait, it's Susan now."

Mike looked at his wife's distressed communication. He thought a minute, and calmly stated, "Ring."

Lucy exhaled and nodded, her color coming back. Sarah was halfway down the aisle, with eyes for no one but Jared, thank goodness.

Tom reached into his pocket and pulled out Jared's ring. Could she catch it? He made as if to toss it, and she shook her head and bugged her eyes in fright. She held out her hand as if to say "stop," and she simply turned to Sarah, smiling, as she made her way to the altar with her father.

TOM HAD THE RING. Thank you, Lord. Everything would be fine. When Pastor Mike, from Sarah and Lucy's home church in Kentucky, asked for Sarah's ring, from Tom, he would hand them both to the pastor. When he asked for Jared's ring, from Lucy, she would pretend to give him a ring.

Once Robert managed to say the words "her mother and I" to the question "who gives this woman to be married to this man," and Sarah handed Lucy her bouquet, she could have passed out with relief. All the planning and work to get them to this point, and it was almost over.

As Sarah and Jared repeated their vows, Lucy didn't feel the way she imagined she would feel. It was as if the stress of forgetting the ring reminded her she wasn't losing her best friend, she was gaining even more friends. It wouldn't be the same once Sarah was married, but when you think about it, it wasn't the same after they got out of high school, or college, was it?

Times and seasons. Life is a series of times and seasons. While there were sniffles all around her, she didn't feel like crying. One thing she did feel right now was joy. Pure, unadulterated joy. And on top of that, humor. She couldn't wait to tell Sarah the story of the rings, once it was all over. Gotta love a good "wedding mishap" story.

They had been serious for so long, with the hurricane, Jared's accident, and the problems at the sheriff's office, that it was good to feel like laughing again.

After the ring ceremony, she took her eyes off Jared and Sarah to smile at Tom, who was grinning at her. Laughter bubbled up in her, and she squelched it as best she could.

The unity candle ceremony over, Sarah turned to Lucy to retrieve her bouquet and turned, with Jared, to face the congregation for their introduction as man and wife.

Brother Mike had it under control. "And now, by the power vested in me by the states of South Carolina and Kentucky, I would like to present to you, Mr. and Mrs. Jared Stuart Benton. Whom God has joined together, let no man put asunder. Jared?"

Jared turned to Sarah's minister. "Yes, sir?"

"You may kiss your bride now."

Jared didn't waste any time. In fact, he may have made up for time he lost while unconscious. When he lifted his head, the congregation stood and cheered, and the music swelled. "Jesu, Joy of Man's Desiring" was played, and once the bride and groom, and then the little girls started down the aisle, Lucy gratefully took Tom's arm to make her way to the front door.

She might not let go this time.

om and Lucy drove the bride and groom to the reception at Pilot Oaks after pictures were made. Along the drive were stakes with ribbon strung from bouquet to bouquet, with candles at each one.

Hors d'oeuvres were served in the double parlors inside the mansion, with a pianist playing Gershwin tunes on the gleaming Steinway for the entertainment of the guests.

The patio and gardens behind Pilot Oaks had been turned into a dream. The summer house was the backdrop for the bride and groom's table, and café lights were strung amongst the trees. The round dining tables were placed within view of the couple and the patio dance floor, and the jazz combo had a small tent near the house.

Lucy sighed as she walked into the house. It was a dream-come-true for Sarah and for her too. To see her best friend find such happiness meant there was hope for her as well. Things certainly hadn't been easy for Sarah. First, a broken engagement, then when things looked perfect for her, the hurricane and Jared's injury. Bad things happened, and God had used every one of those things for good. Tears tickled her eyes, and for a moment, she missed her dad intensely. But this was Sarah's day, and only tears of happiness had a place here.

Once the crowd had moved out of the house and into the area for dining and dancing, Sarah and Jared came in and made their way through the house for their introduction. Lucy had never seen Sarah so radiant, and for some reason, right now it was all a blur to her. They were gathering in the dining room, waiting to be introduced.

"Are you okay?"

A hand gently touched her elbow. It was Tom. She smiled up at him. "I'm better than okay."

"You look a little pale."

She tried to remember when she had eaten last. She twisted her face in embarrassment. "I may or may not have eaten today. I'll be fine."

Tom looked around at the evidence of appetizers that had been deserted for heartier fare. "Wait here." He came back in seconds and handed her a napkin with macaroni-and-cheese bites and a cup of punch. "Carb it up."

She laughed. "And to think I almost missed these. I'm the one that wanted them." She popped the hors d'oeuvre in her mouth and chased it with sparkling punch. "Ah. Thank you. I think I'll live now."

"Good, because I think we're up next."

He placed his hand on the small of her back as they stood at the door, waiting for Susan and Mike to make their entrance.

"You ready?"

"Sure we're not forgetting something?" Lucy arched one finely-tuned eyebrow.

"Not this time. I think we're good to go."

Lucy sighed. "I think so, too. Well, there are the toasts."

He patted his breast pocket. "No worries. Mine is right here."

She pointed at her tiny jeweled bag. "Mine too." She gazed

at him with a smile. Confusion registered on his face. That was just fine. She wasn't holding back anymore.

AFTER THE DINNER AND TOASTS, Tom's work was done. Lucy had everyone, including Sarah and Jared, laughing at her toast. At first she read from her notes, but when she warmed up, she had to share the story of the rings.

He was relaxed now. For the most part. He put his hand in his pocket, fingering the tiny velvet box. All in good time.

"We Will Dance," another song by Christian artist Steven Curtis Chapman, was Jared and Sarah's first dance.

Tom had chills listening to the words of the song, including a reference to a hurricane. This almost didn't happen.

The mood changed a bit with the father-daughter song. Sarah and Robert agreed they did not want a tear-jerker song, so they settled on "You Are the Sunshine of My Life" by Stevie Wonder. Tom noticed Jared seemed grateful to sit down for Sarah and Robert's turn on the dance floor.

Then it was Jared and his mother Liz's turn. Jared smiled when he realized what his mother had picked. "I'll Say A Little Prayer for You," by Aretha Franklin, was the perfect song for a mother and son.

After that, different people made their way to the dance floor or sat and enjoyed the beautiful autumn weather. Who wouldn't want to be in South Carolina in the fall? Well, unless there was a hurricane going on.

Lucy came to sit next to him. "Hey, aren't you going to get out there and dance?"

He laughed. "I'm not much of a dancer."

She grimaced. "Me neither."

"With your coordination?"

Lucy sighed. "I'm afraid it doesn't extend to the dance

floor."

"Good, then I won't feel bad not asking you to dance." They sat in companionable silence for a few minutes when he grabbed her hand. "Are you on duty for anything?"

She looked surprised. "No. Why?"

"Let's take a walk." He stood and pulled her up by her hands. "You might want to leave your shoes behind."

"Where are we going?" She began unstrapping the jeweled heels, carrying them with her.

He led her away from the crowd, toward the boardwalk down to the beach. "This okay?"

"Perfect." She laid her shoes at the head of the path next to his and put her hand in his, draping her long chiffon skirt over her other arm as she walked.

When they got down to the sand, she sighed with pleasure. "Why would anyone not want to be close to this all the time? I don't blame Sarah for moving here."

"Even with the hurricanes?"

She nodded in the twilight. "Even then." She looked up at him. "Did you ever consider leaving the coast?"

He bent down to pick up a rock, throwing it in the ocean. "I thought about it. Did you know I wanted to join the FBI?"

"Really? I mean, that's so cool. I love procedural TV shows." She smiled, more relaxed than he had seen her in a while. Since last summer, in fact, when she didn't have a care in the world. So much had happened in the last year.

"What about you?"

"I've lived in different places. I lived in Kentucky the longest I've lived anywhere. I guess that's 'home,' but I don't have family there anymore. Besides Grandmommy, Sarah's the closest I have to family."

"I met your grandmother again. She's a piece of work, isn't she?" He didn't tell her what her grandmother said, that he'd better not break her granddaughter's heart.

Lucy chuckled. "She is that. She keeps asking me to come live in Atlanta, but I don't feel like that's where the Lord is leading me. You know what I mean?"

"I do. When I went to Blythewood the other week for the deposition, I thought about what it would have been like if I'd pursued either state police or FBI. I would have had to leave the place I love. I wouldn't have been here for my family, or for Jared." He paused and looked down at her. "And I wouldn't have met you."

LUCY STARED UP AT HIM. "God does work in mysterious ways, doesn't He?" The moment seemed to last forever. Lucy could feel her toes tingle, and it wasn't from cold or the sand. She was tingling all over.

Tom turned toward her and put his hands on her cheeks. He shook his head in disbelief, and leaned down to kiss her. When she dropped her armful of skirt and reached up to put her arms around his neck, he pulled her closer, lifting her off her feet.

It was, and it wasn't, like the kiss they had shared last summer. That was an exploratory kiss, saying "I like you. Do you like me?" This was different. They had been through things together that some married couples couldn't survive. Lucy knew there was no going back, for her, after this. She couldn't think about anyone else as long as there was breath in a man named Thomas Sumter Livingston.

Tom pulled back and lowered her to her feet. She stared up into his eyes and said the only thing she could verbalize. "Wow."

Tom threw his head back and laughed. He picked her back up and swung her around. "Wow is right." He pulled her close and they stood there for a few minutes. She could have stayed there forever. In his arms was peace. In his arms was love. She didn't feel alone now.

TOM HELD her close their foreheads touching, eyes closed. "Lucy, I love you."

"I love you, too, Tom."

He opened his eyes to see her beautiful blue ones looking into his. The sun was setting behind him as he faced the ocean and Lucy, the sun shining on her face making her hair glow. He wished he had a painting of her like this. Someday.

He lowered her once again to the sand. He couldn't wait any longer. "Stand right there."

"Okay. Are you going somewhere?" She giggled.

"No, give me a second." He reached into his pants pocket for the box. This time he wasn't making sure it was there. This time, he was taking it out of his pocket.

He knelt on the sand, looking up at Lucy for a change. "Lucy, I've been in love with you since last summer, but I thought, after all that had happened, you deserved more than being saddled with a cop for a husband, and not only that, but a cop with a family dependent on him."

He stopped her when she would have interrupted. He'd better get to the point. Her hands were already on her hips in outrage. "Let me finish." He pulled her hands to him with his free hand. "Luce, what I'm trying to say is that I love you, and, if you will consider it, I would like to ask you to do me the honor of marrying me."

She stood in front of him, one hand still in his, and one hand covering her mouth. When she got over the surprise, she put both hands on his cheeks. "Are you sure, Tom? What if I can't be a good cop's wife? What if your mother doesn't like me?"

Tom threw his head back and laughed. "Are you kidding me? I think she would disinherit me if I didn't marry you." He sobered. "Lucy, you'd make a good any kind of wife. I want you for my wife."

She looked at him, eyes shining. "You mean it?"

Tom opened the box to reveal a vintage half-carat diamond solitaire, his mother's engagement ring. He had taken it to be cleaned and reinforced and had been carrying it for over a week. He didn't know when it would happen, but he depended on God to give him direction. Today was the day.

Lucy put her hands on his shoulders. "Oh, Tom. It's gorgeous."

"Will you marry me, Lucy Dixon?" He tilted his head. Would she?

She leaned down and kissed him full on the lips. "Tom Livingston, you try to stop me. Yes, I'll marry you."

He pulled the ring out of the slot and put it on her third finger, left hand. It fit.

"It's perfect, Tom. Was it your mother's?" Tears beaded her lashes.

He stood and gathered her to himself. "Yes. She gave it to me a long time ago to give to my bride. I think she'll be happy it's you."

She looked up at him. "She doesn't know?"

He smiled and shook his head. "Nobody does, except your grandmother. I asked her for your hand."

Her eyes filled with tears. "Thank you, Tom. That means the world to me. Daddy would have loved you, you know?"

"And mine would have loved you. Do you want to announce it tonight or wait until the wedding is over?"

"Do you seriously think I can keep this to myself?" She shook her head. "Let's go tell Grandmommy and your mother. I've got to tell Sarah. She'll be over the moon."

Tom stood and grabbed her hand. "Let's go and face the music. I'm ready to start planning our wedding and the sooner the better."

"Amen." She hiked up her long dress, and they sprinted to the boardwalk and back to the reception.

# CHAPTER THIRTY-NINE

*One Year Later, in October*

A 1956 Ford Thunderbird on four jacks had two sets of feet coming out from under it: one large set wearing work boots and one petite set wearing grease-smeared pink Converse high-tops.

"Could you hand me that oil wrench?"

Lucy felt around on the garage floor beside her. "Here it is." She handed him the wrench.

"Thanks." He tightened the filter and turned toward her. "I think that does it. Want to see if it'll start?"

"Are you kidding? Let's get out from under here." They rolled out in tandem, although it took Tom longer to roll out than it did Lucy. She pulled a pink bandana from her back pocket and wiped a smudge from her nose and then cleaned her sparkling engagement ring and diamond-studded wedding band.

Tom took it from her and wiped another smudge from her chin. "There. That got it." He leaned in and kissed her thoroughly.

"You taste like motor oil." Lucy giggled and wrinkled her nose.

"So do you, sweetheart." He looked to see if the key was in the ignition. "Would you like to do the honors?"

"Are you sure? It was your dad's car, after all." She was itching to get behind the wheel.

"I'm sure." They worked in tandem lowering the jacks until the tires touched the floor of the garage and then removed them. He opened the door with a flourish. "M'lady."

"Thank you, Thomas." She used her best high-brow imitation and then wrinkled her pert nose when she looked at her dirty jeans and the white leather car interior. "Is there a clean towel over there to put down on the seat?"

Tom found it, and covered the seat. "Now you won't hurt anything."

She sat behind the wheel, reveling in the smooth, hard plastic under her fingers. How her dad would have loved working on this with Tom. She looked up at him and grinned. "Ready?"

He nodded and stood back. "Turn it over."

She turned the key in the ignition, giving it a little gas, and squealed when it roared to life. "We did it!"

Tom looked as surprised as she did. "Hang on." He got in the passenger side of the two-seater. "See if it'll go anywhere."

She reached for the gear, trying to get the hang of the floor-mounted gear shift. It was in the center, like her Mustang, but it still felt different. She looked at Tom, seeing the excitement in his face that mirrored hers.

Foot on clutch, she put it in first and eased out. It pulled forward slowly. When she put it in second, and then third, she was able to drive it around the circular drive. She stopped when they made it to the front door of the house.

"We did it." Pride oozed from her, and she couldn't stop smiling.

Tom reached over and kissed her. "I would have never done it without you."

"Oh, sure you would."

"Nope. It's been sitting there for over ten years, and Dad didn't touch it either."

She scooted over on the bench seat and linked her arms around his neck. "We face things together, you and I. Things like cars, and houses, and hurricanes. There's nothing we can't tackle if we're together."

His kiss left her breathless. "I'm glad you didn't want a long engagement. Life's too short." And he proceeded to show her, once again, why a short engagement had been a good idea. After Sarah and Jared's wedding last October, Tom and Lucy were married in December.

Lucy pulled back to look at him. "You think the car will be ready for a trip down the coast?"

"All we need is a good wax job and detail, and we're good to go."

Lucy smiled as they sat there in the car in front of their house. She had been thrilled to learn Tom was trading houses with his mother and sister. She didn't want to sway him, but the thought of raising their children in the house where generations of Tom's family had lived gave her a sense of permanency she had never known.

Now Mary Ann and Charly lived a mile or so away in the ranch-style house he had bought a few years ago, and they lived in the rambling plantation house. Lucy had used her love of organization to start putting together the family historical items in the house. They had never been cataloged, and some of the brittle paper was almost unreadable. She was not going to let it disappear.

"Do you miss teaching?" Tom still held her in the circle of his arms, enjoying the cool breeze.

"I really don't. I get to use it at church, and who knows,

someday I might want to go back or teach at a private school." She began to play with the buttons on his shirt. "I think, for now, I'd rather take care of my own kids." She twisted her lips, trying to hide her grin, and peeked up at his face.

His eyes were round as saucers, his face a total blank. As her words began to register with him, he continued to stare at her. "Are you . . . are we . . ."

She nodded her head as happy tears began to fall. "Yes."

He pulled her close, holding her as she cried, his tears mingling with hers as they kissed. "I can't believe it. Are you sure?"

"I'm sure. I saw the doctor today, and he says I'm about six weeks along. In two weeks, we can see him . . . or her, if you can get off work."

"If? Try keeping me away." He kissed her again. "Aw, Lucy. We're going to be parents."

"We are. Now I get to decorate a nursery." She laughed at his shaking head.

"Have you told Sarah?"

She shook her head. "Nope. You're the first, besides the doctor. I wanted to be good and sure before I told even you. I didn't want you to get your hopes up."

"Let's drive over and tell Mom and Charly."

"And Sarah and Jared?"

"Yep." He brightened even more. "I beat Jared to the punch."

"What?"

"I'm going to be a dad first." Tom had a very satisfied look on his face. He got out of the car and came around to the driver's side. "Scoot over and I'll drive."

"Mr. Macho, much?" Lucy laughed and scooted to the passenger side. "Enjoy this now, because there's no way we're putting a car seat in this vehicle."

He started the car. When he turned to look at his wife, he was still in awe. "Wow."

"What are you thinking?" She grazed his cheek with her fingers.

"About how much we've been blessed." He grabbed her fingers and kissed them. "God's bent over backward to bless us, and I guess sometimes I wonder, why?"

"Because He's our Father. We may have lost both our earthly fathers, but our Heavenly Father always had a plan for us, and He's big enough to make it happen." She wrinkled her nose. "My dad spoiled me so much I was beginning to think maybe I'd had all the blessings I was going to get, and now look at me." She patted her tummy. "I'm going to be a mother. There is no greater blessing than that, but if my only blessing was marrying you, it would have been enough."

"It's like Micah said, '*He has shown you, O man, what is good; And what does the Lord require of you but to do justly, to love mercy, and to walk humbly with your God?*'" She paused and looked down a minute, thinking. She reached up and placed her hand on the five-o'clock shadow she dearly loved. "You've shown me how to do that, Tom."

He smiled at her, tears glinting in his eyes. "I couldn't have done it without you, Mrs. Livingston."

He started the car, smiling as he revved the engine. "Hey, maybe the baby will become a doctor."

"Maybe. Why?" Lucy looked at him with a confused frown.

Tom laughed. "Then, every time he—"

"Or she," Lucy interrupted.

"Yes, or she. Every time he or she comes over, I can say . . ."

She groaned and shook her head as they said in tandem, "Doctor Livingston, I presume."

# ABOUT THE AUTHOR

Regina Merrick began reading romance and thinking of book ideas as early as her teenage years when she attempted a happily-ever-after sequel to "Gone With the Wind." That love of fiction parlayed into a career as both a school and public librarian, and more recently, as a full-time author. Married for nearly 35 years and active in their local church, Regina and her retired-teacher husband have two grown daughters who share her love of music, writing, and the arts. She resides in a 100-year-old house in Marion, KY with her husband and their dog, Cedric, whose late litter-mate, Oliver, was the model for Sarah's Schnauzer-mix.

***Carolina Dream* by Regina Rudd Merrick**

**A Southern Breeze Series—Book One**

Sarah Crawford wants more from life than to attend the wedding of her ex-fiancée. An unexpected inheritance in South Carolina comes at the perfect time, just as Sarah is willing to use any excuse to get out of town. When she meets potential business partner Jared Benton and discovers that a house is part of the inheritance, she is sure that God has been preparing her for this time through a recurring dream.

But will a dream about an antebellum mansion, many rooms to be explored, and a man with dark brown eyes give her the confidence to take a leap of faith, leaving friends, family, and her job behind?

**_Carolina Grace by Regina Rudd Merrick_**

**A Southern Breeze Series—Book Three**

First-year Special Education teacher Charly Livingston demonstrates God's love on the outside but is resentful that God allowed back-to-back tragedies in her family.

Rance Butler is a top-notch medical intern. He's on his way to the top, and when he meets Charly, he knows things will only get better. When he discovers family secrets and a dying father he never knew, his easy, carefree life seems to disintegrate.

Even in the idyllic ocean breezes and South Carolina sunshine, contentment turns to bitterness and confusion except for God's amazing grace.

Katie McGowan left her parents and their faith behind years ago. However, when faced with a devastating betrayal, Katie is ready to go back to Carbondale, Illinois to help her elderly parents despite their tempestuous relationship. Drained by the constant friction, Katie finds emotional support and encouragement in Austin. His practical, simple faith speaks to Katie, and she finds herself yearning for a new connection to God. As their friendship grows, so does the attraction between Katie and Austin. Before her fledgling faith and thoughts of romance have a chance to take root, Katie's cheating fiancé returns, remorseful and promising change. Can her tentative faith strengthen their past love? And if her heart breaks again, will Katie's journey to faith end before it has really begun?

*Faith's Journey* by Heather Greer.

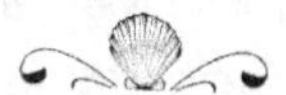

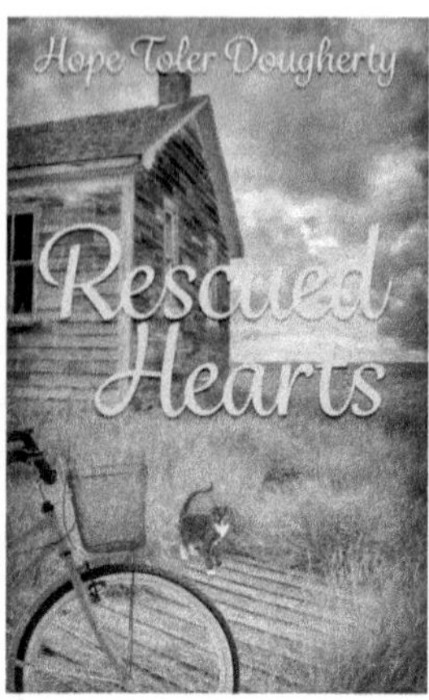

Mary Wade Kimball's soft spot for animals leads to a hostage situation when she spots a briar-entangled kitten in front of an abandoned house. Beaten, bound, and gagged, Mary Wade loses hope for escape. Discovering the kidnapped woman ratchets the complications for undercover agent Brett Davis. Weighing the difference of ruining his three months' investigation against the woman's safety, Brett forsakes his mission and helps her escape the bent-on-revenge brutes following behind. When Mary Wade's safety is threatened once more, Brett rescues her again. This time, her personal safety isn't the only thing in jeopardy. Her heart is endangered as well.

*Rescued Hearts* by Hope Tyler Dougherty.

*Stay up-to-date on your favorite books and authors with our free e-newsletters.*

ScriveningsPress.com